CHAPPENTHING IN TRAVEL ON ''

By the same author

Six Portraits: Wild Birds on a Winter Mountain
Computers and Creativity
Happenthing in Travel On

"CHAPPENTHING IN TRAVEL ON "

Carole Spearin McCauley

DAUGHTERS, INC.

Plainfield, Vermont

FOR MY SISTERS
those I know
those I'll meet
those I can never meet

FOR MEN OF GOODWILL
including my husband

Run mad as often as you chuse; but do not faint.

—Jane Austen

You can't always get what you want
You can't hardly get what you want
You can't always get what you want.

But if you try sometimes
You might find
You can get what you need.

I want to thank these editors for their encouragement when parts of this novel appeared in their publications or anthologies:

Richard Kostelanetz, *Assembling* (New York), "Sex" and "Violence," *In Youth* (Ballantine Books), "Program for a Novel," *Breakthrough Fictioneers* (Something Else Press), "Things I Will Never Do Again;"

Professor Dr. Elisabeth Walther, Professor Dr. Max Bense, Stuttgart, Germany; "Six Portraits" and "Ingrid Is Teaching Us Germlish" appeared in their paperback book series, *rot* (no. 50);

The publishers of *White Mountain Times, New Hampshire Vacationer*, and *Everywoman* for quotations from their journals;

With very special thanks to R. B. Frank of *Panache Magazine* (Princeton); "Program for a Novel" and "Things I Will Never Do Again" appeared originally in *Panache.*

CHAPPENTHING
IN TRAVEL ON "

+ = *POSITIVE NOUN, ADJ., VERB, ADV.*
− = *NEGATIVE   "   "   "   "*
o = *AMBIVALENT "   "   "   "*

RHYME → LINE
  A +*ADJ* +*NOUN* +*VERB* THE +*NOUN*
  −*ADJ* AS −*NOUN*
  A o*ADJ* o*NOUN* *ADVERB* o*VERB* *PREPOSITION* THE o*NOUN*
  +*ADV* −*ADV* o*ADV*
RHYME → LINE

GO TO ____POINT

HAIL → MARY → AIRLINES
  A GILDED BOMBSHELTER AIRRIDES THE FLAMING EGGS
  UNINHABITED AS RAINSTAINS
  A FRIGGIN MOUNTAIN WARILY FISHES UPON THE PLANE
  BRILLIANTLY UNINHABITEDLY TANTALIZINGLY
CROW → IN → THE → SNOW

GO TO IVYPOINT

Only a fool or a coward would have worried at the
start of that trip . . .

In the foothills around the shack-and-hangar, Indian
summer has worn to hazy Thanksgiving. The pilot looks
sober, the small plane sound. Snowed already in the
mountains, somebody says. But it's New England, and
who but tv weather types watches clouds any more?

For a few minutes we're strapped in our seats arcing
high over green and white patchwoods, constructing the
affable maketalk of strangers seated with more strangers
they expect never to see again. I do it too. Seven passengers—three pairs of us plus one woman seated alone—is
just small enough that it seems impossible not to smile
and comment at the pilot's joshing.

He rambles. —All you ladies off to a convention? You
the church group? Or the Republican wives?— He gabs at
us over his shoulder while his hands do the controls.
Smalltown gossip that should have been grounded. He
looks too young for chatter. —Maybe you're bird lovers.
Did you see on tv about the bird societies?—

Hail Mary Airlines. We fly lower and talkier.

As the guesses grow wild, a woman in the aisle seat
ahead of me leans and answers. I lose her words which
are low, of odd rhythm. A foreigner. Her head bears a
white scar on one temple near the cool, dark eyes. A perfect crescent. D for daring, C for coy. Her elegant little
body wears a gold suit.

—What's that, ma'am? . . . Never flown all ladies before. Don't none of you distract a poor man from his job
now.— The pilot rehunches over his panoply of dials and
charts. Close my eyes. Try to rest . . .

I'm still exhausted from my Gray days—my husband
Graydon's dying that ended our gray marriage twenty?
twenty-one days ago. I relive catering to the horde of

useless, sitdown relatives, their uncertain but relieved
faces. Gray died slowly of cancer. Their comfort included
stuffing a collage of egg yolks, coffee grounds, and ba-
nana peels down the garbage disposal we didn't have.
After the funeral I needed two hours with snake and
plunger to unclog the drain and wash the crusted dishes.

Gray's older sister: —Don't look at *me*. Momma kept
cooking. Why don't you call the plumber? Whoever heard
of a house without a disposal?— If the chip on Gwen's
shoulder were any bigger, it would fall and break her leg.

—Leave me alone!— Go to hell with Gray.

Through the coils of the snake her whisper reached
me. —Can't say two words to her. Why doesn't the doctor give her . . .— —But she's been through . . .—

But try to push the gray past behind me. I stretch in
my seat and imagine the interview for a computer job I'm
traveling toward. Gray: —Computer programming? . . .
Don't you feel the baby's still too young? And every day
you would work costs me eight dollars income tax.—
The gray frown.

—Capable young man . . . Do you see the snow down
there?— from the woman next to me at the window. I
open one eye. And focus on white hair. Then a baroque
silver cross against scarves aflow with Indian flora, fauna,
sunheads. High cheekbones, tall ivory forehead. Intrigu-
ing. A Christian Madame Gandhi? . . . I realize she's expecting an answer. Also doesn't approve daytime dozing.
A gilt-edge book (Bible? diary?) sits lightly on her scarfed
lap.

—I guess there's always snow higher up. That's why
people who start out walking in summer clothes wind up
freezing at nightfall.— Her trees and flowers huddle together; my bit of woodslore has chilled her.

—I'm sure I wouldn't let it bother *me*— she boasts. The
corners of her mouth stretch into Mona Lisa composure.

Then why'd you ask the question? This the Twenty

6

Questions Flight? The past months, Graydon's dying, eating me. Her composure irritating? —It's strange only women wanted to charter a midweek flight. *Is* there a meeting somewhere?—

Her eyes perk up. Must have hit one of her better topics.

—Well, ahead of us—the teenager and the woman with the gold suit who spoke to the pilot—I think they do archeology. I heard them say they're off to Egypt.

—And the pair up front left are planning some kind of demonstration in New York.—

I catch tattered jeans on one of the demonstration pair. She's younger than I am, maybe mid-twenties. Her friend is middle-aged, wears pink plastic glasses that keep slipping down her nose. Archeology-demonstration, archdemon . . .

Eyes finally opposite us to the solid woman who sits alone, flipping through *Family Circle*. —She's meeting her husband at LaGuardia. Expecting a baby, I think.—

Is it just sociability that makes her process all this information? She has narrowed it cleverly to *us*. —I'm Ivy Eilbeck.— Accepting discomfort at introducing myself to somebody I've talked with five minutes. And giving Gray's name when I'm no longer . . .

—I'm Chrysta Neff.— Formally takes my hand. Again the bittersweet smile.

Where have I seen her? It zeros in on me. Arguing with a craven interviewer who, by reading other people's quotes, was slyly insisting religious belief really had no place in cybernetic America. So Chrysta—is that her name?—is one who still has time to worry about such things? —Weren't you on a program, Sunday afternoon television? A local station?—

—Yes. I was invited because of a group I belong to. I've also written a book.—

—And he gave you a hard time.—

—Yes. A flip young man. Absolutely sure it's only

7

money that makes the world go round.— A bit of her same bravado, the smoothed white hair, serene face that had impressed me on the screen. Her shoulder squared under the scarves. Knows what she wants and how to get it.

She asks —Your name, Eilbeck. That's Dutch or German? Do you know the Dutch and the Irish have sent more missionaries abroad than any other peoples?—

—It's not my name really. It was my husband's name. When I get to my new job . . .—

Dark. Where did the clouds come from? One second my bones still register the loud forward vibration. Then our machine climbs. An angry roar replaces the engines' evenness. Our seats shudder; we lurch.

Next the plane is blasted straight upward as if blown from a cannon. Our bodies press so hard into the chairbacks that it tears our breath out. My stomach twists and flips. All of us stare wildly out the windows, then at the pilot, whose hands grasp knobs, dials, the steering stick. Chrysta's lips move. Somebody screams.

In another second our bodies sag into the seatbelts. We drop sheerly, rise slightly. Tilt and drop more. It's half quiet—the propeller blades slowing, nearly visible. Quieter. Then more screamings all around me except from Chrysta.

Green and white woods rush by windows. Angry mist, white woods, purple sky, green woods, sky, woods, white, green. Pillows, blankets, coats cascade upon us. I duck.

Close my eyes, brace! It can't be true. Can't, can't. Gray dead. Not me. Holding my breath.

White and green. Firecracker crash, my ears split with it. Pitch forward. Chair in front aiming at my face. Can't control. Grinding, gr-inding. Jolt. Something breaks off . . . Whole floor tearing. We jump up again . . . again . . .

8

When I come to, it's black and white. And red and cold all around me. Is it *my* head bleeding into somebody's lap? Chrysta's? Was that her name?

Or is Chrysta . . . ?

Somehow I'm right side up, but my arms and legs are drained. Immobile with that moment just before waking when you fear your muscles will never move again. But alive. Drag my head off Chrysta's lap. Red in my eyes that runs into the rough seat fabric.

Chrysta unbuckles her seatbelt. A normal action that gives me courage as I dab at my head. But I notice her fingers shaking. And the corners of her mouth as she catches me watching. She bites her lips, slowly masters the horror. The silence now as terrifying as the sudden smashes.

Groaning reaches us. When I've located my arms and legs, I roll out into the aisle floor and begin to crawl toward the others. Forward is somehow uphill. The chair of the —expecting— blonde woman who sat alone on our left has swivelled round. It now points downhill; she's half fallen from it, rubbing her knees.

My neck won't work. Or it's stretched. Like Alice in Wonderland, I'm dizzied at the roof and walls that have crushed inward at me. When I get where the pilot used to be, I'm too big for the space. I cut my arms on spikes of glass. Where the pilot used to be—he's twisted in there red and glassy, his chest mashed into the steering wheel. Panels and controls, wherever I touch, are smeared scarlet, waxy . . . Blood *freezing*?

I wobble around, trying to scramble back downhill. I meet a tangle of blood, boots, eyeglasses, pillows, legs, books. I can't breathe anymore. Slowly I recognize the smell spreading everywhere in the cabin. Raw gas! One mashed apple and somebody's—oh God—head? wig? topples before me down the aisle.

Then Chrysta is somehow standing upright. Touching a woman and a teenager who hug each other; on the other

9

side, two more with arms linked. Then Chrysta has assumed my floor space, her broad hips and bright designs shielding the pilot's body from the five trapped in seats. A moment more we sit, frozen. The worst can't have happened, too quick, impossible, we haven't crashed, it's somebody else, it's a dream.

Then it's Chrysta who knows what to do; I admire and envy her. She unclasps belts, gets the two pairs of women unwound from each other, faced forward. Rubs the knees of the −expecting− blonde woman twisted in her seat. At each place −Don't move, you're all right. Rest, rest, you're all right.− Repeat, repeat, we want to believe. We do what she says.

My watch, the one Gray gave me, has died at 2:13. Somehow should be 3:13. Crystal smashed. Be all right, notice small things—a crescent sandwich on the floor, shine of ragged glass.

Slowly we classify injuries despite our daze and the shambles. Everybody bruised all over, reliving the two great collisions everytime we find a new sore spot.

The archeology pair: the foreign woman's face, arms, and head run red from a long scalp cut. Scarlet destroying her handsome gold suit. But she's conscious. Her friend is the teenager, face crying and streaked. Right arm is bloody and probably broken. She whimpers. Chrysta dumps out the first aid kit for sulfa powder and tries to clean the raw flesh with a wet towel. The girl twists away. But Chrysta and I get the arm bound inside one of her scarves onto the only flat, straight thing we can find—the pilot's metal ruler.

Chrysta asks −Can you stand up?− at the −expecting− blonde woman who sat alone.

She groans. −No. It's heavy.−

Together they paw through her nested pillows and blankets. Unexpected laughter when their hands meet on the reason. Her seatbelt still hugs her. Her knees are bleeding. As she emerges from the bedding, I see more and more round the middle of her. She *is* pregnant.

10

The pair who were —planning some demonstration—:
the middle-aged woman with brassy hair is mumbling,
eyes far away behind the pink glasses. Zeni is her friend
with the jeans, and Zeni rocks her back and forth.

Raw gas and iron smell, spatter of blood, churn my
stomach upward.

Clambering from seat to seat, Chrysta and I make it
down the aisle where the tail of our plane and the luggage
used to live. When we fall out and stare round, we can't
believe it. It's snow and pine trees and singed, withered
bushes smelling all around us. Maybe out is ahead, beyond the crumpled silver nose. But when we've flounder-
ed and choked there through drifts of powdery snow,
flung at us by the wind, we see nothing. Down, sheer
down . . . to more pines, acres, miles before us to clouds
in one direction, to gray-green horizon in the other. No
river, no smoke, no town. Wind currents roaring up the
cliff blow us back toward the plane. Behind us: like a
nest the small snowy plateau, strewn with aluminum and
mist, under the tossing pines . . .

Chrysta and Zeni are arguing already. Zeni, twenty-five
years younger, a waspish creature with stuck-out chin and
flown away hair. Her wild similes and bouncy resilience
make me laugh, despite my banging head.

Chrysta tries dignified authority first. —We'll walk out.
That's all.—

—Yeah? Out where? Nothin' down there but frozen
squirrels. We stay here, light a fire. They'll find us.— Zeni
grins. —We'll eat the damned squirrels.—

On the other side the teenager is crying. —It'll snow. I
know it's going to snow.— Neither Chrysta nor I tell her
what awaits us outside.

Her friend, of the gold suit: —Chrysta's right. We can't
be that far from the airport. But we shan't be found in
thick woods like this.— Quickly with the foreign flavor
I heard before. Her *a*'s broadly British, her *r*'s German?
Her head still bleeds.

11

Zeni: —We can light flares. We'll work the radio.—

Silence. We stare downward at our laps, avoiding the dead pilot. If only he could tell us where we are. Glass-spangled, he's slumped and drunk at the wheel. Are his eyes shut now? But he must have navigated wrong anyway . . . *We welcome flight criticism.*

Me: —We don't know which way to walk.—

Chrysta: —Out is down. I'm sure.—

Zeni: —Dammit, if you wanna freeze, *I* don't. I only got sneakers on, for God sakes.—

After ten minutes of raw nerves and throbbing heads we vote: by Zeni's watch, one hour —down— for Chrysta, Zeni, me, and the foreign woman. Then an hour —back— for us before darkness. The pregnant one will stay and nurse both the teenager with the sling and Zeni's friend of the vacant eyes. They'll try to gather firewood and search the plane for food.

Chrysta shows us how to rip out seat padding and upholstery to make overshoes for those without boots. Then fresh bandages from ripped pillow cases. With her lips the teenager touches her friend's cheek through the blood; the caress is accepted.

We tie plaid blankets on one another's shoulders and set out. You'd think we know where we're going. I feel halfway between a Girl Scout overnight and a World War II movie. Only my head didn't hurt then. Rapid discovery that the places where walking is easiest (flattest) are not the places where it's easiest to walk. Zeni, the foreign woman, and I follow Chrysta's bootprints into the hollows between drifts . . .

Zeni sees it first. Among the black and green shadows a trail—made by animals who seem to know what *they're* doing even if we don't. An unlikely crew, Gray would have said. Why do I care what he would have said?

Zeni: —Pretty good for a kid from the Bronx, huh?—

The foreign woman's name is Ingrid. —Are you a nature enthusiast?— Asks it seriously. Ingrid is *so* serious.

Zeni: —Are you kidding? I can get lost in Central Park on a clear day.—

Down *is* out—not to where anybody will find us for a while but to the trail of large and small tracks that lead to a spring, unfrozen, bubbling from a cracked cement cistern. Over it two-by-fours and a wobbly tin roof. No house in sight. I try to drink with the others, but it's like chewing ice cubes into the fillings of my teeth. We splash the metallic taste over our faces. When I lean over, my head bleeds again.

I try to imagine the brook that made this spring. Only the squirrels know—and one crow that wings away to the trees. For ten minutes we rest in holes tramped in the snow. It's a mistake. When Chrysta urges us onward, our leg and back muscles revolt. One of my shoulders now burns as if somebody had lit a fire under it.

But we've left the wind behind us. The woods have thinned.

Chrysta and Zeni are sure there's a house over the next hill. I daydream a cup of coffee and the New York job interview I'm missing. We progress silently now. Zeni and Chrysta take turns breaking a trail with sticks; the rest of us slide and flounder behind them. What a luxury, being able to panic like the teenager back in the plane. Daze, exhaustion, and the endless effort of thrusting square feet into round holes without breaking an ankle keep us going.

Zeni cheers at the next vision: a fence of carved poles, askew *H*'s leaning into the drifts. Beside it, twin dips that run onward. Chrysta decides these are ruts of an old road. Her optimism astounds me; she's really sure there's something over the next hill.

—Hour's up.— Zeni pants. When she stops walking, Chrysta hikes on ahead of her. The rest of us follow Chrysta, who may not get anywhere but certainly does it with style. Halfway up the hill when I should be panting, I suddenly feel like laughing. I wonder whether the inside of my head got hit as well as the outside. But it's true—I've never felt so free at going absolutely nowhere with a bloody head in the day's last pink sunshine.

But I'm getting hungry, and the sky is too large between the trees.

Zeni plunges ahead now. If there *is* a house, she wants the glory of spotting it first. At the crest we halt. The —road— has died, but a small clearing spreads before us.

—Hey, it's there! See it?— Zeni tears out, flops and rolls down the hill. Her excitement infects us, too. The vastness through which we've marched is channelled now toward a grove of gray trees.

—Let's hope they're home.— Chrysta smooths her white hair and rearranges the blanket over my blood on her dress.

Zeni's —it— is a small peeled house with screen porch and tumbled wood pile. The remaining paint is a brown pox. Over it: a cluster of bare maples and one pine. Behind, a tattered shed looks as if the snowdrifts are holding it up. No footprints or wheeltracks anywhere. Seems bleakly uninhabited as the rainstains under the eaves. So far, Zeni's banging has roused only a scatter of squirrels across the porch.

We test the steps and creep around the flapping screen door. The split firewood is gray at the ends—hardly fresh chopped this year or the last. The front door is stuck; Zeni kicks it. We march through the darkening rooms. Unlike the fresh, clear outside, the interior is stale and incredibly cold. Waves of dampness radiate from the walls and fireplace, two dead stoves, drapes, cupboards. As we enter the dining room, a bluejay squadron takes off through a couple of broken panes. We all jump and sidestep toward the farthest wall. Cobwebs and sprinkled glass. We collapse and shiver in dusty chairs around the dining room table . . .

Chrysta raps the table with one of her rings. —All

14

right, the first thing to do is get more fresh air in here. It smells like a barn.—

Oh no, one of those. She can't be serious! One night Gray left the back door open, and the puppy froze.

—Then we light a fire and look for food. Zeni, you're bursting with energy. It's wonderful . . . Can you make it back up the hill to the other three girls?—

Carefully she avoids —mountain.— Does she have to call us girls? Two of them up there (not to mention the rest of us) are hardly girls.

—Maybe we can find some warmer clothes for you to wear. We're sure you can do it.—

Zeni keeps her face neutral. Chrysta's talent at making a strenuous hike sound like a privilege and a compliment does not pass unnoticed.

—Yeah, I think I can make it up. I'm going nuts without my glasses anyway.— She rationalizes loudly. Her own energy has trapped her. So Zeni's recklessness is part myopia? I like her for it.

—I hope that woman with the cut knees can make it down here tomorrow.—

I wonder why Zeni doesn't mention her own friend of the far eyes and farther mental condition.

Chrysta and I find a sofa in the living room and wrap Ingrid, our serious foreigner, into it; she's pale and aching. Chrysta wants me to sit with her, but it's better to help Zeni dig through upstairs cupboards and cobwebby cellar. In a few minutes we've outfitted Zeni with torn snow-shoes, mouse-chewed matches, two candles, a tin pan, a sugar scoop. —What the well-dressed pioneer wife will wear for spring planting!— She clanks around modelling it. Around the sofa we share our first meal, half an out-size chocolate bar with toasted peanuts. Gift to Ingrid from her teen friend.

When Zeni has accepted the other half from Chrysta, she clomps down the porch and picks up our pothole trail. Silently we watch her black blanket snowsuit

15

grow smaller against the white expanse. As she crests the hill, she turns and waves.

I realize that despite hearty remarks—my attempt to match Chrysta's spirits—I'd hate to be in Zeni's snow-shoes, facing a windy twilight hike, a night in a torn-open plane. She has guts. And Chrysta, who studies such things, has no doubt sized us up way back in the plane—Zeni all energetic, me exhausted, Ingrid dazed—before she —asked— Zeni in the first place.

In the final daylight we tour the pantry peering into dusty barrels, boxes, jars. Most are empty, but we uncover a slab of frozen bacon, three cases of pork and beans, some canned vegetables, a hunk of sugar (salt?), a canister of old tea. While Chrysta fetches water, Ingrid nudges a few warped windows that Chrysta had ordered opened. And I try my first fire of frozen logs and faded 1957 magazines. (Somebody named Harvey Reinholt worries —U. S. science education will fall behind its counterpart in the U.S.S.R. by 1967 unless something is done *now*— and a fluffy woman with curls over her ears is uptight because too much education and —relaxed moral standards— are masculinizing her daughter.) I toss both of them into the warm bright fire.

Somehow we're here. In how many pieces but here.

Gray would have enjoyed it.

Day Two

Well, Zeni managed to cajole, prod, force them and two suitcases down the mountain this morning. It took her three hours. I have to give her credit. The pregnant woman turned out to be the only one really able to navigate although she was forced into careful steps with many rest stops so she wouldn't fall. The last thing we need in our new happy home is a miscarriage.

The archeology (was it?) pair: the teenager's name is

16

Ann. She's totally delirious, lost in her arm and a high fever. Her foreign friend, Ingrid, nurses her now with cold packs on both their heads. (Cold water—we have nothing but.) Ingrid's handsome gold suit is bloodstiffened. Zeni's lent her some inelegant jeans.

The demonstration pair: Zeni's friend is Penny, whose glasses still slide. Nervous creature full of guilts about —doing her share.— Premature middle age. She alternates abject apologies for —my ridiculous behavior yesterday— (whatever it was, Ann's the only one who saw it and Ann's reduced to mumbling) with would-be efficient bustling around. Lifting pails she promptly spills, decorating the linoleum with my open can of beans. If she weren't too young by a few years, I'd guess it's the menopause—or the shakes from some pill she just ran out of.

When Zeni won't help, and Ingrid and Chrysta are too busy to pay attention to Penny (her flitting doesn't bother them), I fix her a cup of tea, find a mattress and bed her down. She quiets obediently like an exhausted two-year-old who knows she's *finally* got your attention. And thanks me profusely as I assure and reassure —No, you're not too much trouble. We all had a tough time, I know you couldn't sleep last night, don't worry about it . . .—

As I stroke her head, she falls asleep. The twilight softens her orange hair, her gaunt face. I'm glad she's back in the world of the sane (compared to yesterday) but I do hope one of us doesn't have to repeat the tea and sympathy routine with her every few hours.

P.m. I've figured out what frightens me about Penny. All those months when Gray was sick, unable to breathe, and my life and marriage got reduced to head and hand stroking, half finished sandwiches on trays, rainbow of pills on shelves. Then hospital and more hospital. Panic and terror during the long days with his bed the sole focus for food, comfort, love, reading, bedpans, dressings, visits from people he hadn't seen in so many years that he had to know he was dying. Nurse, nurse, we all feel

17

worse. Then numbness, entrapment, annoyance during the funeral days. Within fifteen minutes Penny had set off all those emotions, like cluster bombs, in me. I won't give in. I shan't travel that road again, as Ingrid would say.

If Chrysta knew, she'd declare all my nursing of Gray should have strengthened me into *just* the person to cope with Ann and Penny both, while the others tend fires, make food, haul water, repair bedsteads. If Chrysta knew . . .

To puzzle it all out, I pause during a water haul and pace the hill. My fantasies play—a downhill slalom around beanpoles now in the shed. I could stake them out in the snow. Are there skis in the cellar, too? Where somebody found the snowshoes? Let's name it . . . Slalom, Inc.? Dull. Pioneer Women's Slalom Championship Run? PWSCR for short. Pwisker. More tone but still too industrial. And too long . . . Chicks On Sticks. COS it's too male chauvinist, Zeni would hate it.

I glance at the sky. Gray clouds advancing. At the base of the slope the trees are already piling fog onto the house.

Day Three

The fog encloses us. We use the time to lick our wounds, explore the house, meet each other. Penny's condition has improved. After fifteen hours sleep she's at least upright although she still hovers too closely for my work comfort, teetering on her thin legs. Always pushing those glasses uphill to connect with her eyes. Sister Sisyphus who's forgetful as well as accident-prone; the first fog day Chrysta assigned her to feed wood to both black mouths in the kitchen and dining room. She fell asleep. I found her curled on one of the cold sofas, the wood piled around her instead of inside the stoves.

18

But the poor woman *is* ambulatory. Ann is another problem altogether. Except for Ingrid, the coordinates of her world seem to have collapsed. She's feverish at night; Ingrid sleeps with her and gets up to administer aspirin, massages, cold packs. During the daytime we all share reading her stories. (Mildewed Mark Twain, *Pickwick Papers*, and ancient magazines are all we've found so far; whatever they did in this house, they didn't read.) Also share listening to the tales *she* spins. At the age of nineteen she's still picking up pieces of some wretched childhood that sounds like *True Confessions.* Only nobody—*nobody*—loved her until the last year or so when she somehow managed a scholarship to a university where she met Ingrid and has lived (un)happily ever after.

Ingrid's a busy history professor, also an archeologist, from Czechoslovakia (or Germany?) to the U.S. via somewhere. I suspect Ann has more to cope with than she'll ever dig her way out of. An hour with her engenders the same claustrophobia I get with Penny. So I signal Chrysta or Zeni, who both have larger talents for telling jokes and getting the kid to laugh than I do. Sometimes they come, sometimes not.

Overseriousness, worry, fear. All the curses of our closed world here.

I've discovered what troubles me about Ann. If Penny recalls some of my worst marriage days, Ann wheedles me back even farther where I would not walk again—to the trauma and complicated lonelinesses of adolescence. Maybe I am a coward, but I find thirty a decent plateau, if a windy one sometimes. At least I get into less trouble (read this in ten years and laugh!) with parents, men, and cause-espousers than I used to. I need them all less, I guess.

Have I become one of those raunchy anti-community types who don't enjoy being alone but will prefer it to being with helpless, hopeless, awkward people? Ivy, be more clinging . . . On the other hand Zeni, Chrysta, and

Ingrid all fascinate me each in her own way. Ingrid because she is both disciplined and exotic.

Zeni just organized us a christening party. Having dug damp cardboard and crayon from a drawer, we lettered signs and hung a name under each dining room portrait of that elegant group whom Zeni had already called —Grammaw 'n the Patriarchs.— These are five antique oils strung across the wall, flanking the stove pipe. The background of each fades into clouds—a sort of alpine George Washington. Gilbert Stuart rides again.

The two with high foreheads, high collars, stern noses and sterner eyes are now —Isaac— and —Jacob.— —Moses— wears the one-foot beard; —Freud— the string tie and jawline whiskers. —Grammaw— is an androgynous creature whose iron eye, glabrous head, and narrow chin made me suggest —Paul VI— or —Lenin.— But Chrysta's eyebrows rose at the first, and Zeni digs the latter so we settled on —Carrie Nation.— God bless the Victorians; may we deserve no worse when our time comes.

Already Zeni overteases Chrysta. In fact, Zeni and I gain the same delight from twitting hyperserious people like Chrysta and Ingrid.

Yet Ingrid is a capable, gracious and graceful person— as delicate but strong as Penny seems weak and awkward. Learned as she must be, she hasn't forgotten how to work with her hands. Somehow this morning she was simultaneously splitting a log, stirring soup, and telling me of the Arabian —dig— to which she and Ann were bound for a semester's work. It's the gravemounds and mortal remains of an ancient city on the Persian Gulf. She manages to be both transparent (every emotion lights her eyes and face) and yet oblique with a dignity that we Amurricans, especially the garrulous and compulsively friendly, have lost somewhere between Plymouth Rock and Bellevue. I hate to call it European, but it probably is. Even her precise English makes me tone up my loose, transatlantic palate. And her brilliance tantalizes Ann, whose

eyes watch and worship. X times a day she asks
—Where's Ingrid?—

Despite Ann and Penny, the first fog day has an awesome charm of its own. As I yoke myself into pails and
start down the water trail, I get the intimate feeling of
being in a tent; I'm the tentpole. The world is equidistant
from me wherever I pass. Whatever pierces the fog comes
at me close and vivid against our common white.

I sleep badly that night. No matter how many times we
toast and turn the mattresses before the stoves, soon after
we lug them up to the three tiny bedrooms, they're dead
with cold and mildew again. Mine is extra cold because
I'm the odd number seven who sleeps alone. Somewhere
in that frigid white night I wake terrified that I'm sleeping
next to Gray again, and he's dying. When I reach out, he's
not there! When I fumble awake in the cold air, the
mound of quilts jerks me back to here. I lie awake then,
refusing tears, winding myself into smaller coils under the
covers.

Gray, I'm sorry.

While he was ill, I sat bedside and read in order to
avoid thinking, worked to avoid brooding, self pity and
similar destructions. Foolish to imagine some glorious
future with him, had not death imagined first. When we
were good, we were very good. But when we were bad
(two weeks a month), we were awful. And I ranted what
a bastard he was during the days I lost the first baby. And
he ranted about divorce and that if we weren't parents,
what's the use of two people living together and I'd better
just get busy and have another one. And I shouted —Have
it yourself! Who wants your goddamn baby?— And
brought the nurse running to my hospital bed and she
asked him to leave because we were scaring the other
mothers.

And I spent the night crying at one end and bleeding
at the other.

O the sidewalks are made of silver and the streets are
paved with gold . . .

21

Sorry that we ever tangled into each other. He de-
served a traditional little woman of nary a thought beyond his happiness, his house, and the contents of his
babies' diapers.

But, Gray, supermoms went out of style.

And what did I deserve? Surely not all the garbage.
—Why don't you shave your legs? What's the matter with
you? . . . Why are you wearing that dress? You know I
hate it . . . If you're getting sick, go in the other room.—

O the walls are made of diamonds . . .

I was —the coward, the pessimist,— somehow simultaneously —a brick wall— and —a hysterical mess.— I —mor-
tared myself together and didn't let anything out for anybody else.— He never comprehended that years of him
and a small town left me little self to mortar. Just the
resolution scrawled on the refrigerator door DON'T LET
HIM DRIVE YOU CRAZY. Or SHUT UP, SUBMIT.
THAT'S WHAT PEOPLE WANT. And FEAR'S OKAY
BUT DISOBEDIENCE—NEVER. Just guilt. And rage.
At all we might have been to each other and never were,
could be, will be.

Yet I can't repent or kid myself that if he were alive,
we'd get along better. All the strengths (money earning,
business charm and luck, apathy about politics and people) were his; all the weaknesses (fear, intensity about
anybody but him, failure to meet his standards) myste-
riously mine.

Gray, you were right about only one thing—how I hid
scared during all our years. Crept into nooks, fled wherever I thought I could stay Out of Trouble.

SEE THE HIDDEN WOMAN
25¢ ON SUNNY DAYS

Like those dolly figures, beflowered and bonneted, who
peek out the right side of weather houses only when the
sky's blue.

So I camouflaged cigarette holes on the sofa, mold on
the bread, souring milk, religious or political questions

that might prove depressing, our fights
"   "   "   "   , other questions
"   "   "   "   , other women's terrors,
breakups and -downs that truly were depressing.

The unexamined life may not be worth living, but it's
comfortable. Letting Gray decision the decisions, run our
life. His work always more important than mine because
it earned more money. Didn't I drop one job to marry him
and another to produce baby(ies) when he decided we
needed some? And I smiled away the years whenever people congratulated us as a handsome couple with a solid
marriage, charming home, beautiful baby. And petunias
in my flower bed.

He never even believed the hundred ways he terrorized
me. I never fixed the right confrontation that would have
urged us beyond the problems. Hiding from my hiding
didn't leave much time for dancing on the home front,
but I staged a good show, shuffling the soft shoe for em-
ployers and family gatherings. Like the movement men
who, Zeni says, burned down Columbia because that took
less courage than telling their tuition-paying parents when
to shove it.

—It sounds as if you've replaced romantic love with
friendship for us.— Under the blanket Gray propped himself on an elbow and stared at me. —You *might* have told
me.—

—I guess I have.— I hedged. Why did I still fear the company of any idea Gray hated? —The dream is grand, but
we'll never make it as lovers. We humiliate each other.
Why won't you settle for friends and be glad of that?—

Slammed his pillows against the headboard. —It's so
. . . damn anemic! Half a glass of *nothing*.—

—But your kind of love sticks us with rubbish. I don't
want to be worshipped like some art object in fancy wrap-
pings. And I won't be barked at like a servant by you, hungry children, and cocker spaniels when the worship
hour's over.—

23

—Shut up!—

Debt and regret.
Marriage counseling—garbage collection.
Marriage is l(only)onliness.

I lie awake over a trio of crappy sermons Gray and I
heard during our Catholic period. Week I dumped on
—the Executive— for being too absorbed in —the market-
place.— Week II dumped on —the Executive Wife— for no
longer making home —a Home for our poor tired Executive.— Week III dumped on both husband and wife for
not making —Executive Children— into —whole human
beings.—

Gray thought the sermons excellent; I couldn't remember when I'd heard such drivel from a celibate who, if he
were married and had a son busted in a Harvard drug
raid, would be shamed enough not to dump on anybody—
except maybe Harvard.

Me: —Well, everybody's relative in Father's hierarchy,
but some people are more relative than others.—

Gray overunderstood, replied that Father had discussed the situation just right. —After all, the executive
earns the family's money. So his needs should be considered first.—

—But that priest didn't *consider* you. He dumped on
you. Don't you realize that?—

—Well, I didn't take him seriously. Why're you so emotional about him?—

—Then what the hell are we talking about?— Edged our
way out of the parking lot. Politics/religion of the brick
wall.

We are molded and remolded by those who love us.
We are crunched and recrunched by those who are
supposed to love us.

24

Dawn.
Gray's over. You're out now!

Day Four

The fog continues. Penny paces nervously, sure the fog has made the planes stop hunting us altogether. I don't tell her that there's not much chance of anyone spotting that small plane on a mountain side anyway—or our present location even though Zeni optimistically left a note inside the plane for rescuers.

I don't know why, but I'm not fretting. Shock and fatigue, I guess. Our food supply here is limited; the fog increases my claustrophobia; and the pregnant woman's baby is soon due, according to Penny. The woman's name is Joette, also according to P. . . . You delivered your own baby at home. Original do-it-yourself project. Gray's face went wild when he found out.

During —lunch— (bacon, beans, soup; eating —more— at noon instead of evening helps us work, if not sleep, better) we fantasize about life Outside, about the family that must have lived here, when they'll return.

Zeni: —I bet they were hardy pioneers. Grammaw wouldn't have allowed any slackers in her family. Those snowshoes are mended every other thong.—

Joette: —I'll bet they moved away to Burlington or Boston. Raising corn, hay, and a few cows out back couldn't have provided much of a life.—

Ingrid: —From the size of the refuse heap, they were a whole *tribe*.—

Ann: —Ingrid—Ingrid found me a bottle and a military button.—

Ann's first whole sentence to all of us in a couple days. But we laugh, since it's Ingrid who blushes furiously. Because her gift has been revealed? Because her professional interest in civilization's effluvia hasn't abated even here?

25

Chrysta raps the table. —Jokes are fine, but we should begin walking out of here as soon as possible.—

We stare at her. This —business as usual— that's shattered a couple other humorous instants angers me anew. Or is she just aiding Ingrid, her sister Serious?

—Zeni, did you get the pilot's papers? Did you or Joette try to bury him?—

—What? No. He was dead, I mean . . .— Zeni's eyes open wide.

Chrysta twists her lips.

—Besides if we *had* buried him, the animals would just dig him up.—

—Tell me the truth, Zeni.— Her matriarchal I've-caught-you grates on me, too.

Zeni's chin thrusts forward. —Okay, okay. We didn't want to touch him!—

—No need to be so defensive, Zeni. I just asked you a question. You know, people have expectations about what's proper in, well, a situation like that. You mustn't frustrate too many of those expectations.—

—If you're so brave, I didn't see *you* hiking back up the hill . . . Crap!— Her chair falls backward. She stomps from the room.

Me: —Leave her alone, Chrysta, huh? It doesn't do any good.—

When Chrysta's face relaxes instantly into her peculiar thin-lipped smile, I suspect this tiff is a put-on. It went farther than she wanted, but it did get Zeni out of the room . . . The cane chairs creak. We stare at the stove, rainstained wallpaper, fogwhitened windows.

—When the fog lifts, it'll snow more, you know.— Chrysta's calm voice begins to threaten. —So . . . how many of you will walk out with me? Tomorrow morning, if the fog lifts. Ann, you need a doctor. Joette? . . . Penny? Your work—

Penny: —But we still don't know which way to walk.—

Zeni's words. Exiling her to avoid counterargument has made us remember her more.

Chrysta: —We were guided here. I know we'll be guided down to the town.—

Suddenly Zeni appears among us again, carrying two lighted candles. She plunks them onto the table. Her steel-rimmed glasses catch the light. —Listen, all of you. There's no town down there. We all saw exactly nothing off that cliff. If it does snow, we'll just freeze. Here we've got food and a house.— Hand on one hip, boot on Ann's chair. A pioneer general with no troops.

Chrysta has stopped smiling.

—Listen, all those rescues you read about, the Coast Guards, the St. Bernards, the whole bit—they all assume people *want* to get back where they came from. I don't know about you, but I spent the last ten years getting outa where *I* came from . . .—

Chrysta's eyebrows arch. I'm enjoying this.

—Today's Saturday.— Zeni exhales. —I'm supposed to be speaking at a teach-in at Columbia today. Chrysta, I won't bore you with what I was going to say, but it's mostly like, why don't we just spend the winter here? Let the zoning commission kick us out when they find us . . . What's the world ever done for any of you anyway?—

—Zeni! You're selfish and shortsighted.— Chrysta's composure crumbles. Zeni has scored one. A log crackles and falls to the stove bottom. Firelight flares. Elbows on table, fists under chin, Chrysta tries again. —*You* may want to stay. But remember we're six others here . . . Zeni, this demonstration in New York, what was it against? Some war?—

—No. It was *for*. For women's liberation.— Zeni calms. —I teach at a women's college. If you wanna see a bunch of crippled egos, sweet and petrified, just spend an hour with those chicks. They—

I expect Chrysta to shout —Nonsense!— but instead she contents herself with —All right. I won't pass judgment on that. Some people need it, but I've always thought people were liberated from the inside first. Through work, through prayer, through devotion to a community. Then it didn't matter what—

—I suppose you consider your Catholic Church a community?—

—My Christian friends have been good to me. Including the Catholics you don't like. I'm a member of—

—Well, why do you bother with an organization that two thousand years later considers you a second-class citizen?—

—Because I love Christ! . . . Anyway, your question is nonsense. Women have never done more in the churches than they do today.—

—Except run them! Love your bondage. Makes you the perfect slave, doesn't it?—

Chrysta's mouth hangs open. Is it Zeni's grain of truth among all the rhetoric?

Ingrid bangs a fist onto the table. —Zeni! Both of you, stop it. Not to worry about it. Doesn't matter here.—

To my surprise Zeni sits down.

With visible effort of eyebrows and mouth, Chrysta returns to business. —When . . . when the fog lifts, who's coming with me? I assume not *all* of you just want to *sit* here? Ingrid?—

Zeni remains silent. Whatever drives her seems to exhaust itself after short spasms.

Ingrid: —I'll stay. If I can find some paper, I'll work here. We've missed all our travel connections anyway.—

Ann: —I'm staying.— Cradles her arm, glances toward Ingrid.

Chrysta's eyes narrow. —Penny?—

—I'm coming with *you*. My husband and kids must be frantic by now. And I want my doctor to look at my back.— Penny bites her knuckles. —I already had my vacation this year anyway.— She smiles, but the joke flattens as Chrysta presses onward.

—Joette? Certainly *you* should come.—

Joette: —I'd just slow you all down. I better stay and hope somebody finds us . . . I've done a lot of camping. I wasn't raised here in the East like the rest of you.— Annoyed, Ingrid shakes her head. —Chrysta, you're not an outdoor person. I don't think you know what you're getting into. That's all.—

Chrysta ignores her and turns to me. —Ivy, I know *you're* coming.—

—No.— Am I sure? —I agree with Joette. A hundred mile hike's not for me either.— Carefully phrased in the land of geography instead of Zeni vs. Chrysta.

Chrysta frowns. It's her own fault for tricking Zeni from the room in the first place, for making this a loyalty oath session. Has Zeni really unsured her? Or is she so sure it doesn't matter?

—When I got on that plane last Wednesday, I had no idea most of you were . . . *dropouts*.— Tries for drama to shame us. It just sounds peevish.

Zeni: —We're not. Just call us homebodies.—

Ann snickers. For her the closest to a laugh she's ever shown us. Ingrid stares out the window.

Day Five

Fogbound still. Despite Chrysta's bustling around, packing foodscraps, blankets, hunting more matches, a white silence hangs in the house, too. That we've blown something that could have progressed or ended differently if Chrysta were less matriarchal, Zeni less explosive, the rest of us less cowardly or at least more willing to get involved, if—I chuck it and walk about the hill.

But the bushes, posts, well roof, frosted pines, everything that seemed alive in the first day's fog now disappears behind me wherever I pass. They exist only in memory; even there I blur them: was the post painted, does

29

the house look at me with two or three windows? I begin to doubt that any outside world exists, except in my imagination and Chrysta's hopes.

Day Six

Reluctant rising of cold watery sun. At breakfast Chrysta comes on quite her efficient usual self. To continue this mood, we too hustle around the kitchen and onto the porch, helping her and Penny wrap and rope blankets into backpacks. Ann offers Chrysta an orange and the last bit of chocolate from the plane. Minus Zeni, we're a circle on the porch. Penny has linked our arms as if we were class reunioning.

Chrysta and Penny are contrasts—Chrysta silent, her gaze already outward, Penny chattering compulsively. —I'm sure they'll pick us up. The pilot must have radioed our position before we came down. I know they'll see us. Don't worry about us. We'll make it all right. *You're* the ones *I'm* worried about. What if you run out of food before they find you? . . .—

I tune her out long enough to realize she's terrified.

It's Chrysta who interrupts the flow. —Ann, take care. Don't forget what I told you last night?— She smiles, takes Ann's hand.

Now Zeni appears barefoot, barelegged, topped by an Army shirt and moth-holed Canadian Mounty hat from the attic. Shuts Penny up, replaces sentimental goodbyes with hoots and jokes. She's released us from ourselves. Even Chrysta laughs and pulls Penny off the porch toward the white and green. To the road Chrysta is sure exists. Every few feet Penny turns and waves at us.

This afternoon I talk with Ann. Ingrid has found some kind of gloppy plaster mix in the cellar. While she tests it on herself before cementing Ann's wrist, I build a bright bonfire over the living room hearth and try with talk to divert Ann from her swollen arm. The fire turns her dreamy: she doesn't talk or answer questions so much as dip into a semicoherent wordstream that always seems to be flowing under her surface. As if she'd just awakened, and focusing on the world must be unbearable effort, at least unwelcome intrusion.

—Chrysta was so great to me last night . . . really miss her . . . a whole hour. Do you know her faith is so great, I mean it's really beautiful. She really believes God has put us here to test ourselves to learn about ourselves, to test our faith in everything. It makes her so strong. She was so kind to me last night, she said my wrist would heal, I know there's something buried in the bone, I know she wanted me to come with her, do you think she wanted me to come with her?—

At first I'm uncomfortable, trying to devise answers that won't be lies. I relax when I see she expects none, at least from me, although she looks straight at me with each question. She's used to mumbling onward without response; if I left, she'd hardly notice. All punctuated with her peculiar series of precise but vacant tics—a hesitant smirk, shrug of her right shoulder, inhaling, squaring both shoulders under the incongruous scarf, hot pink, she wears day and night. It seems a magical pantomime designed to ward off me and the world, as if we were about to jump her, just as the talk-talk in its own way prevents us from existing.

—Don't tell Ingrid but I'm not sorry now . . . we won't get to Egypt or Arabia. Ingrid's so clever and educated. I couldn't have done the work there anyway.—

—How do you know if you haven't tried it?—

—I have! Why do you say that? Last summer we—

So she has to be injured into talking? —All the better. So why do you think you'll fail?—

—Because I *hate* Ingrid!—

Now I stare at her. Grasp her good arm, try to shake

31

her back to now. The poor kid, huddled roundshouldered in her chair. Zeni in an oversize shirt is funny, but this girl in her own clothes, fuchsia scarf and highwaisted dress, is a dazed creature, a vixen with tiny teeth. Maybe Ingrid can explain her to me. A firstclass crippled ego for Zeni to repair.

The water in this morning's sun fulfills its threat. By dark at five it's snowing. Silent supper, expecting any moment to hear Chrysta and Penny clump onto the porch. But one course of beans is soon over. No one comes. Zeni takes our current candle and lights us up the stairs. Early bed to keep warm as if we'd been naughty. Joette comes to sleep in my room now. She's so much heavier than I am that our whole mattress tilts downhill to meet her. But not being alone any more among the gray shapes is good.

Ann's crying in her room at something Ingrid said. I pull the covers over my head. I can't get involved again tonight. My claustrophobia comes out to play, predictable as the allday damp. We could be so much to each other here if we tried.

Don't know which day this is. Snow has stopped.

They didn't return.

Zeni has assigned us all new jobs. She may not possess Chrysta's accumulated wisdom, but she's a hell of a lot more honest and much more fun. I'm in charge of what we're calling —hunting.— Joette's showing me how to rig ropesnares. Maybe I'll bag a snow monster; we'd settle for a nice deer—the dumb, young kind that walks into such things.

I'm also gathering the right evergreens and birchbarks for these drinks and soups Joette brews. Spruce and pines around a slushy pond with a brook cascading from it. Maybe I can fish it when it freezes hard. Is hemlock really poison?

32

While Joette cooks and dishscrapes, Zeni chops wood, Ingrid fetches water, and Ann's in charge of —housekeeping,— which is mostly rearranging blanket mounds. Without hot running water, it's delightful how much cleaning you don't have to do. May you rot in your dirt unto the third generation. At four o'clock we gather round the table for Joette's latest tea and reading.

Zeni's turning into an excellent first lieutenant. No flattery, no tiptoeing or apparent worry about hurt feelings, just brisk expectations that we'll all keep busy and not plague each other. My kind of woman—or is it boss?! Yet she doesn't sweep things under the carpet we don't even have—she knows Ann's clinging puppiness is increasing Ingrid's tenseness.

Tonight's a celebration anyway. On the animal trail one of my snares caught a rabbit. Strangled it neatly. Joette's stew—our first fresh meat in a week.

Our next difficulty will be Joette's. She keeps her own counsel; so far only Zeni knows just when the baby (ies?) are expected. With our luck it's supposed to be twins. My mattress will believe it. Every time we ask, she just puts a finger to her lips as if the babies might hear. She brushes off any extra concern from us, but Zeni's started dishing up the noon meal so she can sneak extra beans and vegetables onto Joette's plate.

—My— rabbit was tough; maybe the young ones aren't the dumb ones.

Weird Bang-up Night Around Here

Can't figure it out. I thought the strong always win what they want. But sometimes the meek turn out more dangerous if for the wrong half hour they escape their cages.

I'd crept out of my side of the bed, found my icy slippers (Grammaw wore them out long before we arrived) and snuck from the room without waking Joette. My stomach was growling; maybe Joette saved *something* from supper? I continued creeping—the darkness and because I felt guilty. There isn't so much food around that anybody ought to sneak midnight snacks . . . But I work so should eat—even Marx *a la* Zeni says so.

When I reached the hall at the bottom of the stairs, I saw firelight leaping round the dining room. The place is burning? I shivered.

Then I heard a shriek, more rage than terror. I ran in. Crunched broken glass. Ann, that odd little vixen, swinging a poker through the yellow and black air. She's practicing golf?

Next I saw Ingrid heaped on the floor. The mad girl had actually hit Ingrid with the damn thing.

By this time somebody else was clumping downstairs. Zeni beside me. Together we unfisted Ann's poker. Zeni began shaking her until the poor kid's hair swung and her teeth rattled.

—What the hell's the matter with you? It's not enough to follow her everywhere—do you have to kill her?—

While Zeni stood firm, Ann wilted onto a chair. I knelt beside Ingrid . . .

I can't believe the whole thing yet. Chrysta's an antique, but I wonder whether her god could help her make sense . of this.

for Ann

JAY → ON → OUR → WAY
  A WILY ANN ALWAYS HUNTS UPON THE ANN
  UNINHABITED AS CHRYSOSTOMS
  A REDGOLD AMAZON ALWAYS TRAVELS IN THE FIRESHADOW
  CLEVERLY REDCOLDLY WILILY
SPY → ON → THE → SLY

GO TO INGRID WAITS

INGRID WAITS

Ann the Scribbler: Ingrid is a demon
Ingrid is a witch
When the gods stayed at our house—
(Ann could never finish it.)

That venerated and venerable myth by which woman, creating all things, becomes at last the Mother of God.
Male and female she created them.
No god so great but death can kill him.

In Buddhist literature the Arhat or saint is repeatedly described as achieving Nirvana in this life by acquiring its seven constituent parts: self-possession, investigation into the truth, energy, calm, joy, concentration, and magnanimity. These are its content, but hardly its productive cause: the cause and source of Nirvana is the extinction of selfish desire; and Nirvana, in most early contexts, comes to mean the painless peace that rewards the moral annihilation of the self.

Our Oriental Heritage

All the Ingrid pieces—why don't they tear Ingrid apart? (Ann wondered, hanging like a small, humpshouldered animal over the desk, sweating while Ingrid's cool black eyes swept Ann's application.) All the Ingrid pieces had instead interlocked. She's so . . . well, purposeful. Inside and outside and outside at-oned. Her life fits her! She fits it, fits it.
—I mean your work and life, they're so beautiful.—
Confronted with such yearning admiration at the end of a ten-hour day (counseling, teaching, faculty meeting, an hour mediating a student sit-in—"the decline in community spirit has now reached the point . . ."—and what happened to that other hour around lunch time?), Ingrid merely mumbled thank you. And gazed at

<pre>
          the   Henry
    leaning pisas   her research
    of exam papers   assistant's
    unread history   inkspattered
    journals, notes   adolescent
    for a talk she   bungling of
    was giving at   (goddamn him)
    Boston Museum   her original
 transcribed minutes of   drawings and photos made
committee (goddamn them) meetings   at last winter's dig on the Persian Gulf
</pre>

And here stood Ann, messily unraveling tadpole skeins of herself about Ingrid's desk. No, not a tadpole, maybe a halfmade basket that's survived an earthquake or a millennium in the village compost heap. Couldn't these American teenagers rouse themselves more than five minutes from the torpors of *nouveau* introspection (or was it premature exhaustion?) to concentrate on the *work*, the discipline, instead of the personalities performing it? Really this one was brilliant—but hopeless; she regretted having favored her in the first place with compliments, gifts, a trial by fire before her best class. *Ach,* but the child's intensity that she'd interpreted as strength when it was actually misery, a plea for a life jacket in the swamps of self-pity . . .

Whenever she succumbed to one of these rages, she regretted having become an American citizen. (The plastic statue on the judge's bench, the lady with the scales—before her eyes—American justice blinded.) But anti-Americanism was so fashionable these days. How to be against the people who were against America without seeming twice a traitor to herself?

How lucky you are these days! When I was young, there wasn't a good teacher to be found. At least I couldn't uncover one. But the truth is I was rather simple when young, and made one blunder after another. And the fruitless efforts! I don't suppose I'll ever forget those days, if only because they were so painful. That's why I come here every day. I want to teach you how to avoid the blunders I made. How lucky you are these days!
                              Zen: Poems, Prayers

—Why didn't you stay in Europe? Here they promote a man over a woman every time—and five years sooner. Read this letter we've got together for the ACLU about Cynthia's—

—If you don't like this country, why don't you teach in Germany again? It's straight research and lecturing there—no identity crises. Or they work them out slaloming and youth hosteling.—

Hostile youth. If they bug me now (she watched horrified and amused as their slang seeped increasingly into her head, her speech, even her dreams—the persistent one where she was rushing down the dark maze of corridors to her Ph.D. orals and she couldn't find, what was it? . . . the —friggin' room.—) Saddled even in her dawn dream with Henry's all-purpose adjective for the recalcitrant material world. Vivid, yes, but imprecise, unscientific, okay, a vulgar metaphor. *Die Gedanken sind frei?* Foolishness!

SCSCSCSCSCSCSCSCSCSC SC! Sabbatical Coming!

How she'd love to divide it between (1) the Persian Gulf and (2) delving again among the jungle temples and discredited deities of Cambodia or Laos—before the Americans or the guerillas bombed them off the east of the world . . .

Q: —What hope is there for contemporary man to remedy his future unless historians show him the mistakes of his past?—

A: —History proves nobody reads history. That includes historians.—

Q: —Then what, my dear Carlyle, shall we do with our modern historians, especially those who worship at the temples of process instead of personality, of determinism within the social context instead of free will for philosopher kings?—

A: —Why banish them from the state, of course, from corrosive influence upon the sensitive young.—

Q: —And what if these young have already been corroded and trampled, their life circuits shorted, their wires frayed, their only spark the white light of rage?—

A: —Why, toss *them* out too and begin humanity anew with a super race into whose genes the necessary life skills (walking, talking, and the like) have been preprogrammed, including genes for curiosity, love of surprises and of the inalienable rights to life, liberty, and happy pursuit of that bitch goddess—Making Your Own Mistakes.

—What the world needs is scientists with souls or, conversely, romantics with brains . . .

Faculty Meeting

—Now about the coming departmental election, I think we should leave no possibility unscrutinized—

—Does Ingrid want the job again?—

—Okay, Bob, *you* be department head. I got hit by a brick last year.—

—The unrevolting life is not worth living.—

What d'you get when you cross an aging radical with a paraplegic?—

—A kneejerk liberal.—

—What's six feet high and one inch wide?—

—Two schizophrenics side by side.—

—When's a German not a German?—

—When his *Panzer* on backwards . . . Oh, sorry, Ingrid. Didn't know you were here. No offense meant.—

With delight she remembered screwing *him* good last year by assigning him a Saturday eight a.m. class plus a Senior Life Goals Seminar plus a freshman encounter group (remedial sensitivity training, she called it privately). Fun for the Phoebe-minded. Phoebe being the sort of archetypal Lost Student, male and/or female, who, Ingrid discovered with chagrin, seemed ever more attracted (and attractive) to her year by year. The phenomenon made her feel somewhere between a Teutonic goddess and a mother hen. Flattering but, well, futile. Valhalla will get you if you don't watch out.

> Never tussle with a Teuton
> When she's really shootin'
> Though her attitude is teasin'
> Her breastplate is reason
>> And she may stab you in the end,
>> Oh, she'll get you in the end.

Don't get involved! Don't get involved with anyone, whoever he happens to be; rather by ridding yourself of the need for others (which is really a form of self-love) remain in the Buddha-mind.

If you don't fabricate illusions, none will disturb you. Certainly you were born with none. So do not blame them on your parents. Only your selfishness and deplorable mental habits bring them into being. Yet you think of them as inborn, and in everything you do, you continue to stray.

Zen: Poems, Prayers

The boys fell in love with her, and the girls? A harder problem because Ingrid felt worse about discouraging some of their personal attentions to her. The boys could (and did) promptly fall in love with somebody else, but the girls? There were so few women around campus of any staunch and resilience whom the girls could model themselves on, measure up to, rebel against.

Which returned her to Ann, whose childhood was apparently so bereft of proper mothering that she, silent as winter dawn, willingly performed Ingrid's most menial tasks, things even Henry —forgot— to do, like dump wastebaskets, dust the office, file cards, keep library books from getting embarrassingly overdue, mimeograph forms, lie to book salesmen. Her small face alight at the merest smile or nod. Brilliant but so shy her tongue tangled every other

41

sentence. What a ghastly dance the more militant students must lead her. Delicate, soul-eyed creature. How did American small towns still raise girls like her?

Ingrid alternated sorrow for her with passion to see what Ann would become when all her shorted strands finally meshed into a recognizable adult.

> Now it was my turn to begin helping others, and I have been doing just that ever since. That's why I come here to talk to you. It is my desire to bear witness to your satori. You must feel that you have had an awakening, and those of you who haven't had the experience, listen carefully to my words. It's in each of you to utterly change your life!
>
> *Zen: Poems, Prayers*

Ann the Snooper/Wily Spy on the Sly

INGRID URSULA ROSENDAHL
Born September 16, 1936, Stuttgart, Germany
father—industrialist and amateur archeologist, shot by . . .
mother—primary school teacher, killed in . . .
education—primary and secondary schools, Stuttgart
    Stuttgart and Heidelberg universities, Ph.D. in Classical
    Archeology
specialty—Greek and Near Eastern cultures
    fieldwork at Corinth and island of Delos, Greece; Bahrain, Persian Gulf
Her great-grandfather one of original explorers of royal
    tombs at Thebes, Egypt, early 19th century
married October 18, 1960 to David Randall, Pnom Penh,
    Cambodia . . .

Teasing document. How to fix Ingrid, to capture her among these barren facts, the frivolous curlyhaired passport photo, crescent scar camouflaged; the hasty signature, fiercely underscored? . . .

42

Ann's Fantasy for the Fearful

In the beginning the goddess Ingrid roamed the earth
*S*eeking her father
    who was not with her mother because
IT was all over
ALL a very long war long wars having become
    fashionable in those days because all adversaries hav-
                            ing the ultimate
*W*eapon were checkmated   in the art
*O*f war before the war eve-
R began only nobody told them that so they fought on
                                     skilled
*T*horoughly in unartful crimes against unarmed civilians
                                 who were
*H*orribly easier to kill thoroughly or haul off to detention
                                   centers
    compared to armed troops who had a nasty habit of
                        fighting back whenever they
    could which wasn't often
*I*f you bombed them thoroughly then rehabilitated
*T*hem through the Marshall or some other plan that show-
?   ed your basic benevolence
??? and dedication to peace and posterity under justice
?   and prosperity
    or was it despite prosperity   to spite posterity?

    anyway world war ii was everybody's most impor-
                        tant product
    anything else is just exercises to save the world
    from ourselves just start us off
    and we'll reason anywhere   mostly o$_{f_f}$

    Then Ann savored the one evening in two years when In-
grid, drunk and tired on her birthday, made tales of her
personal past.

—For months and months we never heard the least word from him. Then my mother would read a ragged letter to my brother and me. It would be dated two months before and signed *Va*. Well, that's how I get to know my father—from photos and hieroglyphs.— Ingrid smiled.

—One of Hitler's ministries had ordered him to Czechoslovakia in 1939 to supervise Czech textile production in —che.— (Ann couldn't make out the whole name.)

—Yes, my father was a Nazi sympathizer. As far as I know—maybe my mother lied—he never joined Hitler's party. In fact, I still get letters from Jewish families in England whom he helped to escape. Before the Americans bombed, I used to play lookout on the wooden landing outside our door. I'd watch the men who came into the building, especially the rare ones not in uniform. If they had homburg hats or *lederhosen* from our other life. Are you coming to see my mother? I'd ask.

—Once in a crowded tram I stood next to a man's hairy knees sticking out of *lederhosen* and I rubbed them. The man made eyes at my mother—he thought she'd done it. When we climbed down from the tram, my mother's face was pink. She slapped my hands and face and told me I must never do such things. It wasn't ladylike. What would the men think?

—In our flat an oak dinner chair became sacred to me. I was sure my father had sat on it. I cried if anybody, even my mother, used it. I pulled a red velvet rope with tassles off the draperies and laced it between the chair arms like the thrones you see in museums. Oh, I was a sentimental little girl, isn't that so? But that was a long time ago . . .—

Ann continued piecing details. The family lived from rumor to rumor smuggled from Czechoslovakia. That *Va* was captured by Czech partisans but was still alive. His friends were arranging secret passage back to Germany. That his friends or German officials in his company were paying ransom. That . . . During one year's autumn she suffered a nightmare. Her father would be lying on a table under a pine canopy with the velvet rope across his arms and legs. His face would be calm, translucent like wax. Whatever he'd suffered, he'd survived and would wake any moment. If she could just climb up and reach him. With him she'd be safe.

With each rumor her mother retreated farther into the landscape of grief. When she clasped the children to her in front of his smiling photos (every table and shelf was an altar), Ingrid memorized his high cheekbones, long nose, crooked tie. But she squirmed from her mother's arms to escape the blotched face and swollen eyes, the collapsed shoulders. She flung herself on her cot, trembling until her body locked and froze. If her mother touched her again, she'd shatter. Why couldn't her mother see how peaceful he looked (she *knew* it), waiting for Ingrid to awaken him?

At her grandparents' apartment she provoked the worst outburst by asking why her father was talking to the man on the wall. Her grandmother gagged; her grandfather's mouth jabbered away at her. Fresh surge of maternal sobbing. On the wall hung a reproduction of Christ before Pilate.

Every six weeks she lived through days of vomiting, but she'd neither cry before anybody, especially her mother, nor answer anybody's questions. And daily she climbed into the potato bin, the coal cellar, the wardrobe corner, wherever she could curl up alone in the dark with her father . . .

ANN'S DETECTIVE WORK: each incident savored in a time loop of fantasy that began now, journeyed to then, returned to now. She cursed her own background whose chief feature had been not world history but the middle-class American quota of petty tensions, squabbles over money and schoolwork. Nothing of *her* life would ever appear in anybody's history book—nothing there to fascinate Ingrid.

How did people like Ingrid manage it? Whatever happened, no matter how awesome, even their own dying would somehow not defeat them; it would merely settle silklike on their shoulders, wrapping them in further layers of competence and courage. Where did they capture such radiance? . . .

—When more months and months went by without letters, I imagined him in prison camp or escaping alone back to us. But no matter what I did to him in my fantasy world, he was always calm and handsome. Like the photos. Like the letters.

—Then my mother was killed in the summer bombing of Stuttgart. I'd thought I couldn't stand her, but now I missed her dreadfully. I was sorry I'd been so mean to her. My brother and I lived with my grandparents after that . . .

—So at last it was after the war. There was no milk or apples yet, just potatoes and bits of bacon fat for meat, but the trains were running again.— (Ann looked puzzled.) —Oh, potatoes and trains always go together for me. That's the only food my grandmother and I could find for the trip into Czechoslovakia—two raw potatoes.

—The archive office wasn't very helpful, but we wouldn't leave until they told us the truth. In October, 1943—that was exactly the season of my nightmares—they said the Czech partisans had succeeded in capturing my father. They tied him to a tree outside the city.

—They had a whole file on my father; to them he was a criminal. Before my grandmother could shuffle the archive photo under the other papers, I saw it. I had come so far and now I saw it. Now it was near.

—His murder had been a prominent occasion for all German-hating Czechs. One officer, arriving a half hour after the firing squad had done its work, remarked, Oh, I'm sorry I missed it.—

What Ingrid saw: a naked thing, black streaked, crumpled

46

at the foot of a tree, right half of the head torn off, lip pieces parted in a snarl, one eyewhite rolled upward. That thing was *not* her father; it couldn't be. But her grandmother, reading the words, began to cry . . .

The man at the archives was very sorry but now, so many years afterward, no, it wasn't likely that any of the three partisans holding guns in the picture could be identified. He was quite sure they'd been sent to prison camp. No, they weren't from this district, anyway . . .

As a teacher Miss Rosendahl is real neat. She relates very well to our class. History in high school was never one of my favorite subjects because I have trouble remembering dates and names, but Miss Rosendahl makes it clear it's not how much you remember, it's what you know that counts. At first I had trouble understanding her accent, which is Bavarian I think. And also her method—she doesn't teach (like standing up in front and telling us facts to write down for tests). Mostly she sits. Then she meditates about her subject and lets us watch her or come along on her trip. Usually we hardly ever stick only to the past; I mean she talks about the present, too, which is more interesting. Some days she's really where it's at. I hope you don't think she's a Communist and that's the reason for this questionnaire. I feel she is really helping us activate our potential.

P.S. About her accent—I mean everybody understands her okay. Just a few words like "tull" for "toll" and "*Stay*ten Island" are like different.

Interdepartmental Memorandum

Ingrid Rosendahl is a graceful, spirited woman in her thirties. Her face is unusually serene, even severe in repose as she listens to a question. Her smile, however, is extraordinarily radiant. She conducts an interview in the same way she structures her classes—by taking your question and mulling it around for a few seconds. Then she may use it as launch pad for free flow of her own ideas. "I don't talk to students. I get them to talk to themselves, ask themselves questions. Then they pull out of me whatever they want. So I can say anything." Or she may toss your question back at you, preferring to sit silently.

On the day of my visit her office was so neat it looked unused (desk cleared, floor shiny). "Oh, all this is my Ann's doing. The girl's a gem. I've never had an assistant like her," she remarked to the drapes and ten-foot high bookshelves. "Ann, come out. We're saying nice things about you." And from the drapery, puppet-like on cue, emerged a small attractive teenager, her hands and sleeves smudged from a pile of blueprints she was sorting.

Miss Rosendahl smiles at her; Ann responds by looking pleased and flushed at the same time. (Doses of ego-building flattery are also part of her educational method.)

She's accused of being dogmatic about her subject. "Oh, everybody born in Germany has to listen to that charge. It doesn't bother me any more. I'm an American now. Why don't you concentrate on that?"

Miss Rosendahl bristles easily. In the class I witnessed she halted a co-ed who was three pages into a paper on Greek art: "Stop reading! You're boring us. You haven't one original idea in that paper." The unfortunate girl folded it and retreated rapidly to the rear.

Yet she encourages clashes of opinion among students, at times aiding others like Ann who would probably be unable to articulate their own thoughts fast enough to win a discussion round. "Of course, I ask a certain amount of discipline of them, but I give them every opportunity to stand up to me and to each other. I don't like to be surrounded either by yes-people or by those wishy-washy groupy types who believe you ought to be nice to everybody—even if it kills *you* in the process." She laughs.

"Anyhow, I try to give my students an honest crack at

using their own minds. I turn them loose in history with a few assigned readings, mostly the original documents. I won't teach those indigestible survey courses any more; they're for historiographers, not human beings anyway.

"So when they've read a little together, we float a trial answer to a question, a trial model of how those poor fools back when coped with *their* society. I nudge them to see that while this is *our* moment, the human race was off on its goose chase long before *we* hit the scene. Radical new idea to some of them.

"I admit my favorite places are Cambodia, Delos, wherever else I've done archeological work. They're, of course, the realest to me. But I hate the notion of archeology as only artifacts, halfcracked vases in a museum where your feet get sore. Which is what everybody thinks. Any culture excites me if a team of people and I can figure out what their daily life was like, what did they work at, what did they believe in, what did it all mean, in other words.

"I'm not a library researcher. I hate getting lost in other people's time charts and Ph.D. rubbish. What excites me is going there, getting out the shovel, and sifting wherever-it-is through my own hands."

"Your own rubbish maybe?"

"So you rediscovered your tongue. I assume the 'friendly' portion of the interview is now over?"

"Miss Rosendahl, I've heard that you use fieldwork for another purpose. Shall I say an escape hatch from campus pressures?"

She exhales sharply. "Oh, is that all? *Ja*, and you oppose that? Bet you're really a spy from Educational Policy Committee." A radiant smile that lasts an instant. "Well, I believe academic types should contribute to solving social problems, but if you join the sociology binge too young, it creates an identity crisis when you realize there's not an awful lot you personally can do—unless you're a genius loaded with cash. *Are* you?"

There are rumors that students of both sexes attach

49

themselves to her, shower her with gifts, and that far from discouraging this devotion she indeed cultivates it. However, there is no evidence that she has gone beyond the bounds of student-teacher relationships.

Miss Rosendahl's comment was: "If we trusted love, it would not obsess us. If we trusted ourselves, they would not obsess us."

A Sieglinde with a mission
Is a gal with ammunition.
You think she's merely female
But—oh!—that's another kind of he-male.
 Oh, she'll get you in the end,
 Yes, she's got you in the end.

Dr. Heinrich Rosendahl, Thebes, Egypt, 1820

When I had passed through the large hall, the gallery and such wider tunnels as previous explorers had already cleared of rubble, Signor Belzoni and I found ourselves in pitch blackness crawling on our hands and knees through mounds of sand that formed the floor of one small tunnel. Since he is well over six feet tall, such mode of travel was among the most difficult imaginable.

I was creeping ahead of him, vastly afraid that our passage would cause the porous stone above us to collapse and bury us forever with the mummies. These personages waited somewhere ahead of us and after forty centuries were not about to surrender easily either their secrets or their papyri. At one point the tunnel constricted to one foot high so that we crawled belly down like serpents, the dust and sand entering our nostrils and ears, choking our throats. Sharp rocks ripped our flesh and clothing.

After perhaps two hundred yards of such arduous travel, I discovered I could raise my head, sit up, and stretch my arms before me. Expecting the jagged "floor" either to continue or to end abruptly at an impenetrable wall, I was both disconcerted and elated when I groped into the blackness and discovered—a void. My hands could touch nothing!

With much effort during which I was forced to inhale sand, powdery dust, and an increasing stench, I found and lit my

50

packet of candles. It was then we discovered that we were squatting at the knife edge of a black hole. Had I groped forward one more foot, I would have plunged into it and broken my limbs on whatever lay below. Despite these fears and the breathing difficulty I was eager to explore further, if only to ascertain whether the ancients had truly hewn our tunnel or whether it was a more recent excavation made by grave robbers like ourselves.

While Signor Belzoni braced himself and held the rope, I lowered myself over the edge into darkness. About ten feet down my feet reached a porous substance like a forest floor when covered with dry pine needles. Exhausted and near to fainting, I sank down upon it. With a crash it collapsed and pitched me outward into what seemed to be a pile of debris. Such a dust storm arose that I ceased movement for a quarter hour until it subsided.

When I dared again move my arms and relight my candles, I then perceived with horror the true nature of the "forest floor" to which I had sunk so gratefully. It was an immense terrain of splintered wood cases, linen rags, human skulls and bones. I could not refrain from crying out in terror at this charnel house flickering before me, larger than any burial chamber I had ever seen.

And what had collapsed under me? My bruised hands encountered—the remains of a human corpse, the mummy which had made its last protest even as I was destroying it. Everywhere I looked, mummies: a dreadful vista of mummies on the floor, in wall niches, some lying, some standing head up or down against the walls, some in painted wooden cases, others bound just in linen strips. Displayed before me as it had lain forty centuries was the acme of embalmers' art—a veritable horde of corpses, a silent city of the dead. Shiver after shiver racked my body. Wherever my hands grasped for something solid, they were tangled in fetid rags, crumbling ropes, and the eyeholes of a human skull.

By this time Signor Belzoni was shouting in the Italian language, not daring to extinguish his candle or come down himself until I had assured him I was still alive. I had just struggled to my feet and taken one step when I pitched forward again along the downslope of the uneven floor. This time I sank totally into debris: rags, legs, arms, heads avalanching upon me from above. I lost my candles. My throat and lungs filled with noxious dust; my insides smelled and tasted mildewed mummy. I fainted, buried there among the mummies . . .

51

I know not how many minutes or hours later, Signor Belzoni was restoring me to that scene of which I dreamed for so many years afterward. Despite the rolling bones he had already snatched a fair bundle of papyri by pulling them from between the thighs of this corpse, from under the arms of that one, and so on for as many as he could reach. When he saw my shudders, he desisted. Yet I continued to shrink in terror as I had not before that day nor have since during this expedition.

But for whatever reason, I could never bring myself to enter again that room choked with mummies . . .

(translated by Dr. Ingrid Rosendahl)

She never read her great grandfather's words to her classes without a combined surge of pride and shame—that old Heinrich had got far but not far enough, that he had, as the Americans say, —chickened out.— Her own plans for this year had been such a glorious dream when she'd first conceived them: Ann (sturdier now than last year's fleeting chipmunk) and she would fly to Cairo, sail briefly up the Nile to Thebes. She'd obtained a special visa and permit to wander among the antiquities, including some of the rarer masks and gold vessels discovered by Heinrich and not usually displayed to visitors. Then they were to fly from Cairo over Saudi Arabia to the Persian Gulf, the site of her major work for the last ten years . . .

Heinrich at least stayed on the ground. Now after this wild crash—another few feet off Heinrich's —knife edge— and she might be talking history with him and the mummies personally (or was it spirit-ly?) in their Prussian afterlife. Egyptian? Prussian, she decided . . .

And five women moored on this mountain in Vermont (? she wasn't even sure) instead of her mound in Arabia. So the trip was hopelessly postponed just at the start of another winter dig season. So the antique gods would keep their secrets for another spell. She bemoaned her fate and cursed Ann to the group for delaying their trip until that particular Wednesday. Her first reservations had said October 30th.

52

If her head would heal . . . if Ann's right arm weren't broken and swollen to the shoulder . . . if the food would last . . . Whenever she did relax into a dig-like pattern of hard work and grateful solitude, another of Ann's nightmares shattered the icy sleep hours . . . Maybe *share* Ann with the others? *Mutti*, who would want her? . . . Probe Zeni's commune jokes and theories. *I love humanity, it's people I can't stand.*

Face it, as Henry would say, just face it. *Ja.* Ann is your problem. Not Zeni's. Nor Ivy's.

> Ingrid is my lover
> Ingrid is a witch
> When the gods stayed at our house—
> (Ann *still* couldn't finish it.)

for Ann

HATE → THERE
   A HOTPINK GODDESS SEDUCES THE MAIDENNATION
   UNINHABITED AS FREUDS
   A FOGWHITE FISHFOOT ALWAYS BROODS UPON THE
      MAISONETTE
   TANTALIZINGLY BLEAKLY FRIGGINLY
JAY → ON → OUR → WAY

GO TO ANNPOINT

She'd awakened screaming again, racked with fever and
chill, Ingrid's arms about her. Her body plunging into the
crash, her stomach hot and bitter, the twin smashes, twisted smoking metal, awaiting the flames that did not come.
The cuts, her arm and Ingrid's head gushing about her.

—Silly little girl! Why did I ever bother with you? Get
out of my life— Ingrid had shouted. Out, out, out. Zeni
stopped it. Too bad. Loving I. is a trap. All traps. And
what Ann had wanted was to thank, to show gratitude
like some underdeveloped colony for the largesse expend-
ed so unexpectedly these last two years. Giving keeps us
free, having to receive indebts us hopelessly to the giver.

Lounging lightly during the picnic, toying with a wish-
bone. A play day of red and gold. Redgold Amazon. Sun
gamboling at checkers against the plaid blanket. Ingrid's
hair bunned, neck highcollared, pearl brooched, and Ann
wondered, is she really that stiff or is this just her public
personality donned for freshmen? (Ann already, but un-
safely, beyond that catered to but hated category.) Wearing pearls at a picnic—who else but her?

The twins, Erika and Judy, answering earnest freshmen
phrases that they thought Ingrid wanted to hear. Instant
nods at whatever Ingrid said. Hoping to impress the un-
reachable part of her that everybody called her uptight-
ness. But uptight wasn't right; she smiled too easily, that
radiant, inner-lit smile with eyes aglow that plays with
the world and insists if it isn't good, it ought to be. And *I*
know how to make it right. The lessons of history . . .

Erika and Judy giggled when a Henry or somebody else
in sweaty T-shirts and midnight cowboy hats pulled them
to their feet, reclaimed them from the threads of Ingrid's
web. Those little games she played with an elite known
(Ann heard from a new reject) as Ingrid's special people.
—Buncha snobs. You get into her harem, you stop thinking for yourself.—

—Well, see? I lost out to the dating game? Poor me.—

She made questions, summoned Ann and onlookers to support her, solace her. Which she doesn't really need, Ann guessed. Or does she? Infernal puzzle she is . . .

Ingrid trifling with her four students. —Tell me where you come from, what d'you want to study here?— Her controlled English without twang or flatness, foreign-flavored, Germanic but at ease, Ann thought. If Ann's mother, Helen, could hear her? She'd only sneer —That thick accent? The War—what else?— And think she'd closed the subject as unworthy of unexotic mortals who stayed —down to earth.— And trap Ann (*Roseann*, her mother insisted) in yet another untenable judgment.

If Ann continued Helen's game (she always lost, not even hating it now. If lethal, it was nevertheless predictable): —Which war, Roseann? Vietnam, Laos? Korea?— A new one every year, it seemed, how could historians be so sure later?

And Helen would always answer —No, no, Roseann! God you're ignorant. The one before that, before you were born. The big *World* War.— Or —What good's this history teacher of yours if she loses herself in the pyramids and never gets to the twentieth century?—

—You've never even met her! Shut up about her.— Ann's body burning, blaming herself for bothering to try again, to explain anything. Her mother jealous, that's all. Her sallies, the negative courage of spite. How pleasant this fresh reason for hating her . . .

—Why thank you, Ann. Glad to hear you'll be in *my* class. I'll tell you a secret. I asked for you.— Pearly voice, round, playful, perfect; against the light a crescent scar at her temple white on white, her smooth cap of black hair shadowed. Now you see her, now you don't. Her hesitation waltz.

—Asked for me? Why?— Ann tried to sidestep, found her knees shaking. Alarm at this woman who arranged her own human sacrifices without letting the victims know what, if anything, they might

58

expect for it. Again trapped and toyed with. But flattered.

—I like bright students. And you're obviously one of the brighter. With exam results like yours you can practically skip freshman year.— An instant she laid her long fingers, expensively diamonded, on Ann's shoulder. A caress? A trap? Before Ann could sputter a defense, the hand vanished. Ingrid resumed hurrying along the hall, Ann was left staring at the ROTC recruitment sign across which somebody had scrawled FIGHT NOW DIE LATER   IT'S NEVER TOO LATE TO DIE.

Couldn't resist if I'd wanted to. She's so clever. Ann knew. The hesitation waltz—it's one step forward, two steps back that fastens others to her without gifts, money or promises because they follow of their own free will. To let herself be fastened would be to surrender to an Ingrid remote like a hillside statue whom it was safe to love because it would never love back (her profession, her writing, her foreign trips, all those sensible reasons). Finally: to a frightening Ingrid who bridged and didn't bridge the distance, who tore Ann's days apart with yearning, with contriving meetings, with puppylike errands that humiliated Ann even as she performed them.

Their official encounters, like Ingrid's classes, left Ann restless, jealous of Judy's wit, of Henry who had asked the best question. Their —accidental— meetings at cafeteria or mailboxes energized Ann, made her hum and leap, until she realized that Ingrid, always hurrying, hardly noticed their ten-second hellos.

Trying, failing, trying to float Ingrid like a balloon figure, to foster Ann's dream that people really meant what they said during their better moments. (Why should they, when I don't? she wondered too.) That a compliment (—How quick you are!— in return for a fetched newspaper; —God you're a brain, a real owlhead— from her roommate gratefully cribbing Ann's calculus answers), that any hasty praise would magically ward off that terrifying moment

59

when the people around her would decide she was a pest, a brat. Superfluous like torn tissue the day after Christmas to the neat boxes of *their* lives.

I never learn, stay out of people, they don't want anybody. If they let me in, they discover I'll eat them up . . . Resist. People can't do anything to me that I don't want done . . . *But you want it all done.* From an excess of giving everything, give them nothing since they gave you nothing.

—I dreamed I was a brat in my Maidenform bra.— (But Ingrid pierced Ann's attempts at flipness, too.)

Notes

EVIDENCE FOR A DOMESTIC CULT is provided by flat standing female figures made of baked clay or stone equivalents with incised eyes, nose, hair and chin and found in each house . . . The statuettes portray the goddess, and the male occurs only in a subsidiary role as child or paramour. The goddess is shown seated on her sacred animal, the leopard, or standing and holding a leopard cub.

HACILAR

The statues allow us to recognize the main deities worshipped by neolithic people at Catal Huyuk. The principal deity was a goddess, who is shown in her three aspects, as a young woman, a mother giving birth or as an old woman, in one case accompanied by a bird of prey, probably a vulture . . .

CATAL HUYUK

—Victor, *will* you get her down off there? Pest!— Squawk, rrawk. The chicken coop on Saturdays, the weekend marketing and visiting when Ann and her sister, Bobby, were trussed up, pinned down.

Between the rows of Southern highball glasses and the ranks of her father's setter and pointer paintings (dogs whose smart front ends always knew just what they aimed away from), Ann scrunched herself smaller.

60

—Kid, what's red and white and brown and white and loud all over?—

Ann shrank further.

—Haw, a herd of setters. Get it? A *herd*?— He poked a finger among her ribs . . .

Dreaming a larger world like the one in history books. (Victor forbad tv except for quiz shows and documentaries on grasshoppers and salmon spawning.) Fantasyland where people might breathe instead of bicker, might free one another instead of digging bunkers furnished with stale exasperations, unfaced problems, tangled accusations over who was stopping whom from what.

Ann and Bobby playing card war in the pantry, noses in the air, little fingers crooked, runover highheels askew on their ankles. Mimicry was Ann's only weapon but not Bobby's who early learned the value of being a tomboy, of yelling from a safe window —Goddamn you ol' biddies— at a flock of retreating aunts. While Helen smacked Ann in the kitchen for —rudeness,— and because she'd let the soup boil over, anyway.

—God you're so awkward. Aren't you *ever* gonna grow up?—

Bobby was clever. Assessing Helen's weaknesses and taunting her with letting Victor cheat her of free Saturday afternoons by inviting his friends home for dinner, by getting —a great deal— on a dying puppy. —You'll love him, Helen. Best collie in the litter.— Messed the rug, chewed the telephone, died of convulsions one Sunday 3 a.m., Helen cursing him because he wouldn't drink the dish of whiskey.

After secret crying, Bobby flounced around school singing —How much is that doggy in the window, the one with the sickening face?— Five hundred times—I WILL NOT SHOUT IN THE HALL. And twisted Ann's arm until she wrote two hundred fifty of them.

Endlessly resourceful at blaming Ann for accidents and

failures engendered by Bobby's own recklessness: Girl
Scout merit project, decorating ex-pickle jars of no particular merit. —Beautifying— by dribbling molten wax over
them, liquid rainbows from flaming candles.

Then screams from Susan, their sadfaced playmate
whose long blonde hair and rayon sweater exploded in
orange tongues from Bobby's candle. Ann sat horrified
while Bobby tackled Susan, shrieking, running toward the
door and home, and flung an Army blanket over her body.
Smoke and stench flooded the pantry, roiled the kitchen,
alerted shoals of neighbors who poured toward the house.

—Get the window open!—

—Poor child! What happened?—

—Her hair! Helen, get her mother quick.—

—Get Doctor Sims!—

Hubbub of tongue clack, movements automatic but
useless like racing the engine on a stuck car. Meanwhile
Susan screaming, her face one raw hollow sound whenever anybody tried to touch the flesh edges with melted
sweater and singed hair hanging to them.

Until the question —What happened? Which one of
you . . . ?— And Bobby leapt forward, her story all prepared: —It was Ann! She knocked the candle into Susan.—

Ann gasped. —It was not! I—

—It was, it was.—

And Susan still screaming until Ann was sure she and
Susan both would die. She flung herself against Helen.

—Roseann, did you do it?— Helen forced Ann's head
upwards.

—No. I—

—You're lying. I can see it in your eyes.—

The women's chorus, reduced to four neighbors and a
stray cat, continued —. . . must have done it, can't even
explain herself . . .—

When Victor got home, he chased Ann through the
house, cornered her in the bathroom where Helen stepped
aside as he grabbed and smacked their daughter. Helen

62

glad that somebody was being punished for her afternoon's upset, just as well Roseann as Bobby and safer because Roseann never fought back in time . . .

Susan didn't die. (Nothing dramatic in Ann's past compared with Ingrid's, Ann regretted.) But as the horrible days inched by, Ann prayed she and Susan would both perish. When Susan finally told the truth of that afternoon, it was too late. A frontpage article had already appeared in the local paper. Helen collapsed in headaches and vomiting. Victor paid two thousand dollars for Susan's plastic surgery and hospital weeks. Relatives called constantly and crowded the room with candy that Susan couldn't eat, flowers she couldn't smell, and toys she was too old for.

Ann sweated and squirmed to avoid the hospital visits. When she couldn't hide in her room any longer, she stole five dollars from Bobby and boarded a bus for Boston. State troopers caught her in New Hampshire . . .

—We did the best we could for both of them. I was so sick those years. It wasn't easy. But they were such good girls, especially Roseann. She never gave us a moment's trouble.— Darling mother, lying mother, dying mother. Who raised Ann to slink through the house, who made sure Ann would have no self by copying her who had none either . . .

Bobby escaped early. Always clever at leaving others to pick up the pieces behind her. Victor said she was in Alaska; frontier life would be just her style. Ann never wrote her. Decked in cowboy hat and gold lamé sweatshirt, she flew home only for Helen's funeral where she wept vigorously. And had burial guests hiding embarrassed grins when she mimicked Helen's exact exasperation: —Victor, how *could* you? You know—

Bobby loved her and mocked her; Ann hated her and yearned for her . . .

How to know where or why to blame her mother now? Was it Helen's public pretenses that family life was serene, that she loved children, that Victor was the best of husbands compared to what her sisters had bagged?

Was it her ailments? Who else could combine asthma, heart attacks, arthritis, insomnia, ulcers, varicose veins and breast cancer—and live for God sakes?

—Who's this *Bruce*? Your boyfriends are such weirdos. Why don't you find a nice one?—

Nightmares exploding inside her. Always things hot and metal—a car, a wet razor, a robot that she loved and hated, cramming her into a black hole, always a burned child with bloodied clothes and tangled legs. Again the plane crash. Piece of shrapnel, a glowing crescent, in her wrist. Her fear, not of pain or dying, but that when it was over, the first image she'd meet would be Helen, eyebrows knit, lips bitten, who'd hiss —The part in your hair's crooked.— She'd failed again. —What right have you to die when we're your parents? Be grateful . . .—

Ingrid had Xeroxed one of Ann's papers on goddess myths, the Amazon women, and archeology. Enjoyed its teasing title, *Maiden Nations—A Strange Arrangement*. Praised it to senior history majors and graduate students and invited Ann to a circle of fifteen, her disciples, to read and defend it. An annual winter elite, brilliant returnees from studies in historiography, philosophy, and linguistics in France, Germany, or Italy. Long heads, Mensa minds, flashing verbalisms. Dark, witty cabal of special intonations, inverted eyebrows, sentences half finished because —everybody— knew the jokes. Codes and riddles. Ann hated and envied them.

Surrendering her chair to Ann, Ingrid strolled to the back of the room. Ann began her paper . . .

—Read louder— from somebody daisychaining paperclips . . .

64

She strained, feeling her written arguments fall apart. She cleared her throat, finally stumbled through the last page. Ingrid's profile stared out the window.

—Your paper's incomplete.—

—I—I know. It's only a beginning. I've only been here a few—

—How about reconsidering your method? All you do is set up straw men—or shall I say *women*—and knock them down.— From a knitter of green stitches. Ann saw her counting heads at the French Revolution . . . Method! How do you acquire that?

—What were your sources?—

—Why did you choose this subject?—

—Not valid.—

Ann squirmed.

—Question's not valid. Deal with what she's done.—

Ann relaxed. If she could only get them to fight each other, they'd leave her alone. How does Ingrid do it? Like the others her face hard at Ann, eyes squinted, lips compressed. Ann hated Ingrid's professional moods. Worshippers of scholarship, she's another of them . . . More questions.

Finally: —Ann, you could answer these questions if you'd read more widely. Remember that next time.— Game must have pleased her long enough. Rose, dancerlike from her seat, and shooed Ann to the rear . . . The tower bell.

—Hey, kid, you made it.— Bruce, standing over Ann. Her head pounded; the slippery pages scattered about her. Bruce gathered them dirty and dogeared, faced them up on the table.

Tried to slither out the door, but Ingrid caught up. —Ann, it's really nice to have discovered you. Hope today wasn't too bad?—

—Oh no. I got along fine.— Liar. Bitch she is for burning you at her stake. Hotpink goddess.

—I knew you would. You're an exceptional student.

All your tests say so. Don't let the seniors frighten you.
They're all head and no heart. Come to the office later?—
    Betraying her own proteges. What Alexander has build-
ed, Alexander will tear down.

    Bruce said later —Are you writing a whole history of
women? Myths and stuff.—
    —Feminism lives!—
    —Yeah.—

    If I do as I want, people don't like me.
    If people don't like me, I can do as I want.

    Wandering. Her body steps. Walks. Awakening to
        the edge. Snow crust. Trust. Never trust
            herself. Ingrid. She's empty, burned out
                bombed, her edges dried and curled.

    If we can't be happy as women, why didn't God make
us men?
    If we can't be happy as men, why didn't God make
us angels?
        And if even the angels weren't happy . . . ?

    —You come to me now for a little *schnapps*, yes? To
warm you. Come.— Ann still noted how Ingrid, when
tired, reverted to Bavarian word order . . .
    They'd worked late in Ingrid's office. Not all of Ann,
just the rational, problem-solving surface that didn't mind
poring late over blueprints at a low table under glaring
bulb. The rest of her shrinking rabbitlike into its corner
burrow, hiding, begging, notice me, feed me. Her white
sweater bluesmeared despite the apron. Ingrid still had
the only soft light and comfortable desk in the office.
    Ill-mooded, Ingrid had knocked over a mug of rancid
coffee that Ann toweled off the desk, notebooks, Ingrid's
lap and the wool dress over her firm breasts. She expected

Ingrid to grab the rag in resentment either at her slowness
or at being touched.

—Will you look at that? I'm so clumsy!— Ingrid insult-
ing herself, treating the touches matter of factly as if Ann
were the mother and she the child. The usual roles deli-
ciously reversed and the first time she'd ever dared touch
Ingrid higher or lower than an elbow. And maybe more
to happen that evening if . . . if she just didn't blow it . . .
Ingrid disabled and Ann her only savioress.

—No, you're not.— Ann dug again into the glary
blueprints.

Every few minutes Ingrid raised her arms from the
lighted desk circle and massaged her neck and shoulders.
Tired but what . . . ? Flirtatious, skirt at high thigh, as she
crossed her legs and rubbed them from too long at her
own charts, dots, and graphs. Cramming her share of ma-
terials to be presented at a New York conference with her
—colleagues.— Europeanly phrased. An American would
have said —my co-workers— or (current academic drivel)
the —archeology community.— The first time Ann had
heard that phrase on tape, she imagined some rare mummy
group or a circle of fertility figurines, all facing inward. Always made her mind laugh, but she didn't tell Ingrid . . .
Who still marveled at Ann's —seriousness, your *calmness*—
toward mountains of work that drove Ingrid to furrowed
forehead, ruby eyes, tense muscles, and wornout typewri-
ter ribbon.

When Ingrid considered it at all, it seemed a lucky, if
sometimes annoying, byproduct of the girl's natural skill
at drawing, painting, and detail work. Yet it made Ann
seem weary or cold, apathetic.

Not apathy, Ann knew, but careful disguise, affected
to conceal the tearing, unraveling strands of her. Someone
else's project! Her —slackness— merely her rejoicing at
somebody else's awful mess and she needn't get involved,
needn't ever be blamed when it failed. But then she did.
She always did. Bruce's organizing. Ingrid's India ink . . .

Then surprise: Ingrid leaning on what she took as —confidence,— Ann's —Yes, we can finish, yes, it'll look good.— Ignoring her own inside muddle, fearful as and at Ingrid. She'd learned never to speak the muddle; no one really cared about what happened inside her because it always scared hell out of them when they discovered what she was truly like . . .

—Jesus, Ann, if you got that many problems, you're sick. I'll get somebody else for the job.— —No, Bruce, I . . .— And to prove them wrong, busied herself mornings before classes, noons without lunch, evenings after dinner. And everybody thought, God what's Ingrid's secret? She's slavedriving that kid.

But Ingrid's not doing it just to get promoted. She really cares about the stuff she's discovering. She's promotable, everybody knows, no family or house to bother with, just work, work, and summers free to work more. If she doesn't work to get promoted, then maybe to escape terror? Idiot! That's *you*. Ingrid's happy—that's why you love her. Doesn't need anybody, people don't terrify her or she can hold them away until she's found the sword to slash them. But there must be a chink in her armor . . . must be. She's so . . . innocent. She really believes these snake goddesses and stelae fascinate you as they do her. She never guesses you've made them your own just so you can live and enter *her*.

Snake! Will she be the only person you hurt deliberately because she took the trouble to get close to you? —*Baby, not today. It's too hot, huh?*— But she can take care of herself . . .

The *schnapps* was taking care of them both. Ann should have eaten. Apartment room oozing into dark green planes around the gold cone that bathed Ingrid. Better than smoking Mike's grass that tore up her lungs and throat for the first half hour. Now her whole body warmed and flowed.

68

—Ann, I hardly know you. You're the first student I've worked with closely who didn't involve me in her identity crisis. You're quieter, more mature somehow . . . Well, no identity crisis?— Ingrid teasing, toying, Tilted her head at Ann.

—I *am* an identity crisis!— Blurted it out, blushing. She giggled. They both laughed. —Goddamn. It's not funny!— But Ann's vehemence proved only more embarrassing. Opposite Ingrid, she squirmed in the armchair, hanging her head in panic and rage at how three words from this woman could stampede everything she wanted concealed. Hadn't she learned with Bruce and Mike that pity didn't draw anybody to her—for long? The trials of her life so . . . paltry compared to Ingrid's tales.

Triumphant, Ingrid reigned from her polished throne, African spear as sceptre above her head, surrounded by a court of statues, plaques, photos, mounted coins of the world. Ann stared at the gold and turquoise figurine twins that floated, miniature mummies, above each of Ingrid's shoulders. Ladies in waiting? The house idols?

—My father's. Ceramic from Thebes.—

—Are they goddesses?—

—No. They're called shawabty figures. They were made as homes for somebody's spirit if the embalmed body was ever destroyed. Later somebody else got the bright idea that these little statues could substitute if the deceased had to do any ugly jobs in the hereafter. So some rich Egyptians ordered one for every day of the year—with a foreman for every ten. Good idea, yes?—

—Like bribing your draft board.— Attempted joke.

—*Ja-a.*— Reluctant Ingrid. —They were my father's. I take them everywhere.— Her fingers caressed both heads.

Silence. Except for Ann's leather armchair which wouldn't cease squeaking. Did she put me in it on purpose?

—Ann, come here— Ingrid murmured.

Ann's stomach sank. Suspecting a trap, she suddenly

69

couldn't imagine a more velvety way to go. So she hadn't blown it! A time for everything, including shutting up. Half drunk, she was sweating under her arms and between her legs.

Ingrid pointed to the stool at her feet.

At first Ann refused, wanting to seat herself on the arm of Ingrid's chair, to get above her just once somehow, to preplan a move before Ingrid got her own way. But Ingrid jerked her by one arm onto the stool; she found herself leaning into Ingrid's knees. Even without stockings, Ingrid's legs felt like marble against Ann's arms, not five days' stubbled like her own. —*Watch out for the hand on the knee routine.* — Who said that? Bruce? But it was *her* hand on Ingrid's knee. Ann smiled.

—Come on, dear. If you don't want to talk— And Ingrid swooped, hugged, kissed her on the cheek. Ann prayed to hold her and return the affection. Ingrid drew back. Ann terrified she'd be kicked out into winter, again relieved she hadn't blown it by responding too fast. Who the hell's running this seduction, you or her?

Ann's head blurred. Now she seemed to be enticing not Ingrid but a close warm part of her own self, in the bright circle uncovering a hidden being that she could love without thinking or calculating. To whom she might surrender later the other self she couldn't bear? Too much to believe?

Ingrid was laughing now. —You're afraid of me, aren't you? Why? You know me well enough after all these weeks and months.—

Ann gulped. Again outguessed. Ingrid so clever. Her head haloed against the light now. Her rings sparkled, and Ann wondered to how many others of what sexes she'd appeared like this. She'd been married. (Ann hadn't dared ask about it.) You're not married, so again she's one up on you. One up on you . . . how sexual all Ann's metaphors grew in the right mood. But fool she was, made love with Bruce for six months and never had an orgasm

70

(*he* came every time) because she hadn't even understood
how her own body worked. Bruce thought it *her* problem.
Like the contraceptives, nothing *he* should worry about.
And fancying herself so liberated all the time. Fool! Her
roommate had to tell her what was supposed to happen,
what could happen if . . .

But loving Ingrid would be like making love with herself, except she was so glorious compared to Ann's wretched interior.

Now Ingrid's fingers caressed lightly under Ann's breasts.
She worried, fearing Ingrid would notice how small they
were. Then relaxed, realizing Ingrid would understand.
Bruce never did, but she would.

For a moment Ann sat quietly on the stool and let it
be done to her, every nerve ecstatic, her face and body
flaming, the hairs electric on her arms. She marveled at the
workings of Ingrid's hands, how she could draw from Ann's
back, neck and underarms such feelings in those places
she'd never imagined she could experience. And stored
them for the delightful moment, already dreamed, when
she could do such things to Ingrid.

She rested her head in Ingrid's lap, closed her eyes, and
the last embarrassment magically subsided. The wand of
Ingrid's fingers had banished that, too. She opened one eye
to Ingrid still silhouetted against the light and couldn't believe she was the same woman she'd drowned in blueprints
with for five months. The first unclocked, unscheduled
tenderness . . . she wanted to lap it up, preserve it, stretch
it out, kill Ingrid's cuckoo just about to blast eleven.

Ingrid's hands at play again under Ann's arms, Ann
ashamed of the wetness. Helen's sarcasm: —You smell like
a football player. When are you gonna take a bath?— Ann
not daring to touch her for fear she'd take offense, slap,
scream, vanish, any number of foul awakenings.

Ingrid's skilled fingers explored down Ann's blouse
inside her slip . . . and bra. Not venturing to look, Ann ex-
tended her own arms (not your hands, they're cold) and

rested them around Ingrid's neck. Ingrid kissed her once, twice lightly on the lips. Not hungrily like Bruce. For the first time Ann sensed her decorum, the exquisite, dance-like rhythm Ingrid seemed to follow to calm, to relax as if they both had hours and hours, all night.

The minutes wrapped about her, soft, warm, full of delight and discovery. Still Ingrid said nothing, continued seeking Ann out, warming the cold places, melting every tension. Tomorrow, tomorrow you'll never be able to face her or believe this midnight, but right now you don't give a damn. Right? Right now.

Ann's hands fumbling over Ingrid's face, the planes of straight nose, moist lips, around her neck. Ann wondered what Ingrid would do if she suddenly began to choke her. Then it rose. *Ingrid trusts you.* The first human being who ever has. Not to hurt her, not to talk. Waves of gratitude washed through her.

Now she kissed Ingrid eagerly, smoothing the neck of her dress, touching warm skin, velvet cheeks, nape of her neck where the soft hairs grew.

When Ingrid arose from the chair, it hardly surprised Ann. Her stomach sank. It's all over.

But Ingrid continued moving, clasping Ann close, drawing her step by step, hip by hip, into another room. The bedroom, that Ann had never seen, flicked into light. She wondered if now was the time to undress. Why the hell did nothing she'd learned with Bruce seem to apply? Uncertain, she hung on one corner of the silk spread while Ingrid stared at her.

—Come on! Fight back!— Ingrid ordered. —I want you to grow up. To know what you're *inside for.*—

Inside *where*? . . . Oh god, she's getting metaphysical. What do you do now? Ann drooped. Terrified. Ingrid had caressed her hot out of her mind; now she'd kick her out, replace her with a more experienced number, next September's model. (—Among the sculptures found with the skeletons in mass grave no. 203 was the figurine of a kneeling child, hands together in supplication, while on its face you can see its extraordinary smile. The only figure we've found with such facial modeling, a sort of early Mona Lisa fifteen hundred years before Leonardo, perhaps a sacrificial figure. At any rate this child seems totally aware, controlled . . .—)

Gathering her arms and legs, Ann stood up, pulled, eased Ingrid backward onto her own bed. She resisted not at all, which shocked and delighted Ann. Drugged sacrificial maiden. And she realized she was about to —know— Ingrid just as the Good Book on Helen's dusty shelf had said. Why had the Bible no goddesses . . . ? From her last lit class the Song of Songs sang through her. In the tossup between God and love, she knew what always won.

Now she and Ingrid stretched full length together. Not even worrying any more what her hands and/or lips should do. Ingrid sighed deeply, closed her eyes; Ann relaxed in Ingrid's arms, ecstatic in total, certain delight (her first at last) of finding somebody who wanted what she wanted at the moment she wanted it . . .

for Zeni

HATE → THERE
   A BRAWNY ZENI SOMETIMES SEARCHES INTO THE
      MAIDENNATION
   FRIGID AS SHOTGUN
   A FOGWHITE LADYBUG WARILY DREAMS FOR THE
      ROPESNARE
HOW?
   REDGOLDLY REDCOLDLY FRIGGINLY
SPY → ON → THE → SLY

GO TO IVY IN THE HOUSE

IVY IN THE HOUSE

Day?

We think today is December 15th, but with 1957 our most recent calendar it's a little hard to tell. Anyway, we declared it our preChristmas Christmas. A warm-up, Zeni says. And a holiday from hunting, work, mattress lugging, and general low spirits that have sat on us these past days. Dinner is a fest with two trout that I lured from the pond. After the fog the —ice— has been odd: circles of gray slush, winter water lilies, too thin to walk on. I should stop annoying it and let it freeze until I can icefish without falling in.

We pass the last of the whiskey and rap the table for Zeni's speech. She hoists her glass and toasts —making it together . . . Yah know, kids, Ah loves commoonity, it's *pee-pul* Ah can't stand!—

Three of us burst out laughing. Zeni's talent for banishing gloom is probably what has kept us working for each other. Even Ann manages a weak, embarrassed smile. She's a living lowpoint—the only one she speaks to any more is Zeni. She's become a wraith in white sling about the house. Timing her life so we barely see her. She's just begun eating with us again.

Ingrid is a marvel. All we can figure out is that Ann was so drunk or sick that night that her poker arm strayed. Joette shaved the back of Ingrid's head again and dressed the new horizontal gash in addition to the vertical one from the crash which is still healing. Zeni's mouth got loose one day and said —I know what we can call you—our Hot Cross bun.— Joke flopped—a rarity for Zeni. Ingrid's front looks normal; the back view, however, does resemble an apprentice Buddhist monk. I haven't dared tell her this, of course.

Both Ingrid and Ann are mortified that their private affairs got splattered this way.

In our warmup spirit we continue something we've

77

lacked time or energy for. Which is getting to know each other (not to be confused with living together.) If you're as task-oriented as Ingrid or even me while coping with Gray, you forget other people. I'd thought Zeni a wild radical, for instance. It turns out she's more disgruntled than wild.

Her hypnotic way of holding court with her topics makes you certain that if things aren't structured correctly *now*, they could be *if* people would spend more money here, concoct something better there, toss out something else . . .

Ingrid: —So you're doing women's liberation now—I mean before we came here.— (No matter how we live here, there's still a —before— and —after.— And it's —we *came* here— now. Everybody seems willing to forget the crash like a collective bad dream.)

Zeni: —No. I'm *doing* women's liberation *right now*. But I hate movements.—

Ivy: —Then why do you move us around all the time? "Lift that pail," "stack that pile . . ."— Laughter.

Zeni: —Just keepin' you busy. It's good for you . . . No, what I mean is I hate the garbage that goes along with movements . . . Living here with you people is the best thing that's happened in years.—

We all stare. Another joke?

Ivy: —You're kidding.—

Zeni: —It's real, that's all. No theories. Well, okay, don't jump on me. So I do want to see what women can be and do . . . I even used to think women had some special talent for community. They don't, any more than men. They've just been forced to meet more basic needs for so many years.—

Joette: —But some women enjoy that, Zeni. It's their whole life.—

Collective focus on the arc of Joette's stomach.

Zeni: —You know our cold beds, cold water, cold everything here just make me glad I'm not my grandmother. I

78

see what she put up with. But ninety-five percent of humanity's scientists who are supposed to be alive and thinking now ought to get beyond Grammaw with houses.—

Ingrid laughs. —While you wait for science to rescue you, what have *you* done about it?—

Zeni: —Okay, before we came here, I drew up a model suburban neighborhood for when cars will be banned from cities. Plus a house of the future. No junky expensive furniture to make you panic if your teenager drops a Coke. All built-in stuff, off the floor, disposable dishes and clothes, suction floor and wall cleaning, infrared oven, all fixtures preinstalled, fiberglass walls you can bolt together. Ingrid, I'm saving you a year's song and dance with carpenters, electricians, and plumbers. Or maybe you think houses should still be put together brick by brick the way the Egyptians did it?—

Ingrid: —So it's true. You don't like people. Here you are taking their livelihoods away.—

Zeni: —Well, who feels any solidarity with masses of people like Chrysta's "mystical body"? I don't. I just feel people can make it in small groups if the artificial pressures are lifted.—

—I don't think people will *ever* understand each other!— Ann's first public words in days are blurted out. She blushes. Ingrid tightens her lips and throat, stares out the window.

Zeni: —You can do it, Ann. Remember we talked? We're *for* you. Try.—

It's too late. Ann's eyes and face are dripping. She flees the table. We all shift noisily to cover her exit.

Ingrid: —I'm sorry.—

We finish the meal, subdued by a family camping tale Joette is telling.

I caught a couple catfish today—not nearly as tasty as last week's trout despite Joette's best efforts. I'm glad Gray and I fished during all those summer vacations. I

79

never dreamed I'd be doing it seriously for food. One end of the pond is frozen tight now; the other, where it becomes a brook, remains slushy. But I still don't like walking on the ice. The hardest part is keeping warm. If I prop the pole and do something, I may lose a bite. Already the fish are wily; I'm Pisces Enemy No. 1. But if I sit, after fifteen minutes my blood gels. Not to mention my feet. I've constructed a new poncho overcoat—an Army blanket lined with a flannel sheet and sided with raglan sleeves. It keeps my upstairs warm anyway.

This morning I rooted through the attic. Ingrid has visited there too. No wonder; it's an antiquer's treasure trove—of junk. Broken rockers, a wooden bathtub, a cradle that we're sanding for Joette, mildewed clothes, stained photos whose bearded visages make the hippies look like children. I play the faces like cards across the rough floor in the chartreuse light. Dogeared comic books; Zeni's reading an old Wonder Woman to us.

How simple a universe—when you *know* who the enemy is.

Anyway: a stuffed deerhead of elegant antler and saffron eye, a rusty shotgun for which I ransacked the place (Grammaw cursing me) after cartridges. Not even a BB so far. I practice my aim onto the hill —in case a wild hippo stumbles in— Zeni says. We wonder if this house is ever used by hunters. When is deer season?

Some of the inhabitants were called Figgins. A Lionel and a Cabell inside some primary readers. Grammaw's name seems to have been Effie. Joette: —Short for effete.— Hardly.

As the days get colder (or dawn later—however you want to look at it) we linger round the woodstove in the mornings. Zeni and I entertain with dramatic monologues from an old history review text.

After initial relief at not hearing daily news about fire, flood, famine, and fighting, Zeni and I find ourselves nostalgic for bulletins from the outside. Even a campus riot would cheer us. We seem the only ones interested. Ingrid writes; Ann suffers; Joette cooks and waits.

Joette and I also pore through a warped green tome called *The Boy Mechanic Who Represents the Best Accomplishments of the Mechanical Genius of Young America.* "A boy would be an old man before he could make half the things described in this wonderful book."

Besides the Homemade Bed Warmer, we're experimenting with A Pair of Wood Foot Boats which Waldo Saul of Lexington, Mass., swears will let me walk on water. Zeni has built an ingenious Spiral Mouse Trap (two lengths of coat hanger) on the assumption that we can eat them if we catch them.

What we really need is a cheap and easy candle because we're running out of them. We're reduced to sticking wax dribbles back onto each precious stump. Supper is 4 p.m. now. Maybe I can kill something with more fat on it. Or burn moss like the Eskimos. When I remember that *one* of Louis XIV's many chandeliers at Versailles burned a mere four thousand candles, I get sick.

How quickly my suburban mind has acquired frontier ways of death and destruction. —Nature— has already been reduced to unecological visions of baked bluejay, stewed squirrel, roast mouse. The squirrels are particular teases— they let you get eight feet away and *then* they scamper up a fifty-foot tree. And in college I thought I was a vegetarian.

It snowed last night, and besides the patter of little feet (which except for rabbits I can't seem to snare) I saw hoofs! around the pond. Deer? Elk? Hell, I don't even know what an elk looks like. Maybe I saw one at the Bronx Zoo?

Joette and I walked there and experimented with a large noose trap of the heaviest rope we could find. We stretched the noose across the trail between a bush and some higher pegs nailed into a tree. From there the rope

81

ascends over a limb and gingerly dangles a large fireplace log above all unsuspecting antlers. It took a trio of Zeni, me and a ladder to hoist the log up there before each test of the noose. If an animal runs along the trail and steps into the noose, he dislodges the pegs (theoretically) and is assisted from this callous world by the weight of our log.

Arr-rrgh! Something with hoofs ran by all right but played real smart and went *around* the bush instead of between the bush and our deathtrap tree. Zeni and I spent an hour dragging pine branches and underbrush to line the path with four-foot thickets so Rudolph will have to run just where we want.

Nothing.
Nothing.
Third day of nothing. Joette thinks thick rope is too visible. It snowed again.

A kill! This morning I checked the trail and there lay— at first I thought they were sticks—but they were antlers, a head! A moderate-sized deer, snowfrosted. The noose was firmly round its hind end, and the log must have broken its legs. I couldn't get nearer then. The poor thing was alive and made a dreadful scrabble in the snow and bushes trying to escape when it saw me.

I dashed back for Zeni. We set out silently, she with a knife, I with a two-by-four. Dreadful sickening job. At first I couldn't near its head at all for the antlers slashing at me. Suddenly I recalled my simpler, humaner traps (total failures), and I got mad. While Zeni threatened it from one side, I moved in and bashed it somewhere on the head and neck with the plank. Its beautiful eyes glazed. Zeni couldn't do a thing with the knife; her face had turned quite green and white. As the wind powdered the snow all about us, she stared at the blood around the deer.

—God, is this what you go through with every rabbit or fish you bring home?—

I remember that I used to weep tears of outrage at what they did to Bambi and his mother.

When the deer was quiet, Zeni and I tried to figure out how to drag him home. Pulling didn't work— his legs kept getting caught on rocks and branches. When we tried to bind and lift the stiffening animal between us, the noose failed. Snowy, frozen knot wouldn't slide.

When he collapsed on our toes again, we stood above him sweating and fuming until I got a brainstorm. African movie? Girl Scout manual? I found a heavy clothespole to which we tied all his legs upside down. When we'd yoked ourselves to the pole, we began a triumphant, slippery stagger back to the house. By this time Joette and Ingrid were cheering us from the porch.

After hugs all around, Zeni and I dropped in front of hot cans of tea. My head is still woozy with hunger.

Ingrid: —How did you think up tying it to a pole? I've watched Bedouins in the mountains. That's how they transport a wild goat or anything they're lucky enough to shoot.—

Ivy: —Why didn't *you* come out? We could have used you . . . I don't know. Remember that sadistic African movie with Cornel Wilde? The one where he gets buried in the mud?— Ingrid shook her head. —Well, the natives carried people around like that before they ate them.—

Ann gulps. I shouldn't torment the poor kid this way. But she's so fragile you can pull her leg on anything from —Beautiful blizzard this morning, huh?— to —Of course, I poisoned pigeons on my street.— And she won't get the joke.

We've hung the deer in the woodshed, and Joette has volunteered to clean and carve him. His insides will make my first decent fishbait. Hope the funny little devils aren't wintering in the mud by this time.

Snow blows deeper. Today we played a trot up and down game. Tramping a giant SOS and arrow on the hill in case an airplane should wander over us. It's Ingrid's job to keep the letters deep and clear.

Exhausted when we dragged back from just fifteen minutes of it. No sugar and little fat are telling on us. To get off beans, we've begun the row of dusty jars filled with stewed tomatoes, bleached string beans, and corn. Ingrid worries about ptomaine or botulism (just two glasses of those germs could wipe out the planet, she says), but we haven't died yet. Tomorrow we begin the deer. Joette has been seasoning him.

I hear Zeni chopping firewood. If only we had some coal. All those Appalachian miners sitting idle while we incinerate the forest and still can't raise Travel On (Zeni's naming from an attic sign) above a cozy fifty-two degrees.

This morning I huddled awake an hour under the blankets imagining the —great rejoicing throughout the Kingdom— that would happen should Chrysta return. Of course, she won't now or she-plus-they can't until it stops snowing and somebody sights the airplane.

If it had been a 747, they would have scoured everywhere for insurance pieces of three hundred of us. But because we're only seven, they ceased rapidly. And with a 747 we wouldn't be alive anyway. What a shame Indira Gandhi, Norman Mailer, or Barry Goldwater wasn't aboard. Then they'd be looking harder. Just think—six months in the wilderness with Norman Mailer. Give me an ax and I'll follow you anywhere. Zeni's zaniest nightmare.

Why Are We in Northern Vermont? (If we are.)

We Are in Northern Vermont because . . .

It's probably easier to retrieve moon missions than search *our* ol' rugged forest.

Absurd fantasies: Chrysta and the Mounties arrive by dogsled with steaming styrofoam cups of coffee. I never knew I was a caffeine addict until deprived of my daily fix. (Sure, birch bark tea is great, Henry David, but . . .)

2. Reporters pop flashbulbs about us and the newsprint reads *Find Five Lost in Forest*. Next day housewives collage coffee grounds and egg yolks over our rescue.

3. Environmentalists sign us up for a lecture circuit on *Female Thoreau* or *My Stay in the Woods*. Fame. Glory (i.e., medium steak, peas, french fries, red wine, apple pie, cheese, seconds on everything at the local hotel)˙with a coffee and cruller hour afterward for the ardent questioners.

What's the plural of Thoreau? Thoreaux? Thoreaus? Oh well. If they ever do find us, all we'll probably get is K rations at the local Boy Scout hut. Yeah, as Zeni would say.

I remember reading about (*Time* delights in such gruesome irony) the poor mother and daughter who starved to death and were eaten by bears in some California woods just *ten miles* from a superhighway. If they'd only known which way to walk . . .

> I think that I
> Shall never see
> A blizzard that
> Truly pleases me.

A doggerel in the hand is worth two on the hill.

As I get hungrier, I lapse into my nonconnectable state that I experience in restaurants just before lunch. People become objects to me, like Gray during the baddest married years when he was sick or I was sick. I notice somebodies; with great effort I can imagine they're hungry, tired, paining. They're flesh and faces, wrinkles, bulges, but they might as well be cement.

Gray's three questions in museums of the world:
    What does it all mean?
      Did they love each other?
        Was it all worth it?

But the price of continued involvement here is swallowing my annoyance at Ann's adolescent trauma; at Ingrid's saucy bossiness as if there was only one right way to pour tea or make a bed, which of course *she's* known for years; at Zeni's uptight reformist moods; and my sadness at Joette's soon-motherhood without a doctor in the woods, because she wants one.

If we ever do get out of here, will I someday nostaligize at reunions over all that fresh air and healthy country living?

Zeni says her latest assignment—why she was coming to New York—was to teach a woman studies course. She believes women have acted too long in reaction to men. And you can't be a person if you're nothing but a reaction . . .

Would this have helped Gray and me? Don't know. Sometimes he thought I was too much a person in —wrong directions.— But why did I let him convince me that anybody else's direction for me was better than my own?

On the length of marriage: Ann claims the idea of marriage to *one* person for her whole life terrifies her. —I won't want the same person at forty-five or seventy. They won't want me . . . I won't live that long anyway.—

Joette cocks a quizzical eyebrow.

Ingrid toys with my idea that if people just waited, they'd be so self-sufficient—say by the golden age of thirty!—they'd not need marriage at all. Down with marriages of desperate loneliness, of —make me a person because I haven't figured out how to do it myself.— Then there's my (and Joette's) contradictory idea of Believing Makes It So—if you believe you're in for life, as I did with Gray, it helps you over the inevitable chasms, the urge to cut and run, even if it's off a cliff.

86

As usual, Zeni has a better idea: five-year marriage contracts, renewable publicly and privately only if both parties are satisfied. If a couple cracks after five or ten years, both people should share child care alternately and equally year by year. Now Zeni's really revved up. —What a revolution! See? And I haven't even mentioned communes.—

Ingrid laughs.

—Seriously. No more articles on "the unmanned mother" who "didn't work hard enough" to "hold *him.*" If you were a man, how would you like *your* psyche stuck between a Tide ad and a rhubarb pie recipe?—

Ivypoints

How we scrutinize photos of us at nadirs and zeniths (doesn't matter which) like graduations, weddings, parties to see how we've aged and in what directions.

Why on knowing people better, we wonder what they looked like when they were younger without lines about the mouth (Zeni), or vein-backed hands and legs (Ingrid), or shiny crackled skin a la chicken feet (me), puffy eyes (Ann), grizzled hair and bifocals (all of us in a few years).

Why Zeni's acne has cleared out. —All this wild God's country.—

How we jostle into an airplane knowing this group will never travel together again in the history of the world. True, too, for us postplane and clinging to the mountain.

Why we scare December bluejays, obscene reminders of summer so far behind—or so far ahead. They should all fly south and stop screeching.

How I hunger for May air, red silk, autumn leaves, violets.

How I hunger.

How tired I am of brushing my teeth with soap.
washing dishes in snow.
plates with tawny flecks of previous meals.

the kidney-chilling outhouse, a two-
seater, with rearview mirror and
air conditioning.

How *Reader's Digest* makes neat sanitary napkins as long
as we don't lose Grammaw's safety pins. —Effluvia unto
effluvia.—

Why Ingrid smells of perspiration all the time now.

How everybody's legs are bristly, except for Ingrid (mys-
teriously).

Someone is being born. Someone is being dying.

There's a big place in the Southwest sun for YOU!

Today I ranged outward. Powder crunchy snow, but a
blizzard is tuning up. We need dead branches for kindling,
Zeni says. I decide to strike out along —the trail— and past
the pond. I expect endless evergreens and oaks but over a
bump I stumble into a white pit. Gnarled trees gnash in
the wind above it.

I kick odd shapes. Old ice chest, horde of crushed cans,
rowboat skeleton, bundle of rolled snowfence. Under the
gray sky a melancholy, antique lot that would set Ingrid's
palms itching. Whenever the wind drops, the pit is totally
silent. Not even a rat. I scour the ground expecting Friday's
footprints. Too much debris for a single family. Maybe a
whole commune beyond somewhere? It has been one century since our last holy bonfire . . .

I must have hoped for something picturesque or inspir-
ing (Grammaw Moses' *Winter Landscape*) when I started
out, but this place is evening's bleak dump.

Grammaw's 1940 washer, its tilted wringer sprung and
grinning. If I dig deeper, will I meet handblown bottles,
buttons from Civil War trousers, Ethan Allen's keyring, a
gravestone of wornout angels and mordant epitaph? And
if I lie down here . . .

Nobody lives here. Uninhabitable exterior. This house
we found, it's not fit either. Abandoned because the mod-

ern world flunked it. NO lights, running water, toilet, garbage disposal. Waste is our most important product.

My seat is freezing to the ice chest . . . Are the five of us intruders here or part of the process? I'll bring Ingrid. It's something to see. Lightning or trash fire blasted all those trees? . . . Doll's drowned body in an old trough. I won't bring Ingrid; Ann's enough wasteland for now.

Red and gold rifts among the clouds, fireshadows on the snow as if the place was still burning. Corpse of an apple tree creaks at me. Once this was a summer meadow of daisies, cows, clover.

I huddle my elbows farther into my lap. I need to whistle but it would mean inhaling more cold air. I'm half asleep with my wool-tasting scarf across my nose when I remember Zeni's firewood. As I try to rise, my legs complain that they're asleep. I sink onto one knee. Pain! Shout. Mistake. Dig from my knee the black shard that has torn my blanket-pants and cut my leg. A rusty can.

Fantasizing a future rosy with lockjaw, I throw some branches together and get the hell out of there.

A dull, dispiriting, disillusioned day that tears me inside. Sometime before dawn the world swept another gray blizzard upon us. Came the whiney wind, the insidious snow that seeps under door jambs, through window frames, down the chimney. The five of us huddle on boxes and stools, stirring mugs of the weakest tea I've ever tasted. Joette has failed to disguise its condition, poured it into white cups instead of the earthen mugs. There's no question of my escaping the kitchen half-warmth to hunt or fetch water until the steel curtain lifts. So I sit. We all sit, surrendering to exhaustion, boredom, fear, pain, whatever is painting a still life of us this morning. Joette says we should save the rest of our deer, so it'll be a vegetarian lunch followed by a vegetarian supper. Annoyed consensus: we look everywhere but at the stove (where nothing's cooking) or out the shrouded windows.

89

But the fog inside me isn't thick enough, can't prevent my staring at all of us. Zeni's Snow Squad. Refugees from the late late show's last bombing mission in unglorious black/white/gray. Bandaged and dirty, we slump here. Then I nonconnect again as at cheap lunch counters with flies in the meringue, grease on the griddle, and fluorescent people munching plastic hotdogs and chemical french fries. The drawn faces are the same, but the overstuffingness is not. Except for Joette, we run to leaner and hungrier.

I imagine us a pack of miscellaneous canines.

Joette—something large, blonde, furry. A collie.

Zeni—snappy, scrappy, intense, a Pacesetter for the Cause. A grayhound? Our . . . terrier.

Ingrid—European, elegant. One of those tall poodles. Or a wolfhound that condescends to garbage pails.

Ann—a mut with a thorn in its paw.

Me—I'll probably do as a chocolate Weimaraner. Or an old bitch basset hound.

Chrysta and Penny—gone and not to be forgotten although we've stopped speculating. After these weeks it's just depressing.

Chrysta—a flowing russet retriever.

Penny—something small, patient, and ridiculous. A Pekinese. A dachshund.

Not for a moment would I compare us to cats. We're more varied, and we're trying to learn running in a pack because we must. A return to childhood perhaps, a life again among sisters, near-equals, among people who don't yet know or have forgotten it's men who run the world, armies, churches, governments, corporations, universities, computer companies like the one I was to work in. So people like Zeni can rightly blame them for the way they've botched it up.

Here we have none of them whom we must console, bolster, bribe with food, flattery, sex and affection so they'll be nice to us. Here we have nobody but ourselves

90

to blame for mistakes. It's liberating and frightening. If we blow it, they'll find us someday. *Search Party Locates Tea-Drinking Skeletons.*

If we make it here despite food, cold, and festering tension, we'll have proved something. But we don't pull as a group yet or run as that pack. Ann, Ingrid, and I resist groups. In our other lives privacy was our god-good. By it we strengthened ourselves to get to work, teach classes, give talks, be gal Fridays on blue Mondays. Without privacy or with the less of it that's possible here our foibles and exasperations, hatreds and childhood hangovers, our neuroses begin to crop out like fleas in the sunshine.

Ann's wrist continues to ache. Joette misses her (other) children.

I can't believe it, but already the dailiness of our strange life has become ordinary. Our other lives now seem the fantasy. I say *we* because we do act like one of those sprawling family reunions, overhearty or bored by turns, drunk or sober, anything to camouflage the truth. That we haven't been—and aren't—to each other what we might be.

I expect too much of the others—or not enough. I begin to love and hate them alternately depending on (a) whether Zeni makes a breakfast effort to get us talking about something, anything. The skiing we could do, how to rent this place out as the ultimate in lodges (no heat or running water but there's fresh squirrel and plenty of oxygen). (b) Whether I make an effort. But so little about the Great White Beyond is amusing. Hunting has again become a euphemism for the ill-equipped (me) trying to outwit the well-camouflaged (all the finned and furry thems).

Of course, I understand the conservationists' ravings on clean air and water, on deporting urbanites from rundown cities and paying them to populate rundown towns. But now I also appreciate why my great grandmother and a few other pioneers damned it as —the godforsaken wilderness.— As farmers, they knew that this rocky land don't

91

give away nothin' that you don't scrounge from it with a lot of effort.

Item 2: as one of Zeni's women types said of a California commune —The climate was great, but I took a good look at who was in the kitchen.—

Item 3: After years of marriage I discover I prefer solitude to always stumbling over bodies in some —community.—

Shut up. Time to check the fishlines at the pond.

I	shall	"	"	"	"	"	"
You	"	"	"	"	"	"	"
She	"	"	"	"	"	"	"
We	"	"	"	"	"	"	"

A good sentence for some pioneer immigrant's Basic English somewhere between *The butter churn is in the tool shed* and *Lightning has struck our position. Prudence, fetch Patience.*

NOTHING. Gr-r @† $%*!!

Tonight we discuss food dreams. And discover we're all having them, the variety depending on what our favorite edibles are (were). Mine is a turkey banquet of wall-to-wall cranberry relishes, sweet and baked potatoes, peas, milk, coffee, olives, salad, mince-blueberry-apricot pies, etc. etc. I salivate as I fantasize. Just last night attended this feast (not one I cooked for Gray and his family because that was ever an allday pain in the everywhere). It was the feast my mother cooked for the two of us once when my father and brothers had driven to Montreal. She and I talked long that weekend about school, the wars, the Rosenbergs whose trial she followed avidly. When they were finally electrocuted, we didn't eat chicken for a year because chicken had been their last meal. That was the only good and private talk I ever remember. The other years seem full of dirty dishes, homework, sick headaches, frayed upholstery and nerves, yells of —Where is . . . ?—

and —Why can't I . . . ?— Somehow I never missed her until now, today, and I'm ashamed that I think of her mostly
in connection with food.

Joette is the coffee and apple pie generation: —I was
baking and baking, but I never got to eat a single tart or
muffin or pie. They were all too hot. Then I woke up.
Isn't that the darnedest?—

Zeni: —I remember the best meal I ever had. I was, like,
fourteen. My best friend invited me to her house, Italian
style. I was starving so I stuffed myself on the first three
courses—you know, soup, salad, antipasto, wine. I thought
that was the dinner. Although I wondered because her
mother hadn't sat down yet, she was still in the kitchen
steaming, stewing, frying, and boiling.

—Well, then her mother walks in with this tray of lasa-
gne which was like half this table.— Zeni's arms flail about;
we all laugh. —She never could have baked it in the oven.
She'd have needed a *furnace*! . . . Anyway, after the lasa-
gne was veal parmigiana with escarole. By the second bite
I was bleary. I had to leave and run around the block.

—You know how long that dinner went on?— Her eyes
widen and interrogate us one by one. Collective headshake.
—*Four* hours by the time they finished with spumoni,
demitasse, and fruit. And a couple uncles not only ate it
all, they packed it away with hunks of Italian bread. I remember one uncle with this white on white necktie shouting across the table. *Silvio! Basta! Stupido. Do what your
Mama say, eat nice!* By the end they were all crying and
laughing into the wine.—

—Did anybody get sick?— Joette's over-practical mind.

—That crew? No-oo. They ate like that every Sunday.
Bet they all had heart attacks at fifty.—

I smile. Ingrid says nothing.

Chilled walls of air hang in the rooms now, partition-
ing them from one another. Our bedrooms are an ice-
cube tray. But I mind it a little less than the others

93

because I'm outside so much. Outside is better, lighter, less sodden with staleness.

Chrysta walked toward me last night. So real I thought she was standing beside my bed. My Chrysta babble woke Joette . . . It was gold fall like the days before we boarded the plane. Her scarves flowed merrily; her cross shone. On the runway she paused, threw back her head, squared her shoulders, and announced —The old ways are best.— Then the wind and a jet engine drowned the rest.

The dream disturbs me because my subconscious has it wrong. *I* never thought Chrysta a relic. Zeni did. And somehow I was Zeni, seeing through her eyes. Yet through my own, too. Puzzling. Why must we become the people we live with, summon empathy real or feigned, in order to make it with them at all? I'd like everybody stronger. We're all too important to each other. If as children we didn't need people so much in the first place . . .

December 23d (Zeni says)

Joette's babies were born this morning. The girl, then ten minutes later a boy. We stoked the kitchen and dining room stoves the grandest ever, next moved Joette's whole mattress and pillows into the kitchen for the final countdown. I've got so used to a gigantic Joette, arms folded across the shelf of her stomach, that I can't picture her with the babies outside her.

Zeni and Ingrid officiated. Ingrid has even delivered another birth once; one of the women who wash pottery fragments at one of her fieldworks got caught suddenly. The birth went well; this is Joette's third time and the heads were positioned correctly. I should have helped. I wanted to brag that I'd delivered my own baby (true) because I hate doctors (true), but I was afraid so I shut up.

Birthing and dying share the same smelly, relentless biology, the same irreversible spasms (Gray's coma throat

94

arattle and choking) deflected not at all by tubes, pills, injections.

The new babies' noses are twisted and, of course, there's the fierce red skin. Joette is sitting up now. Ingrid cooks while Ann and I improvise diapers from cold-washed curtains, old newspapers and World War II frocks from the attic.

Something new wrong with Ann. She's red-eyed and trembly. Hides in her room again.

Joette worries about —our— baby girl whom she's named Sara. The girl is smaller, doesn't cry or suck as hard as the boy. We're hoping for the best.

for Ann

HATE → THERE
    A REDGOLD AMAZON ALWAYS TRAVELS IN THE FIRESHADOW
    DEAD AS WEAK TEAS
    A FLIRTATIOUS ANN ALWAYS FISHFOOTS UPON THE
        MOUNTAIN
    FREE ALONELY DANKLY FLIRTATIOUSLY
FEAR → HERE

GO TO ANN MINUS ANN

ANN MINUS ANN

If we trusted love, it would not obsess us.
If we trusted ourselves, they would not obsess us.

Steps. Her body steps. Awakening. To the edge. Can't
find the ice. Dark, it's dark. Slate blues. Blues. No
edge. Ice cascade, frozen fall. Dead fountain.

What she's done must be . . . unforgivable. No more
shared room. Ingrid out. Gone healing love touch. Ingrid
no longer comes to read or tell stories of the outside. Or
rub her back and arm. Must be ashamed. Strangers know.
It all (Ann imagines) being, well, splashed about this way
so people can't help but . . . —Did you hear what she's . . .—
    Ivy avoiding too. Only Zeni still creaks the stairs. The
story of how they dragged the deer home. And Joette every morning weaker and weaker tea until one snowing time
just a cup of hot water.
    Pain. Watched by the gold and blue statues Ingrid's lent
her and not taken back. Egyptian giver.
    Pain.
    Then wakes to bustle from the kitchen, mattresses stair-
bumping, shouts and cries. And knows Joette's baby is born.
It's babies, Zeni says. And not enough food for every . . . In
the rush they forget about her, let her lie dirty all day under
her blanketmound, assuming it's what she wants . . .
    Staggers to the curtain rags. Tries to read Mark Twain
but the drafts from rattly window frames chill her. Rats
run at night. Creeps back barefoot to bed. The statues float.
Bribe one to suffer for her. With what. She has nothing but
the pain. Tell Ingrid. Don't tell Ingrid.
    Pain.
    Hate them downstairs all. Glad to be punished somehow
but how to punish them? She deserves it for being a drag,
for eating too much, for not helping with cooking, water-

99

gathering, hunting. —If only it were her *left* arm maybe—
If she lit a candle, she might read in bed but she doesn't
deserve a candle. The others need it.

Ought to drag herself down to congratulate Joette, see
the new babies. Standing dizzy. Now her arm throbs so
much she vomits on the floor. Falls back. Never make it
downstairs unless Ingrid helped. Doesn't deserve that.
Chamberpot full again.

If she can pull her arms above her head on the pillow,
the fire stops a few seconds. But her arm gets cold. Again
the cold and fire everywhere. Has to drag it undercover.
Hide it, hide.

. . . falling down the stairs. So they'll notice. Imagine
she's done it but—landed just on Joette who will die now.
And the babies . . .

. . . must be so evil. Can kill anybody who touches her.
Poor Ingrid, I love her. Wrist's a slimy poison metal whose
fumes she breathes all the time. Ivy sees and smells. Smart
to stay away. Piece of shrapnel in her wrist. Piece of Ingrid.
Pulsating crescent.

One evening (knows it evening by shadows from the
right window) her legs unfreeze, her body all a hot poker
she'll never cool. Where to thrust it? Around the mattress
ticking, outside the blankets, onto the floor? Her wrist is
four angry wrists—black, blue, red, green. Gleaming oozing
crescent.

Pain. That begins in her legs, climbs her stomach, sits on
her arm, makes her lungs gasp, ends in popping light behind
her eyes, inside her hair. Will not cry out, will not . . . cry
out. For what has she left of herself to prove she exists except this long hot pain? That she fights alone. Not to trouble the others. Not even Ingrid, who doesn't care anymore
. . . Must be unforgivable after all Ingrid . . .

Zeni touches her that lies outside the blankets. Tries to
cover Ann who tears the wool from Zeni's hands and hud-
dles at a bed corner. Again Ingrid's bedroom . . . Zeni asks
her how she is. Mocking. What answer? If she tries, she'll

100

scream. That would just scare them; they'd all run to her room. Then away if she writhed in front of them. Zeni's eyes stare, her hands drop, she walks away. Ann tries to beg for water, but her throat burns. No words come. Parched pain. Closes her eyes. Bouquet of red flames from her mouth instead of words . . .

Steps. Her body steps. No edge. Pond snaps at freezing.
   Freeze her arm. Water for her head. To water her head.
 Steps. Her body steps. To water ahead. Molten red.

If she could get cool . . . a few minutes . . . she might sleep instead of toss inside the strewn, sweated blankets, her left arm and legs numb and prickly under her. Fails at the knots in her pink scarf; it rips.
   Dark. Pain.
   Drags herself toward the gray window and bathes her face against the frosty glass. Frost melts and runs along her chin and neck. When her tongue licks the droplets, they taste hot, red, salty. Not green and cool as she dreamed. She wishes she could cry but now she has no tears.
   Watches her fingers inching the window up. One. Two. Warped. Jams! But the night wind cools her at last. If she could get outside . . .
   Feels for her shoes, is surprised—they're stuck onto her feet. Doesn't remember putting them on—when? Staggers along the iron bedrail to the door. Surely her clumping (—God, you're awkward!—) or the poplights ahead of her in the darkness will awaken somebody. Joette . . . babies will cry. She'll trip. When she bangs the night table, something shatters on the floor. Ingrid's baby twins. Good. Laughs.
   Lurches along the hall, down the stairs by sitting every few inches. Ingrid sleeping . . . where? If she can make it into the living room, she'll reach the porch without passing through the kitchen . . .

Just before the door onto the porch, she wobbles, collapses toward oakpanels. Bonfire in her chest now; she's positive somebody must hear the gasping. What . . . is it? Noisy! Her own breathing. She coughs.

Forgets the downstep to the porch and slams into the uprights and torn screening. Wrist screams. Now they'll come. Must come . . . No one comes. Show them she's not a burden any longer. Rosy ball, molten pain. Burnt, blasted bush. Roasted animal. Can't see any longer . . .

Compare and contrast the legends of the Amazon women warriors with

    (a) the legends of Persephone and Andromeda
    (b) " " " Athena and Atalanta
    (c) modern characters such as Wonderwoman.

                       1 Hour. Open Book.

Still she couldn't finish it.

FEAR → HERE
   A GILDED FLAMING EGGS QUESTS THE MAIDENNATION
   MILDEWED AS ABEND DUMP
   A FLIRTATIOUS ANN WARILY FISHES UPON THE LADYBUG
   VIGOROUSLY BLEAKLY FOGWHITELY
HATE → THERE

GO TO GNASHINGS

Ann has disappeared. When she hadn't appeared by nine this morning, Ingrid built a cup of tea. Ann's room was frigid because she'd somehow forced up the window. The raggy drapes were sailing in the gale. When Ingrid poked the blanket mound, it was totally cold. Ann wasn't there. Ingrid's two dolls lay among their cracked heads and arms.

At first we were sure she'd jumped out the window. But no dents in the house drifts. Last night's fresh snow in deeper swirls around our clearing. Joette remembers hearing stair noises; she thought they were mice.

Ingrid is sure that if Ann has wandered off, she'll be too sick to trace her way back. Ingrid seems suspiciously eager to dispose of her. Is it to rid herself of guilt? Or just her usual business-like self pronouncing the possibilities (—Ve dig *here*. Yace. Zare ist nott zo goot.—)? Yet her forehead is wrinkled and her face, that had seemed so tan compared to the rest of us, has blanched.

Ann's disappearance doesn't surprise me. Daily she was limpening into an unmoving heap like somebody's old doll. But in the breakfast silence each of us knows we could have done more to keep her afloat. We couldn't cure her infected arm, but keeping her mind together should have been possible. If I'd read to her more, if Zeni had talked with her more . . .

I map out search directions while the sun still half shines. There's back toward the airplane, down the —road— Chrysta and Penny traveled, out to the pond along my hunting trails.

Ingrid will search around the house, Zeni to the pond. I'll try Chrysta's —road.— It's a nervous job. At every wind-whipping branch I jump, thinking, there she is. But the gale dies, and silence besets me again. Another few steps, and my own crunching feet betray me. Surely she's following me? When I look around . . . nothing. Snow-crusted trees.

105

When we first came, I tried to guess their kinds . . . maples, oak, elm. Now I hardly differentiate bare ones from evergreen. Endlessly they flow on.

Finish of the —road.— Dies. I plunk down on a fallen something that's a great chalkstick in this white and blackboard wilderness.

If I were Ann, where would I go?

I'd get my arm fixed up.

I'd travel the way Chrysta went . . . But there's nothing here. Not a print. Then I'd probably get lost, I'd wander, call . . . the wind . . . I'd lose my voice on it. Silence. Squirrel skitters up a tree; snow shower fans from his tail.

But I wouldn't kill myself . . . intentionally . . . would I? If all my days and nights were pain? Inside pain, outside pain. If even Ingrid and Joette were walking again while I lay useless in bed? . . . With a bad arm I couldn't dig a snowhole, couldn't hide against last night's fall . . .

I realize if I sit here longer, I'll get as loony and frozen as Ann probably is. Worrying about her fate frightens me. Somehow I blame her for taking the easy way, surrendering to the cold, the silence, the damp, ourselves that the rest of us are still fighting.

Ingrid and Zeni have no better results. One section of the pond ice near the waterfall is mushy, Zeni says, but the snow looks intact all around the shore.

In the kitchen we pass the afternoon slumped about Joette. Her girl baby is bright red, ailing and squalling. Fever like Ann's and we seem equally helpless against it. Ingrid makes a few commonsense questions: do you suppose she caught cold? Have you got enough milk for her? Does she feed well?

Then we're reduced to sitting and watching. Joette wipes the baby's head with a cold cloth. If only we had
    aspirin
    penicillin
    thermometer.

When I'm half frozen to my chair (should always sit on the stool; the balancing act keeps me alive and awake despite leg cramps), I challenge Zeni to a game of Travel On checkers (buttons on charcoaled table cloth). I get two overcoaters crowned, but she wins.

When a log tumbles onto the porch floor, we fall over each other rushing out. It's Ann! . . .

But outside is only windy getting dark. We retreat inward and slam the door. The kitchen shakes.

Ingrid is trying to glue her idols with pine pitch.

This morning five minutes of total—and ridiculous—fiery rage against Gray who is dead. Joette and the babies unleash all the phobia to reproducing that I developed while living with Gray. That didn't abate even when my baby was born.

Why did he suppose I or anybody would have wanted his children when nobody could love him without getting (at best) bruised, (at worst) destroyed by his nagging, insults, rages, moods?

The male is by nature temperamental. If only it weren't true. His —strength— always superior to my —weakness,— nag, nag. Who proved superior finally? Who endured your pain, your delirium, your choking, your —accidents—? Your diapers and dressings? Who buried you, Gray? And who paid your last doctor's last bill before crashing on this hillside?

Sage Zeni say: Man marry to expand the services Mother
provided.
Woman marry to achieve an identity—in
service.

No trace of Ann. Not even a note. Only a patch of her rosy scarf in the soil under her blankets.

Well, the weather has worsened. Sleet squalls that leave all my paths, right from the steps, more skating rink than fishfoot trail. No go even with snowshoes now.

The little girl Sara remains ill, but it's the boy that yells all day long. Joette worries about her milk. I've retreated to the attic. How does Joette stand it? I ought to go mumble something comforting, but I've always considered babies other people's problems. Defective maternal instinct—if there remains such a thing.

Gray accused me of hating children. Well, anybody who hates children and Gray can't be all bad, to paraphrase Fields. I wouldn't admit it to the others, but Zeni's idea of eugenically inserting into kids at birth the abilities to walk, talk, play nonlethally, be toilet trained, avoid all the other painful, boring lessons of anybody's first five years has much to recommend it. We might actually get evolved somewhere valuable instead of doing a repeating decimal on Grammaw's mistakes . . . and Grampaw's wars.

My head aches and the sky just set.

Horrendous day. The babies' squall and Ann's vanish have us all edged up like knives awaiting a victim. Ingrid is a walking bundle of raw annoyance; she stomps room to room banging cups, tossing newspapers, claims she's —keeping warm.— I'd like to toss her into the fireplace.

Whyever Ann fell in love with her is certainly not evident. Oh she's different, all right, but take away the exotic accent and what have you got? A spike-ish, astringent autocrat with stiletto tongue. This afternoon (also in keeping warm) I cross the dining room where Ingrid hastily pretends to be writing at the table.

Ingrid: —Yes? What're *you* doing here? . . . I mean, I thought you were outside.—

Me: —I live here . . . And knock off that tone. I'm not another teenager you boss around.— And she's in a helluva mess if Ann is really . . .

She allows me an exasperated sniff, the familiar clouded, crosshatched forehead.

—Ingrid, why are *your* moods allowed? Why do we all have to take them when you don't allow us the merest complaint? . . . You run a tight ship, you know.—

She looks up curiously. Reminds me of the mule you had to hit with the 2 x 4 to get its attention.

I sit down opposite her. Maybe I am annoying her purposely. But if she's innocent of Ann's disappearing, then why so defensive?

—*I* don't *run* this place, as you call it . . . How can you be so . . . flip, Ivy?— (Must be some nice German word she wants to sic on me.) —Whatever your talents are, you've no sense of community. What's the *matter* with you?— Glares at me. Just when I think she'll soften, she adds —You treat people like chess pieces!—

—Well, at least I don't seduce them so they kill themselves over me.—

—How . . . ?— Stops. She scribbles round and round on notepaper until she's gouged a hole in it. Sits erect, cheeks flaming. She is glorious when angry. Most people satisfy themselves with petulance, arrogance, or socking somebody. She comes through like one of her winged bulls stabbing the earth before takeoff.

—Community's all right. I envy people who know how to keep it going. Like Zeni. But I'm a loner. I feel no matter how much time people spend together, they meet each other's needs so poorly. Like porcupines needling each other . . . If you have to spend all that time fighting or appeasing, you might as well live alone.—

Now she returns my stare. —Was it your marriage or your family that made you such a pessimist?—

Now my turn at jawdropping. Surprise, embarrassment, plus crazy desire to shake her hand, clap her on the back for good guessing. —My husband died. And the dying was horrible. I still have nightmares about it. I have them here . . . Well, you've been married, too?— She nods. —What do you think? Is it all worth it?—

—You don't expect an answer. You want me to restore your faith in human nature. Only you can do that.

109

—It's too late.— I laugh. —Anyway, you didn't answer my question.—

—Everybody doesn't have your experience. I mean so much illness so early in living. Ann . . .— Her face contorts.

—You can tell me . . . if you want. I don't talk around much.—

—Ann had . . . no resilience ei . . .— (Is it —either— she wanted to add?) —No . . . self-confidence. Nobody ever taught her very young that people should be loved. Life is worth trying even if you fail.—

—Failure's not allowed in America . . . But you still haven't answered. My other question.—

—What? Oh, my marriage? It worked for a while. Too many things we should have settled finally overwhelmed us. It was too late to talk somehow. But I don't remember it with bitterness. We were both staffing a dig in Cambodia. We just organized our work schedules so we saw less and less of each other.—

—Just like that? You buried yourself while you were un-covering the ruins? I don't believe you. Nobody gets out of loving or hating that easy.—

—Maybe . . . but it wasn't like that for me.—

—Then you really didn't *love* him in the first place.— Score one for Ivy. Now Ingrid's jaw drops. Flashes angry black eyes at me.

—Why must you . . . *soil* everything?— (Try the good ol' Anglo-Saxon word, Ingrid.) —All right, I guess he did love me more than I could love him. He came courting me; I didn't even encourage him at first. Maybe he was right. I do work too much. But something was missing in him, I don't know. *Largesse,* a talent for the big fling, the unlike-ly chance, whatever it is that keeps people from being sat-isfied with just being cozy. So they lock out the times, the history they belong to.—

—So his ideas on women were medieval? He wanted you to play cozy *Hausfrau* and . . .—

—Ah, no!— she explodes. —You're as simpleminded as

110

Zeni. Still in Spain or Germany that may be true but no longer in America. That's one reason I like it here . . . You don't let people get away with anything, do you?–

A dreadful, dreaded day. We live on riceandbeansbeans-andricericeand beans. I write that to distract me from what actually happened today.

Despite Joette's devoted nursing of all kinds, small Sara died today. Wheezing and coughing until she finally couldn't breathe anymore. All along she'd been apple red with fever and pneumonia; today she turned blue and cold and at the last, her skin was purple. Choking to death. Every time I think about it, I stop breathing. A hospital might have cured her with two shots of penicillin.

If I expected Joette to collapse utterly, I was wrong . . .

Ingrid, Zeni, and I had been sitting around the kitchen tossing those silly tongue twisters.

> *The sixth Sheik's sixth sheep's sick.*
> *Strange strategic statistics.*

Hot blush from Ingrid when she couldn't make it through either of her German contributions. *Fritz Fischer fische frische fische.* And something about –putzing a post coach– which she couldn't reconstruct at all. To save (flushed) face, she threatened to teach us more German later.

And Zeni fell off her stool doing *A skunk sat on a stump.*

–Zany Zeni's Zesty Zoo– I chanted as Ingrid and I picked her up and dusted off her raggy denims. It was the most frolic we'd dared enjoy since Ann disappeared. And most briefly ended.

–She's stopped breathing!– Scream from Joette.

Bewildered, we stared around. Zeni stop breathing. Who? Grins faded from faces.

Joette had taken the baby from the orange crate, was shaking the naked blue body upside down. Then she clamped her lips over the tiny nose and mouth. We slumped onto our stools and watched. One, two . . . five silent minutes. Then

111

Zeni tried to give the baby breath . . . Joette . . .
Zeni.

But the eyes never moved. Sara watched the whole
attempt blankly as if challenging us to get her alive again.
Finally Ingrid bent over Zeni's frantic effort inside the
orange crate. Pulled Zeni off, straightened the baby's cover, and closed her eyelids.

Joette attempted to yank Ingrid's hands away. Ingrid
firmed them onto Joette's shoulders. Then Joette's eyes
overflowed; Ingrid's face twisted to restrain her own tears.
Sobbing in Ingrid's arms.

The boy baby began to wail.

Zeni hunched over his box and tried to quiet him.

Tasting my own face. Wet and salty. Escaped to the
back hall, up the stairs, the attic. A red curtain and papers . . .

In the dining room away from Joette, Ingrid and I
wrapped the baby and settled her into the paper nest I'd
made. Then I carried the crate to the back hall. Heavier
than I expected; mothball smell. The red velvet must have
been Grammaw's finest when it hung between the dining-
room and parlor from those bone rings.

I couldn't get myself to put the box outside. It's snowing again . . .

Gray and I walked the hospital corridor . . . when our
own baby died . . . Ian. And loved the tenderness we saw
at last in each other.

> All the white I'll ever see
> Is far too much of white for me.

112

for Zeni

MOUNTAIN → KNOWS → SNOWS
  A TEASING JOAN DARC QUESTS THE VIN VITAE
  A GILDED JOAN DARC CHOPS THE FIRESHADOW
  A RESOURCEFUL MAIDENNATION SEDUCES THE AMAZON
  REDCOLD AS OTHERHOODS
    UNINHABITABLE AS OTHERHOOD
FEAR → UP → HERE

GO TO IVY'S GONE HUNTING

IVY'S GONE HUNTING

January ? (*must* be).

I haven't written here for a week. People day-draggy again. I've taken to the outdoors and found a new foot-warming technique. As usual, Ingrid pops my balloon by saying the Eskimos already invented it, but anyway it's wrapping my feet in plastic bread bags before donning Grammaw's socks.

Today as I slammed the door to knock Ingrid out of my head, Zeni shouted —It's Christmas! You can't stay mad on Christmas. Go out and get us a tree!— And that's how Christmas came to be.

At first we were all skeptical; with our recent failure(s) we didn't *deserve* Christmas somehow. But I hoisted the ax on my shoulder, cut a small hemlock, and dragged it back to the porch. In the kitchen Joette had readied a stand and pan of water; Zeni and Ingrid were hanging slivers of silver balls and sprigs of plastic mistletoe. Ingrid had even crayoned a few Merry Christmas signs in a bunch of languages.

More marvels: on the dining room table stood: a half-pint of ? water? ah, *gin*! four glasses and a hot pie whose steam rose fruitful. All the California groves weren't sweeter than the smell from one little six-inch pie. Days ago Zeni found the gin behind two living room bricks and has been plotting a party.

Zeni: —Hey, Ingrid, cut us some stars for the tree. It's naked.—

Ingrid: —Is there any more tinfoil in the attic?—

Ivy: —There's pink tissue. Go see. I left it on the trunk.—

Ingrid: —Okay.—

Zeni: —Caught ya! First time you ever said "okay" instead of "yes" or "*ja*."—

Ingrid: —When in Amurrica, be an Amurrican.—

Zeni: —*Ja, ja.*— She salutes —for good measurement.— Another Ingridism.

Ivy: —Hey, that's the first time Ingrid's Germanic reserve's down.—

Zeni: —She made the pie, too.—

I was awed, a domestic Ingrid being a new blip on my radar screen. I'd assumed that anything tasty must be Joette's work.

During the next half hour: joy, expectation, unity. All those impossible items I thought had vanished from the world pulsed through the dining room. All because of a five-foot evergreen, a batch of magazine covers, and moldy tissue.

Ingrid ripped while I glued. Soon the table, floor, tree, and fireplace glowed with rose snowflakes, angel wings, poinsettias, stars and chains. When Joette opened the door, our pink avalanche raced across the floor. Shots of gin on an empty stomach made Ingrid gayer and gayer into risque verses for Christmas carols and absurd toasts.

As the liquor disappears, Zeni declares it time for presents. —You guys are way behind. I got mine all ready.— And she draws from her shirt three mangled hunks of fishline-tied tissue, which she spins across the table. —Okay, you have fifteen minutes.— Checking her arm for the watch that's not there.

We all scramble toward our rooms and the attic. I ferret out a vintage 1957 *Woman's Day* for Joette, an ancient bottle for Ingrid, and an iron cross for Zeni. After we reassemble about the stove, Joette and Sammy get the best haul in presents—a pearl necklace from Ingrid, my *Woman's Day* done in white ribbons, a dollar plus a certificate, hand inscribed from Zeni, for Joette's —valorous services to the republic.— Ingrid gives Sammy a hat she's knitted with orange ears on top. When Joette fits it on him, he looks like a Halloween koala bear.

From Ingrid I get a copy of *Hunting Life* (also '57), from Joette a pack of fish hooks, and from Zeni a sort of trophy construction whose base is a candy box on which sits a pink pipe cleaner figure holding her head in her

116

hands. Across the front in Zeni's sprawly handwriting: *And I thought community was possible!* This creature we savor and pass around.

Zeni gets my iron cross and a pair of large barrettes from Joette. —Whatsa matter? You don't like my shaggy dog special?— From Ingrid a plastic globe and sceptre: —Of course, Zeni, you're our ruling monarch.— At which Zeni pales and squirms. Ingrid does know how to hit the sore spots because Zeni's regalest illusion (may be what keeps her going?) is that we're all equal here.

An awkward moment that Ingrid tries to gloss by clutching her glass, fingering the ribbons on her presents, devising effusively correct compliments. —Oh, they're beautiful! Thank you *so* much.—

When she opens her presents, we find we've all attempted the elegant delicate for her—my shimmering bottle, peacock feather earrings from Zeni, a —jeweled— pencil sharpener (rhinestones) from Joette.

After bedding the presents beneath the tree, we share Ingrid's strawberry jam pie and try to follow her in German carols. Every time she forgets a second verse, she stamps her foot like a little girl who's just had her pigtails slammed in the door. Then she lectures us all on the fine art of superspitting our *ch*'s. Finally whatever we sing sounds like *Edelweiss*.

Ingrid plonks onto the parlor sofa, muffles her laughing in the cushions. Zeni is sitting on my lap, and Joette dances Sammy atop her head. His great blue eyes watch us impassively from the tiny face. Bigger than his sister.

Next Zeni kazoos a number on a comb and whistle combo she's devised and then we're dancing. Me with her, Ingrid with Joette while Sammy wiggles on the dining room table, watching us upside down.

When we're wholly winded, three of us pile onto Ingrid on the sofa, choking and giggling, with such force that two maple legs collapse. We list to starboard, a mass of cozy confused limbs and torsos. Ingrid's blouse is askew,

117

and I see some of why Ann enjoyed sleeping with her—if
she did.

Ach ja, that we never have to work or freeze again.
Just stay here stoned forever on dancing, gin, and strawberry pie.

Lord, let me be a country girl again.

Funny how when we're (at last) doing well here I don't
write much.

XMAS INTO NEW YEAR'S HIGH

And it's grown into new willingness to help each other
through the dark morning's cold, the watery noon soup,
the waterier evening soup.

Afternoons Zeni has begun what I call the Children's
Story Hour. At first we tried the Bible, but the plot was
a drag so we switched to Mark Twain. And now are happily escaped into *Captain Stormfield's Visit to Heaven*,
that I found in the attic, waterwarped and spidery-inscrib-
ed: From Caleb to Henry, Christmas, 1926.

May we continue our spirits so spritely . . .

A day of intense mental talkings—what I'm reduced to
when it's snow outside (more) and tension inside again.
Christmas truce is over.

Wander aimlessly about the house like a ten-year-old
at the end of a rainy vacation. When I open the kitchen
door, Joette is propped on her mattress, clutching and
feeding the boy baby. I ease the door shut and meander
onward, imagining how I might have cheered her up if I
were Chrysta or if there were anything cheerful to say
about Sara.

Upstairs I stop at Ingrid's closed door. A toddler asking,
Can Ingrid come out to play? I chuck the notion and progress onward, upward, imagining the conversation Ingrid
and I might have about archeology—if I knew anything
about archeology.

118

Zeni is nowhere, or rather she's probably applying herself to one of our myriad practical problems—checking the mousetraps, stuffing more newspaper around windows, de-icing the steps—as I should be.

Although it's noon, the narrow stairs behind the attic door rise eerie black. I recall Zeni trying her best subject last night over rice and beans and sand. —What's wrong with our *interpersonal relationships*?— Certainly Gray and I never settled this dilemma: does love mean accepting somebody the way he/she is—or working industriously to subvert him/her into *your* ideal? But talking about it never helped somehow; that's what frustrates Zeni—that horrible gap between word and action, idea and reality.

The weather under these rafters is amazing. How it manages to be both frigid and stuffy simultaneously. Probably some new law of thermodynamics which nobody but me will ever know:

$32°F. + 100°$ Stuffiness $= 132°$ Fahrenstuff

Yesterday I tried to open a window, but ol' Caleb or somebody back in 1900 'n donkey's years had nailed them both shut.

I've been wandering through a stack of *Life* from the Forties. Envying that last generation of lucky people who felt they had a national challenge that could be met if we all work together. Is a hero's death by Fascism better than malingering with emphysema or getting stabbed by a junkie? Or will the deaths of today seem equally envious, luxurious, to the next generation who'll be living on rationed water, rationed air, rationed food and rationed space?

Must be 3 a.m. This is the second night I've awakened awash in sweat. I hop to bed iciclecold under so many Grammaw quilts that by dawn I smell like an Arrid ad. Now I know what Ann must have suffered with fever. But I fear unwrapping even to use my basin because I'll catch worse than cold. So I've taken to sleeping with the basin inside the covers.

119

Today Zeni reports similar hot flashes and sleepwakes. Wonder if it's a new rice- or sand-induced disease? Ingrid says her head still aches so much every night it keeps her from getting hot or cold.

Optimistic note to interior decorators: I've finally swallowed the mildew odor on bedding and walls that used to keep me sick until afternoon. I haven't noticed it since ? even in the attic.

Found my coat belt and tried it on. Despite three hunting shirts I've shrunk two notches down to the smallest hole. A shock for some reason. Zeni and I had both boasted how glad we'd be to lose a bit of flab.

Zeni and I are alternately woodchopping. Ingrid has started foraging for small kindling.

This morning in the kitchen around Joette we raged for two hours over the women's movement. Joette had just finished nursing and bubbling Sammy and was bundling him into his reupholstered crate. She's twitted Zeni before on being —against marriage.—

—Zeni, why *do* you think marriage is outmoded?—

Zeni, who is handing around peas as half our unhearty pioneer breakfast, flinches—unusual for her. Too early? Exhaustion? Yesterday's continued futile Ann hunt?

Joette repeats the question at Zeni and settles into Grammaw's rocker. (Is it the double chin, the still-maternal middle, or the clear eyes that always seem to announce, *I* can cope. How about you?)

At the stove's other side Ingrid stares from some canned rhubarb she spoons. I'm stool sitting right before our slowpoke oven.

—I don't think it's outmoded for everybody.— Zeni hedging? —Like I just wish people would *do it* as two tall wholes instead of two little broken down halves seeking each other in the wilderness.—

Ingrid: —Zeni! Everybody doesn't get married like that. I . . .—

—Okay. Not always. But people often—okay?—get married for the wrong reasons.—

—That's not why *I* married!— Snap from Ingrid. —How can you generalize so?—

Zeni: —'Cause I see the facts behind all the nonsense.— Sudden vague smile toward the floor, not toward us, as if she's remembered that riling us against each other is not a recommended survival technique.

—Ingrid, why did you get married?—

Pleasant to see Ingrid before Zeni's firing squad. Usually she reveals as little of herself to us as I do.

—I don't care for that weary tone . . . My husband's name was David. We were married in Cambodia during some fieldwork we both did there. We made it *good enough* together—as you would say.— Glare at Zeni. —But the years . . . we just had less living in common. But we didn't hate each other. *I* certainly don't hate men. That's all I care to say about it.—

I decide to join the fun. —When did Zeni say she hated men?—

Zeni smiles at me. So I have one friend left in the icebox. The baby gurgles, spits. Joette turns aside. Ingrid ramrod on her stool; her throat and head jut forward. Reminds me of Nefertiti—with a bandage. Egypt and Berlin meeting somewhere around Czechoslovakia.

Zeni inhales. I hope a harangue isn't in the works. —Okay, I think everybody needs a new deal. But how the women's movement got shaped, how it isn't *run*, like it founders along all busted up into bitter little segments, isn't the way to do it—

Ivy: —What happened, Zeni? Did they purge you?—

She nods. Spreads her fingers, which seems to mean I should shut up. But she continues. —So I quit the group I started with, but there's ten other groups.—

Ivy: —But what did you *do* that outraged everybody?—

—Oh hell, all I did was answer two *New York Times* reporters during a Union Square demonstration. It was like the sisters had been waiting for months to get me on some misdemeanor. So they did . . .—

Und so weiter with an insult or two (Zeni vs. Ingrid) for another hour. It's the warmest I've been in weeks since the Big Fog!

Are the four and a half (Sammy) of us here *really* Zeni's most promising social experiment so far?

Joette our True Believer: —Who wants to be equal to men when we're superior?—

Joette is a female chauvinist. Parlor graffitus.

It's true we're all equal here—equally hungry, equally raggy . . . But we're not identical or even similar. Our histories, marriages, lives have been too different. Zeni ignores that when she talks about some unity we're supposed to share automatically just by being women. If she'd hand-picked us (instead of falling from the sky with us), I'm sure she'd have preferred us more desperate, more persecuted—black and bitter maybe, potential bombers, dedicated despisers of the System.

And what's beyond sisterhood? Motherhood? Just try Ivy for the finest in old-line reproductive thinking. Zeni has met the enemy and he is me.

FREE PAPERBACK BOOKS! FREE!*

Love by Mary Jan and Lawrence L. Losoncy. Gives students a hopeful realistic picture of a healthy marriage. $1.35.
Creative Suffering: A Ripple of Hope. Exploring suffering in its broadest meaning. $2.25.
I Will by Urban Steinmetz. The present and future of marriage. $1.35.
  *with a two-year subscription, choose any *one* title.

Zeni: —Ingrid, you're the historian. Why don't you write a history of women?—

Ingrid: —I'm busy enough with a history of civilization.—

Zeni: —Think about it. What about matriarchies, the Amazon myth, Atalanta, the Virgin Mary?—

Don't mention Ann.

Something—the cold, the sparse food, the house demon, the way station sort of life here—is freezing our brains (Ingrid's and mine). Meals used to make me sleepy, but now my only spurts of mental power last the hour after lunch or dinner when my fingers are warm enough and the fire high enough to thaw my head.

Ingrid says she can't work at all on her charts because her room is too cold and our din-liv rooms too communal. She can't think at airports either. She still lets people bug her too much. Disliking them is her dependence . . .

Ingrid is teaching us Churman phrases (euphemism for laughing at Joette and me as we try to wrap our mouths around *ch*'s and *r*'s that are never the right *ch* or *r*). She says when she first came to this country, she taught at Berlitz.

I continue collecting words and stanzas that I can have fun with when I return to a computer. I no longer imagine us as dogs . . . How about birds? Six Wild Birds on a Winter Mountain. Six Portraits. I try a few phrases between Ingrid, the German grammar book, and the fireplace. The effort warms me.

NAME	OCCUPATION	AGE
Ingrid Rosendahl	Professor, archeologist	35

DATA: Ingrid is teaching us German. *Der schöne Flamingo.*

PRONOUNCE CAREFULLY: *Gemischtes Eis*

                  Wir kommen nicht mehr so jung
                      zusammen.
                  Hals und Beinbruch
                  Der Verlust ist vergessen.

TRANSLATE INTO GERMAN FOLLOWING THE EXAMPLES GIVEN IN YOUR BOOK:

    Twice a day she gathers eggs in her basket.

Attract all sizes.

Sexually demanding and possibly insatiable.

This museum owes a great deal to archeologists.

Just show me a rich archeologist.

Bumps and lumps

Ingrid is our witch—our richly bewitching witch.

NOTE: One should keep in mind that most words of non-Germanic origin have German counterparts. Examples are animal = *Tier*; kitten = *Putty*; mantrap = *Fussangel*; plague = *Pest*; courage = *Mut*.

While conversions will definitely increase the student's ability to communicate, her ability to understand will not necessarily increase at the same rate.

Ivy Eilbeck   Computer programmer   30

DATA: *Hausfink.* Yellow-shafted Flicker. Great Blue Heron.

PRONOUNCE CAREFULLY: *Wir machen einen Drache. Diese Männer!*

TRANSLATE INTO GERMAN:

> Help! Lightning has struck our postilion!
>
> The bitter lemon is in the tool room.
>
> It is snowing, was snowing, will snow, would snow, has snowed, had snowed—oh hell, let it snow!
>
> Watch your weather!
>
> Send nature on a memo.
>
> I hate these dull foggy days.
>
> Palm Coast is the kind of place where you can slip your boat from its moorings.
>
> Can I persuade you to come hunting with me?
>
> No distinction between willingness and compulsion is possible.
>
> —Do you want a baby?—
>
> —Why can't I have a puppy?—

Lugging wood in. Rammed against my stomach to stop hunger. Finger splinters and the burnt smell of wet wool round my wrists . . . Running to keep warm. Running, running. Lump of terror hard inside me. Brilliant with coal's sharp facets . . . When I discovered I was pregnant; Gray's humping had been —successful.— When the doctor told

124

me Gray was dying. When I buried Gray. The old temptation to cut and run . . . to cut and run the terror.

Damn the cold! Have to use the pail again. And Gray
sneered —When they blow up the world, you'll be in the
ladies' room.—

Terror of being trapped, of having my body beyond
my control, strapped on a table with white lights ablaze
as if I were a mental patient, rubber digits and stainless
steel prodding my insides . . .

—Ivy? Dr. Campbell. You know, the baby's two weeks
overdue and you haven't come to see me. I should check
you over.—

—There's no need.—

—What do you mean, there's no need? You haven't
done anything foolish, have you? You *are* my responsibility, you know.—

—Nothing foolish. Just the baby is six days old, and
we're doing fine.—

—Wha-at? . . . Who delivered it?—

—I did. At home. Last Wednesday early.—

—Has the clinic seen him? He needs . . .—

—Yes. I brought him there Friday.—

—And you delivered him *yourself*? . . . Young lady,
you're a damn fool. You attended enough prenatal classes
to know the dangers. If anything had happened . . .—

—It didn't.—

—Are you hemorrhaging at all?—

—No. The bleeding's stopped.—

—Are you breastfeeding?—

—Yes.—

—Good . . . but foolish. I deliver 350 babies a year and
in ten years I've never had a woman deliberately play a
trick like that on me. What did your husband say?— I
didn't answer. —Well, I must check you over. Can you
come tomorrow afternoon? . . . What, Cindy? . . . Oh,
my secretary just reminded me I'm playing golf . . .—

Quietly, firmly I pressed down the phone. Dr.

125

Campbell's office called twice more, but my mind was out.

Terror strapping me into the house.

Awake, my body unable to move or dress until noon, to heat soup and baby food and stay alive until three, to get up when Gray arrived home. —I'm sure it's the flu— he said. —How's the baby? What're we having for dinner?—

My mind unable to hinge one thought to another. Just stark winged terrors, disheveled crows, that perched on my chest, pecked and cawed at me.

You want to kill Gray . . . Caw.
You wish you never started the babies . . . Caw
You want to cut and run . . . Caw.
Crow in the snow.

I try some Ann:

Roseann ?   Student   19
DATA: White breasted Nuthatch
PRONOUNCE CAREFULLY: *Wo ist der Fussboden?*
                         Was ist denn los?
                         Das Vermogen ging verloren.
                         Das Füttern der Tiere ist verboten.
TRANSLATE INTO GERMAN:
    Brat. Pest. Frightened sprite.
    Put a bird together.
    It's enough to drive ya outa yah tree!
    Do you find it difficult to speak English on the telephone?
    An orgy every morning.
    Too much Freud brings no joy.
    —My mother made me a homosexual.—
    —If you give her the wool, will she make me one?—
    The woods are full of rabbits this fall.

Mustn't let Ingrid see this.

The trouble with passivity, dependence, fragility, delicacy, and the other —charms— of women is that people later hold it against you that you weren't —there— when they needed a formed personality, order in the chaos.

Zeni said during her first talk on women's history her students begged her for a definition of "femininity," and she refused to give one. I should ask her whether they were just baiting her for an authoritarian statement to knock down—or whether they knew already that having other people define you is more annoying but less frightening than having to do the job yourself.

Zeni Abbott   Assistant professor, revolutionary   26
DATA: Chickadee. Bohemian Waxwing. Birdsongs in your garden.
PRONOUNCE CAREFULLY: *Dort sind die Schweine! Der Bär*
                hat Fänge.
            Übermüde Brüder.
NOTE: Germanic agents derive feminine agents in the same manner, if a feminine agent makes sense at all. Miscellaneous masculine agents.
TRANSLATE INTO GERMAN:
    —What can I do for you, Madam?— he said with a smile.
    To earn your living, you must first find a job.
    Those who teach school are training the citizens of the
        future.
    —I love teaching—It's students I can't stand!—

Mustn't let Zeni see this yet. Nervous birds.

Lugged too many logs this morning. Wound down exhausted, wracked with cramps, started on a tear jag that has me cold, sweaty, and shaking. If I'm afraid, of what am I afraid? That we won't be found? That we will? That Ingrid hates me? That I failed my parents and Gray also?

If I'm nervous, of what am I nervous? That life here is claustrophobic? That I just can't *sit still* like Joette or Ingrid?

If I'm horrified, of what am I horrified? That we're not

—making it— as a group, that we're not more or better to each other?

Go chop some more wood.

Don't know whether talking with Zeni energizes or enervates me. Probably both. I can't believe that my struggles with Gray were —inevitable— just because we were male and female. I'm not that determinist. I believe *any* two people will probably fight when they try to do *anything* together. Which Zeni declares is —far more determinist. God, that's a lockout before you even start.—

Gray and I were just the wrong two people of whatever sexes. And I won't hack it over further. There's no need to fight or hate men, parents, anybody—if you can only ignore them long enough to do what you really want. Make a lifestyle that looks happy enough to disarm the critics ahead of time.

Zeni sounded a subject I'd thought was taboo—Ann. If I've considered Zeni somebody who always blew off instantly whatever was bubbling in her head, I was wrong. She's waited . . . *The woods are full of rabbits this fall.*

After dreary lunching on corn-rye cakes with flour soup, she lashed into us all for saddling her with the problem of —what to do about Ann— before and after she —walked off.—

—Especially you, Ivy. You came to me complaining, what are *we* going to do about Ann, when what you meant was that *I* ought to do something because you couldn't take looking at her. She depressed you too much. Right?— Zeni's arms and legs cross on Joette's mattress, eyes aflare.

Ingrid stares at me. No expression yet that I can read. All right, Lady Flamingo, if I get it, you're coming with me.

—I never pretended I knew what was wrong with her, but I felt that together . . .—

—So you're the last of the bigtime groupies.— Sneer from Zeni. Ingrid smiles.

—Zeni, what the hell's the matter with you? If you need somebody to blame, try Ingrid. She's the one who fucked the kid over!—

—*Must* you use language like that?— Joette.

—Who're you? Emily Post? . . . Make Ingrid talk. She saddled us with Ann.—

Zeni sighs. But three of us are now regrouped toward Ingrid. I see how these days have shaken her. Bits of gray hair previously tucked into crisp waves or hidden under the bandage straggle at the sides of her face. Her hands are dirty, nails broken. I'm sorry for her. Losing both Ann and a whole work season must be hell to her *ordnung*-oriented soul.

But it's misplaced mercy. Her salvo is all ready. —What Ann and I did is my business. Is that clear? I won't have it referred to again.—

Zeni: —Yes, you will. I agree with Ivy that because of you we all got involved with Ann. But, Ivy, you go too far. What Ann did to herself isn't *all* Ingrid's fault.—

Ingrid's teeth grit. Is it only embarrassment and guilt or is she truly not used to accounting to anybody for her actions? Ingrid lived alone, Ann said. And liked it, I bet.

—All right. Peace offer. I won't mention Ann again to you, Ingrid, or behind your back. Which is what you think I've been doing. But I want something. I want you to stop cutting me off—like a bug—when you see me.—

—Are you that delicate?—

—Just a humane answer next time I have to ask you something.—

Today we all got flaked by Zeni—with special accusations against me. The hassle consumed an hour, left us drained but pacified somehow. On one point she's right: accused us of not making or maintaining any *act of will* to cooperate here. With particular annoyance toward me

129

for—spreading a *gospel* of pessimism about people ever getting along together.— (Is Zeni an ex-Catholic? She *must* be.)

Ingrid hops on that one. —Ivy, you are a sad sack from one week to the next.—

—So I don't smile every other minute. I bring home the rabbits, don't I?—

Joette laughs.

—Look, Zeni, the trouble with your Grand Utopian Dream is that none of us ever *chose* to live here. We're just making the best of bad circumstances, that's all.—

—That's shit. You *did* choose. All of you chose. We chose to take that plane. Then we chose again to stay here instead of walking into a blizzard with Chrysta.—

At Chrysta's name we silence again. The Unresolved Problem Category that's already crowded with Ann and the baby. Winddriven snow sprays the kitchen window, silting the cracks; the water pot hisses.

—Ivy and Ingrid, hey, you both talk as if out *there* wherever you came from, you have infinite choices, all kinds of free will to live whatever you want. You know that isn't true. —

—I think here on the mountain is freer . . . and better. We see each other face to face. We don't have to hide or run; we needn't play cute games conning each other into little pigeonholes.—

—Then what're you doing now?—

—I'm trying to form us into a group instead of a bunch of isolated igloos. We've already chosen each other; we just need to work harder.—

—Maybe we don't like groups. Why don't you ask us what *we* want?—

—Okay. Fireside chat time . . . Joette, what do *you* want?—

—Well, first I wish you'd all *keep quiet.*— (Ingrid laughs.) —Why can't we just do what we're supposed to do? Why these discussions? Whatever your problem, just don't upset other people.—

130

—Okay. One bid for repression. Do I hear others? Going, going . . .—

—Gone!— We all yell to break the tension. Zeni now bangs the counter with an impromptu gavel—one rotten turnip that Joette was fixing for lunch.

—Joette's right. We do waste too much time sitting and dreaming. The main reason I stayed here is I thought I'd get caught up with half my articles for this year. And I haven't done it because my notes and photos, everything I need, is in my office. And Ann . . .— Ingrid stops.

The U.P.C. looms again. —Look, we don't blame you about Ann. She was ill but it was your own business. But I am curious. Why did you pick someone like her to work for you?—

—I— Ingrid frowns.

—Cut it, Ivy.— Zeni glares at me. *The bear has fangs.*

—No! We should talk about it. You and Joette want everything shoved under the rug. Or is it the stove? Whatever destroys your little Utopian vision. Ann was sick, she took a poker to her best friend, then she wandered into the snow. Where does that leave us? *I* feel responsible. I don't know about *you.*—

—Shut up about Ann. Ingrid and I have talked about Ann. Frankly it's none of your business, Ivy. Let me handle it, will you? Worry about what *is* your business—the raunchy comments you make all the time.— Zeni squares her shoulders at me. —And keep the agreement you made yesterday.—

Joette: —Somebody else has hurt you, Ivy. You have to work that out yourself. You can't take it out on us.— So . . . she and Ingrid have been whispering together.

—Why not? You dump on me about Sara and Sammy, about how you miss your husband, the kids, and the house.—

Zeni sighs. —Jesus, I wish I had a cigarette . . . Okay. So we all hate each other.— She smiles. —So what do we do now?—

Through my enraged exhaustion I begin to measure her

method. She operates by deliberately provoking a quarrel. Defuse the sizzling monkeys on our backs by chilling them out in the frosty air. I've been had! Don't know now whether to anger or sigh with relief that somebody is still running this show, has a plan for us.

Zeni: —Enough. Why don't we do something practical for an hour like get some water? And then come back with maybe one suggestion each for making it together here.—

Scrape of stools and it's over. Does she really think such kindergarten group dynamics will get us anywhere? Zeni is a peculiar puzzle. I feel like scrawling it on the living room wall next to Grammaw's portrait . . .

I can't believe it. After yoking and hauling the sieve-y wooden pails, we meet and it goes right. I expect renewed blasts from both Ingrid and Zeni, but the community has somehow in the hour's release of stumbling uphill under heavy buckets progressed away from four disgruntled solitudes through one disgruntled solitude to ? Respect for each other, willingness to start over, forgiveness for what we aren't to each other, acceptance of what we are.

A delicate see saw. The cliff edge where Gray and I teetered for years always falling off, back into our wretched habits, negative thoughts, self-pity. Ah the life I could lead if I wasn't stuck with YOU. Then inching upward to teeter again. And I'd panic, wondering why the work I did, the love I gave in good moments, couldn't buy freedom from criticism, insults and vengeance of the bad moments . . .

We meet again; it flows. I promise to tone down what Zeni calls —my negative comments.— Ingrid phrases hers delicately, but it amounts to how she'll stop brooding afternoons in her room, using wood she hasn't chopped to heat her own fireplace. Zeni promises to spot trouble and get —anyone of you to talk it over with me before it blows up.— Joette agrees to get food into Sammy three times during the long darkness instead of twice to make our pre-

132

dawns more peaceful. And all of us (including Joette!) confess anti-Sammy thoughts. Sammy, destroyer of our sleeps hard won against clammy mattresses, creaky bed-steads, arms and legs that fall asleep before we do.

Zeni's right about one thing: our first —covenant— concerned only outside work, who was doing what. But it's the *inner* attitudes that can tear us apart.

Joette Winton   Housewife, mother   37
DATA: *Die Taube*
PRONOUNCE CAREFULLY: *Es ist Geröll im Gewölbe.*
                         Eine Schneeballschlacht.
TRANSLATE:
    Gamebird placemats. Birdsong playing cards.
    Add cheer to family dinners.
    We do everything ourselves except the very heavy work.
    Do you serve lunch on this flight?
    I was an unwed mother for the FBI.
    My son's diapers are wet.
    Go to bed quickly—I shall call the doctor.
    This house is haunted.

Day of fishsitting. Nothing (caught).

What Zeni's —consciousness raising— is raising in me is acute and useless (postoperative) guilts. I react to it as if I were still married, Gray alive, as if my listening to Zeni's rhetoric on how women need a variety of life styles is somehow traitorous to him. Or is a part of *me* surfacing— that Gray hunk he nagged so hard to place within me, a cold nugget of guilt that would —make me think twice,— see everything (even how much to open a bedroom window) through four, six eyes. His, mine, two more labeled what he thinks of what I think of myself.

Predawn mice woke me up scampering and gnawing through one of my corners. They've not fallen for Zeni's universal mousetrap. A phalanx of them has redecorated Ingrid's archeologizing; her notebook now has smart deckle

133

edges. I envy mice. Their whole life, like ours, is a food search. But they have fur coats, instead of rags, and generally seem to make it.

House, teach me how to live in you.

Help me not to answer fear, suspicion, and paranoia with f.s.p.

—Zeni, I have a confession to make.— Passing what used to be her room (she now sleeps on the horsehair sofa), I catch her thrust headlong into the dusty closet. —You know, I agreed to stay here for all the wrong reasons.— Smile and try a light tone, hoping she'll laugh. She doesn't. Backs from the closet and sprongs herself onto the empty bedframe.

—Do you have to tell me now? I hate people unloading on me when I haven't eaten for six hours.— She anchors both flanges of her hair behind her ears. —Okay. Sorry.— She sighs. —What is it, Ive?—

The —Ive— is new. —I don't know. I guess I've been stuck in the snow too much.—

—C'mon. Don't pretty it up. What're you trying to say?—

—I agreed to stay here— I'm about to admit: because I was between lives anyway. Cancel it to —because I needed answers. How to live . . . So I was impressed with all your energy. And with Ingrid as the kind of woman I was never able to be.—

—She's not, you know.— Her words tumble at me. —She got so hung up over Ann.—

—Okay. But *you're* a raving bundle of energy. You can't deny that.—

—Yeah. No. Look, I don't think about it. I just *do* it.—

—Joette strikes again!— We both laugh; I relax.

—So you *have* been studying us?— Mock horror. —That's funny because you've got something I want. I'll bet you know. It's like you're impervious to people. Half the time they just don't reach you. So you're free not to get all sticky and thrown by them the way Joette and I do. The

134

way Ingrid does even though she hides it more. You're free to do what *you* want.—

Now I'm laughing. —That's crazy.—

—Is it true?—

—It 's what my husband used to say about me. A cool perimeter I developed to live with him. I never thought I was good at it because he called me hysterical, too. But it's true I can work no matter what trough I'm trying to climb out of.—

—C'mon. Stay in it and slosh around with the rest of us.—

(En)treaty. We shake on it. *Translate into German: —What can I do for you, madam?— she said with a smile.*

A helluva battle with, of all things, the dining room wall. To be precise, the gutter on the dining room wall. Yesterday's ice storm slicked and silvered our already white world. Would have stayed minor if it had only stayed frozen. But not *our* ice. Before dawn, cylinders of it began clunking onto the tin roof, a festival of cymbals followed by a finale—one great crash behind the dining room. After this forced us from the sack at six, I tiptoed through the dining room straight into an icy puddle two inches deep, four feet wide. Our private pond, table to window.

To Zeni: —You go out.—

Zeni, yawning: —*You* go out. I can't find my sweaters.—

Sammy began yelling. I went out.

Reddish-gray dawn smearing the white-weighted branches. *It is snowing, was snowing, will snow, would snow.* Transparent turd-like ices everywhere. The storm's spoor . . . From the shadowed entrails I thought at first the whole wall was collapsing.

Finally I spotted the trouble. Half a glacier had moved down the roof, shattered the wooden gutter onto the ground. Leaving the melting free to inundate the room for twenty feet along the wall. The roof is flatter here; snow collects and stays.

135

Ivy the guttersnipe. To the woodshed for hammer and nails and a length of corroded aluminum something. Nail the rotten, warped gutter together. Hoist one end; it topples onto the chimney. Try again. Prop it slo-owly with the aluminum something until it's horizontal back under the eaves, left of the chimney. Support the drip end with a tree limb so the water drains down the corner of the house instead of into the living room fireplace or dining room.

Pausing to wipe my nose (on my sleeve), I see that my arms to elbows and knees to toes are covered with ice. By dawn light my fingers are purple. If I stand here, I'll soon be cemented to the ground. With the stirring wind ice pellets bombard my head and neck, melt and trickle down the warm flesh of my back.

For some reason I begin loud, long laughs to the dribbly trees. I want to tell Zeni how women's liberation in your cozy home on a $700 Karistan carpet is one thing; the liberated woman out here is something else.

I land a kick into the aluminum something which jars the gutter which jars the chimney which jars the branch just enough so the gutter creaks out from under the eave . . . and balances . . . and catches the drip.

One more huge kick at the house—near the door so I won't unseat my new trapeze sculpture. An icicle wall cascades down. I retreat inside.

At breakfast Zeni presents me the perfect ad:

136

Tear the tiny tots to tiny shreds.

We've homegrown a variety of new family jokes. Zeni
began one with a flourish by leaping up and pulling out
my chair for me at the table, meanwhile announcing —And
what would uh Madame fancee *pour dinaire?*— Now it's And
what does Madame want for breakfast?
                              tea?
                              bedtime?
                              woodchopping?
                              _____ (fill in the blank.)
            Correct ans/s: FOOD!!
                            Filet mignon avec truffles
                            a hot fudge sundae
                            dripping roast beef
            or a three speed electric blanket (because ice
                              cubes are our most important
                              product.)
When Ingrid absentmindedly hummed a German carol,
Zeni desecrated *On the First Day of Christmas My True
Love Sent to Me* with

            A blue jay-ay in a snowy tree!
            Two broken windows
            And a blue jay in a snowy tree!

Now it's On the forty-first day of Travel On
            Jack Frost sent to me
            Fi-ive frozen noses
            Four dull axes
            Three dirty plates
            Two broken windows
            And a bluejay in a snowy tree.

Our first singing frightened Sammy. Now he coos along
with us from his orange crate. (I can see him twenty years
from now chasing any woman who yodels or smells like
fruit. The womb, dear Sammy, doth make fools of us
all . . .)

Ingrid's *Stille Nacht, Heilige Nacht* a la Zeni:

> Windy night, horrible night
> All is calm but nothing is bright.

Joette has been reading the Bible except for the food sections. Milk, honey, manna, mama . . . I consider reading my Bird Portraits to everybody, but *chicken* out. The desire passes. I'll organize them as a present for Zeni. Group Portrait—Dove to Hawk.

Chansons de Notre Chalet

> *arrangees par les Mountain Four*
> *Allegro andante*

> *Bitch! Bitch! Bitch! The girls are marching.*
> *Cheer up, sisters, they will come.*
> *And beneath the starry flag*
> *We will breathe the air again*
> *Of the free land in our own beloved home.*

Sigh. Zeni hates the first line.

> *In this mountain house I set*
> *Thinking, mother dear, of you*
> *And our bright and happy* (yuh, let's hear it
>   again for *happy*) *home so far away.*
> *And the tears they fill my eyes*
> *'Spite of all that I can do*
> *Tho' I try to cheer my sisters and be gay.*
>   (*. . . Sexually demanding and possibly . . .*)
>   Ingrid wants to hear it again for *gay.*

If at first I was tempted to dismiss Zeni as a garrulous activist or worse—somebody who mistook talking and theorizing for acting and living—it appears I'm wrong here, too. Today she claims it's precisely to *escape* such evils that she's glad we're living here.

Me: —I don't believe you. You'd like us to warm the

stools around the stove all afternoon with you. Doesn't your seat get numb—or your feet?—

Z: —Okay. They're trying to tell you something.—

Me: —But you're not listening.—

Z: —Remember what I came from. People building walls of words to shut each other out—with the tower of Babel on top.—

Me: —But there must have been one group you liked. What about your women's collective . . . action cell, whatever you called it?—

At the rhetoric she winces. —It should have been, but it wasn't. I mean there were too many of us—nine. I even started the group. We were good friends. We'd known each other two years. We met once a week, which looks like plenty, given everybody's insane schedule. But it got like therapy hour. Instead of people dealing with problems, fights, slights whenever they cropped us elsewhere, we saved it all for each other.

—For instance, Joan, who lived on the upper West Side, got mugged on the subway. So she was hot to talk about violence in society. But we could never penetrate her defenses and make her see her own violence. How she terrorized her child. The kid was five years old and still had to tell Joan every time she wanted to use the bathroom. And Joan's husband used his ulcer to keep everybody in line. If we met at her apartment, she had big QUIET signs plastered all over.

—Nine people was too many. I mean, each person would try to say her thing. Even if she finished it, she'd go away feeling, they really didn't listen to me. Because instead of responding to what *she* had said, somebody else would start: This may be off the subject but . . . Jesus, would I like to stick that sentence up every classroom in the country!—

—Spoken like a true fascist!—

—Fuck you. Anyway my friend Marty . . . we were skiing together for Thanksgiving. She saw me off at that dinky airport.— Zeni grimaces. —Marty and I and this beautiful girl named Shana were the only single women in the group. Whenever the married members planned anything, we'd never be invited. You just don't want loose singles messing up your cocktail hour. Or potted palm raising.

—But Shana wasn't the best groupie either. If she brought a friend, she'd respond only to what that person said or did. We couldn't budge her into any interest for the rest of us.—

—Were the women happily married?—

—*That* was the problem. Their defense—which was very flattering to them—was that finally they didn't need all of us anyway. So they could be dishonest, they could tune us out whenever we hit a sore spot.—

—But you must have confronted them?—

—They denied everything. Deny, deny . . . So here we're four. Without Ann.—

—Which brings its own claustrophobia.—

—That's *your* defense, Ivy. You don't want to let anybody in either.—

—No. I just insist on not being defined. Which means shunted aside by you pasting some label on me. "Oppressed," "enslaved." I heard you with Ann and Chrysta.—

—Well, if you haven't figured out by now I'm not a Marxist. If you play power politics, you wind up . . .—

—Powerful.—

—No, dammit! Full of hate . . . Ivy, don't shut me or Ingrid or Joette out of you. We're not the people you would have chosen for your country holiday, but we're not horrors either.—

When she grasps my hand, hers is warm and mine is cold.

Lurching down-mountain today, I stared back at —our— house. How long ago we stumbled from the plane. And at this distance our life truly seems a crazy interlude to which it's silly to dedicate ourselves because we're leaving soon. We must leave *soon?*

A white birch nearby intrigues me. Its power to outsnow

140

the snow by being whiter, upright, alive and struggling in the wind. I see why the sign Zeni found in the attic says Travel On. This valley doesn't shelter; it just funnels all the arctic blasts down upon us.

Zeni has rationed our evening candles. Only people who want to read aloud at night to somebody else can have one. She who does not commune shall not read. Wicksputter.

I've foiled the order by dragging back two pine branches. Chopped the pitchy knots from them. Burn them in these iron standy things I found. Ivy's incense. What a shame we've lost so much of how antique houses operated. There's a jungle of other tools on the cellar walls whose uses we can't begin to guess. If we knew even their names, it would dignify —that doodaddy near the stairs— or —that thingie next to the mantel.—

Found an empty coffee can and have coiled strips of newspaper, forcing them, cut edges up, into the can. If I just had some kerosene to baste them with . . . Joette nags me about burning down the house.

Now that I can see: Grammaw, for all her probable energy, didn't expend much of it housecleaning. The dining room has the manure of ages ground into its cracks; posied wallpaper was curled and fingerstained long before our arrival. Near the ceiling a herd of flies petitpointed the paper borders. Pink plisse tablecloth is a collage of unnameable substances. Small panes of several windows are tarpapered. Maybe some horseplay by Caleb and Jacob? Or Grampaw making free with his rifle butt?

Dining room stageset: poor but unhappy rural sitting room, a midafternoon of 1932. Grammaw in her rocker dozes over some mismatched socks she is darning. Caleb and Jacob play checkers on a horsehaired, lion's footed settee around which the newest litter of kittens gambols. On the wall between the two windows are cheap reproductions of The Last Supper, The Angelus, and Noah beaching the ark on Mt. Ararat. Grammaw won't admit

141

it, but she passes more and more of these middle winter days just a-settin' and a-thinkin: (mostly settin'). Her darning egg clatters to the floor . . .

—Take that torch to the fireplace!— Joette is nervous.

Hate to admit it, but we pass our days hewing wood, drawing water, and patching rags. Just like Grammaw. Because somebody's got to do it. And poverty is next to equality.

This afternoon Zeni worked us round to her conclusion (pre-decided?) during cup of hot water time. About how we lean on her too much to assign us work (Joette), cheer us up (Ingrid), fight the snow and woodpiles (me, I guess).

Ingrid, gaily: —Zeni, you should be glad we respect you enough to let you order us around.—

Z: —Yeah. It's flattering. But when the crunch comes, everybody to her own mistakes.—

Me: —You mean you're abdicating as *gruppenfuhrer*?—

She nods. —Look, I want us all to be *gruppenfuhrei*. I don't want to be the group nag, the only one who checks on are we half alive? do we have enough wood or water? all that household jazz.—

Me: —These are the times that try women's . . .—

Z: —And pack up the smartass remarks, Ivy!—

Embarrassment settles. We wiggle in the cold. Zeni's such a jokester we had no idea she'd got so mad. —Why didn't you tell us you were simmering? It's as much your fault as anybody's.—

—Because I was testing. To see if anybody ever does more than they're ordered to.—

Ingrid frowns and purses her lips. Joette shakes her head in dismay. —You expect too much. People can't read your mind.—

—Okay, I'm the last of the bigtime idealists. And you all flunked . . . Now what're we going to do about sharing responsibility better? Like I'm sick of telling you watch the fire, save the candles, dump the bucket.— The last items are chanted litany-style and Zeni seems on the road to recovery.

We total all jobs from banking the fire to stuffing the window frames and decide on a more rotating task force. The list hangs publicly upon the wall—nobody's supposed to nag. Ingrid and Zeni will be outdoors this week on water, wood, and hunting. Joette and I will stay on fire, cooking, lampmaking, bedding, and Sammy. Next week we switch.

If mother could see me now—a damp baby in one arm and a hunk of frozen bacon in the other . . . *Add cheer to family dinners. Do you serve lunch on this flight? My son's diapers are wet* . . . The Dove and the Hausfink. New regime also to include getting up in the morning, which I was finding the colossal struggle.

Somehow this afternoon (result of this morning's conversation and yet a violation of our new work code) we fasten on a subject I've thrust from my mind because my opinions thereon are hopelessly ambivalent. Like one of those places you can't reach from here, and if you do, you can't get back again. It is, of course, our childhood(s), that biggest sack of worms the human race ever had to deal with.

Naturally Joette's comes out simplest, sunniest; she doesn't deny tensions with her sisters and brother so much as she's forgotten them. —And I could do anything I wanted as far as my father was concerned. I was his little girl.—

Zeni's raucous laugh. Joette drops her staring eyelids, replaces semi-rapture with embarrassment.

Z: —What about your mother?—

J: —She said we could do anything we wanted as long as we didn't get either pregnant or arrested.—

Me: —Well, let's hear it for sex and violence.—

J: —Keep quiet, Ivy! You're so cynical.—

I nod goodnaturedly at her.

Z: —So you really felt *free*? Your whole childhood.—

J: —Of course. But I must have been a good child. I

mean teachers trusted me to ring bells and march kids across the street on time. Once a boy and I ran away and spent an afternoon in the woods, but we told them we got lost and we never heard anything about it.—

Z: —Ah paradise!—

J: —What about *your* childhood? You've been grilling me.—

Z: —Okay. Mine would have been great except for two problems—my mother and my father. Actually I'm from hardy French Canadian stock that got totally debilitated living in this wicked country. Like the first thing to go was their farms when the men got jobs in paper mills. The next thing was their language when the kids refused to speak French at home. Then their religion when the kids married nonCatholics and had babies that never got baptized.

—But when their women started getting out of control, *that* was the last straw. You know, sinful luxuries like being entitled to a new dress and a noncooking vacation every year and how American doctors had little devices and foams so you could stop at three children instead of thirteen. And if somehow the wife could get a job, they could replace the icebox with a frigidaire, the black stove with a white one, and the horse with two cars.—

Me: —Who won?—

Zeni looks puzzled. —Nobody. That was the trouble. There were happy moments but generally they all went around plaguing each other. You know, one of those large families where people have "fun" together, but what they remember afterward is the poverty, one can of tuna to feed thirteen on Friday, dresses made from flour sacks, a lifetime of foot troubles from wearing your sister's shoes. And your mother winds up the best madonna martyr you ever saw.

—But how would I know? I was raised by an aunt in the Bronx.—

Joette and I laugh.

Ingrid fidgets. —Well, at least you *saw* your parents. My father was killed when my brother and I were very young. It was during the War.— (Zeni opens her mouth; I expect —Which war?— to come out, but she holds off.) —My mother I hardly knew. Nobody in our building had much leisure during those years; everybody was in military training or civil defense, mostly in addition to regular jobs.—

J: —Women, too? I thought Hitler wanted women in their homes.— Joette is shocked.

I: —He did at first. But so many men and boys marched off. Then women ran hospitals, schools, and offices. They worked on damaged buildings. They worked in factories. Everywhere.—

Z: —But they were kicked out as soon as the men returned.—

—We never thought it like that!— Ingrid snaps. —Already every family was just surviving together. If you think the food is sparse here, you should have seen what *we* lived on. A basin of potato soup per family per week. And a few carrots if you knew somebody on the land.—

The conversation is taking a certain poorer and self-righteous-er-than-thou tone that annoys me. And sticking safely to the past. If we're really telling secrets, what about Ann? *Frightened sprite.*

Zeni changes the topic. She must be working on Ingrid in some way that doesn't involve angering her right now. —What about you, Ivy? You don't say anything, but we see you there drinking us in.—

I laugh, glad that the right and contemporary —we— has reasserted hersel(ves). —Okay. We've had one positive, one negative, one *nolo contendere*. But this will really foul you up—I'm somewhere in the middle on everything. I remember my father as a fool who hadn't the least notion how people's insides worked. He was a Victorian paper tiger who thought people ought to do something *and* enjoy it just because he'd ordered them to. The real great jobs like spending the morning at the garage on your day off, waiting thirty minutes in a bakery line to get the special rolls he needed for Sunday breakfast or he'd throw a fit. He could brood as much as he wanted on how things "shouldn't be like that," but he lacked the talent and warmth, the cleverness, to intrigue people into acting otherwise. The other side of authority should be some subtlety. And he was a flop at that.—

Z: —How about your mother?—

Me: —I think he terrorized her. Every few days I'd find her crying. Whatever warmth there was in the house did come from her, though. If he terrorized her, he just annoyed me. But they both raved how children no longer respected parents. No matter how many times my brother and I reminded them they should be something or do something to earn respect, if they wanted it. They ignored that.—

J: —What about when you married?—

Me: —My husband was much older than I was. He said the same garbage about what I owed him was obedience and self-sacrifice. He even censored my hair and clothes. I didn't react to it any better than with my father.—

J: —But he died. How awful!—

Me: —Yeah.—

J: —And your child died, too?—

Me: —Two. I had one miscarriage and one meningitis.—

Ingrid: —How can you talk about it in that tone? It's shocking.—

Me: —Exhaustion. All those years of coping with impossible situations. Well, you know—you were married.— And divorced, I think but don't say. —I hoped my husband would turn out better than my father. But I really had no more choice about it than about the family I was born into. I mean it was a small town. If you didn't marry, you taught school and I'd be damned if I'd spend my life behind a spelling book.—

Zeni: —Aha, you don't like kids either.—

Me: —They're all right. But tell me the last time *you* cooed at Sammy.—

He cries. Zeni laughs. We all laugh.

Zeni: —Okay. Let's think up something *good* that happened to us.—

I shake a finger at her. —Zeni, you're copping out. Getting positive in your old age.—

—What d'you mean? I'm younger than you.— She hops a one-footed dance. *Chickadee.*

My reply gets submerged in the voices.

Today another round in one of our meagre entertainments, Refugees' Special, the Game of If:

Zeni: —Y'know if we hadn't taken that plane, we'd never have met each other.—

—*Ja.*— Ingrid frowns. —And if all of us hadn't chartered the plane, we might have used the train.—

Me: —Vermont and New Hampshire don't have any more trains.—

Ingrid: —No. That's Maine . . . So—the bus.—

Zeni: —But we're lucky. To find this house and catch food.—

Now I frown. —If only we had skis, we could get out of here. You know that?—

Joette: —If only they continued searching for lost planes. But they don't. Even in good weather, they stop after two weeks.—

Me: —Because it costs too much.—

Zeni: —Yeah. I read about these people who crashed in North Carolina. In a swamp. They gave them up fast.—

Joette shudders. —Were they killed?—

—Nobody ever found out . . . I bet with all these hijackings, little bunches of people get held and *never* return home. Hijack Class of '75.—

Ingrid: —When does hunting season start?—

Me: —It's over.—

Zeni: —C'mon. Let's work.—

Hey, maybe I'm getting what Zeni calls —radicalized.— Me a feminist?

Zeni can't believe me when I tell her (for the last time) I was raised not knowing I was female, that it made little difference in the middle-this and middle-that life my parents provided for all of us—me and my brothers. I recall skirmishes like being rejected as (aim high!) a caddy at age nine when my brother was accepted at ten dollars a day tips. How he justified such discrimination: she who shall not caddy also escapes his regular chores, like washing cars, mowing lawns, shoveling snow. And I guiltily agreed, yes, cooking wasn't nearly as strenuous.

If I was brainwashed, I agreed to it because it gave me leisure for tv, books, and music.

And cowarded out of my next first job, "research assistant" for a company magazine. My boss wore pink shirts and specialized in mislaying everything on or near his desk, accompanied this by bellowing at anyone in view. One day I set a report high on his heap and tried to score a point by joking —How do you live with that desk?—

—Because I'm surrounded by fools who never do all of a job. They leave half of it to me.— Mutter. —Now why didn't *you* put an index in this report, for instance?—

Still a bona fide brownnoser, I nevertheless screwed my courage together. —It's on page three if you'd take time to read what people give you.—

—I don't need to read! That's what I pay you smart little girls for. Right?—

I walked out of his office. And out of the magazine a month later after an argument with him. Gray and my parents agreed I'd taken the —wisest course . . . Oh well, your job isn't important. You'll be married soon.—

Coward Ivy . . . For all my mother's own trauma she never ceased believing in Mr. Right and Mr. Special who were, of course, Gray.

In the dining room Ingrid practices the other pair of snowshoes. Fishing with me tomorrow. To reach anywhere now in the drifts, we need the fishfoots.

148

Ill. Foul sleep, couldn't get one obstinate hunk of my back warmed no matter how I burrowed and rigidified. After our canned onion and birch bark tea (Zeni: —Whatsamatter? You don't like a real Russian breakfast?—) this tingling ache. Then ear chimes and chills. Lie down, lie down, lie . . . down. Escape my body that's become one throb, make myself so small and silent that pain can't find me.

Hour of chills. Hour of burning. What the hell have I got? Illness now inescapable. I relax and almost enjoy the masochism of summoning pain on command. Move an arm, a leg; just swallow. Except for the trouble it will cause the others. Ingrid will have to carry *your* water . . . Oh hell, get up . . .

Lunge. And fall over. Eyesight's drowned in a swimming head. Floor is frigid and splintery.

—Hey, what is it?—

Suddenly Joette is there, mumbling comfortable things around my chest. Then I'm laid back, quilted, onto the sofa. I could be six again, measled or mumped, with the cat snoozing under my elbow, my mother in the kitchen making me an egg sandwich and hot tea. Except that my mother's dead, and we have no eggs . . . the gifts that parents give, beyond the terrors.

Newly appreciate Joette as SWNB (She Who Never Bitches). Who figures out what she has to do, then does it. Were my grandmothers like that? All I remember is whitened women with droopy dresses and funny jewelry.

My head commences dripping. I blow it on a hunk of newspaper (bread 24¢ a loaf and hamburg 39¢ a pound). Collapse on the hard horsehair and discover my seat and back are numb. Then I revel in being cared for, a joy I haven't tasted for five? ten? years . . . Hard frost line glints and slants across the windows, opaquing them; a diamond perimeter encircles me.

Suddenly Joette is back, and I'm rolling six-inch squares of newspaper around a pencil. Crafts for the invalid? Brown things crunch in her hands.

149

—Here's hemlock needles I've saved. We'll smoke this. It'll clear your stuffy nose.—

My stuffy nose gags. Now I know why the old folks were —never sick a day in their lives.— The cures were more appalling than the illness. Light up the thing she's just rolled.

The acrid smoke chokes me. My T-zone already raw out of its mind.

—That's it. Keep trying.— She soothes. —You'll see how good it feels.—

My eyes now run down my cheeks. Ears and head a simultaneous throb. —Where the hell did you get *this* idea? The Indians?— Breathe and cough. Breathe and . . . cough!

—A cookbook I got at an auction. I tried it once on a campout. It really works.—

—You don't say.—

—Just keep puffing. Smoke! Don't just look at it. I'll roll you another when you're through.—

I vow this one will last a long time. —Hey, didn't Socrates *die* of hemlock something?—

Her front, busy in the woodbox, doesn't answer.

Between coughs I relapse onto the sofa. Odalisque of the horsehair and hemlock. Shame it's not opium.

Fifteen minutes later my throat is a total rasping disaster, but the nose has stopped!

Zeni stomps in from the porch. —Hey, you guys, smells great in here. You burning the furniture?—

I gesture toward Joette who's tending Sammy. Maybe if I eat snow, or hang my flaming mouth out the window . . .

Post-lunch. The invalid rises. I wander upward, hoping to comfort myself with a favorite haunt—the attic. We *womenfolk* (mustn't call us *family*, Zeni hates that) have decided my illness is flu + exhaustion and that I deserve a day inside (before pneumonia sets in).

I forget —my— attic lies about minus 10° on this frosty

afternoon. So I hurry to the game trunk, riffle through icy packs of Lotto, Old Maid, and Author cards. Poor George Eliot. Looks so sad. Nowadays people would just congratulate her for doing her own thing.

Pack of ordinary cards, box of dominoes, an antique bottle. Liquor? Flowery inscription intrigues me, coughing, over to the window. Label is smudged, deckled, irregular-printed on fake parchment-like reproductions of the Constitution:

> VIN VITAE, THE WINE OF LIFE, is a preparation combining the curative & strengthening powers of celebrated vegetable elements, procured from medicinal South American HERBS, with invigorating tonic effect of the prest & finest WINES of Southern California. The HERBS supply needed food strength for the blood & nerves, the WINE counteracts the disagreeable nauseous property of the HERBS & gives just the right fire and life to the preparation.

> VIN VITAE MAKES WOMEN STRONG. Weak women, easily tired, worn out by household duties, should take Wine of Life regularly. VIN VITAE is giving thousands of women health, beauty & freedom from the dragging pains which have made their lives so miserable. VIN VITAE corrects all ailments peculiar to the sex, regulates the system, tones up the nervous organisms, brightens the eye, clears out the complexion & rounds out the figure.

The bottle is empty.

And I'm shivering with hunger cramps by the time I finish reading. Cards and a couple of *Farm Journals* into my pocket. Tuck the bottle under my arm for Zeni's Chamber of Discriminations. I retreat downstairs, nursing my *dragging pains.*

Joette is scrubbing Sammy's calico diapers in the kitchen tub. I help her hang them behind the stove.

Drag to the woodshed. And vomit . . . *Was ist denn los? Where is the floor?*

Blurry days. Loll on the couch. Spasms *en route* downward from head and throat to chest, stomach, abdomen

151

ending in the wracks of diarrhea and more vomiting. And guilt that others are hewing the wood, drawing the water. We eat, gathered around me although it means an extra fire in the living room for Joette to build.

The grand outdoors is changing Ingrid—she no longer combs her hair and straightens her bandage four times a day. Her clothes are now early ragbag like the rest of us. Her knuckles are wood-splintered in little red patches. So this is her *alfresco*, archeology self—disciplined core, no frowns, no Lolita flirtations. Has the softie, intramural self of pouts, moods, solitudes really vanished?

By the fifth day (notches on the walnut arm of Grammaw's sofa) I can't stretch here any longer. My head is still a twisted yo-yo, but I tune up my cough and drape an outer set of rags over the inner. Strap on fishfoots and try gathering firewood. Frigid air bites my face and throat. I pant; five days and I wheeze like an old crone. Drifts look twice as high.

Woodsled catches a rock. The trees close about me again. This is my first time through here since we hunted Ann. Chrysta's —road— dies just as before at the pile of boulders. Graceful breastshapes under the snow. Next the ledge with the snowchoked ravine below. Only a few rusted machineries, thrust at odd angles, visible now.

There must have been a road here, must have . . . Did they tear it up? Maybe a bridge *over* the ravine? Maybe there was a road here until they quarried the hillside and dumped the junk. How did Penny and Chrysta get through it? . . .

Chilled. Wood. Turn back. To look useful, I gather a few stiff black apple branches. Get them tied onto the sled.

Halfway to the house, my chest aches, the wood spills, and I want to cry. I vomit instead.

Joette: —How did you get to Cambodia?—
Ingrid: —David and I had spent years working on Greek

152

and Near Eastern cultures. We wanted a complete break. We had a friend in USIA service who sent us letters that positively raved about Cambodia, the people, the monuments.— Ingrid's eyes glow. Our flaming Flamingo.

—Zeni, did you know that Cambodia has a Citadel of Women? It's an ornate temple with five-foot-high doorways and celestial dancer statues. Lovely yellow stone. It's north of Angkor, the old city and tomb area. If they bomb there— (she frowns) —*no* one can replace those buildings.

—So we spent a month digging and climbing around the stones. Took half our skin off on the lichen and tree roots. The banyan trees—just the roots are fifteen feet high. Grow right up through the paving and tear the shrines apart. At night you feel wind and it's bats flying through the rooms. Acres and acres.—

Zeni taps her foot.

—And, Zeni, I bet you didn't know that women controlled all the commerce at Angkor about 1300 A.D.? Each had her own little shop, and if men married, it was so they could profit from one of these industrious little women . . . You don't like this story? It doesn't fit with your . . .—

—Yes. It does. But I'm sick of you baiting me . . . Your cute little stories.—

—*Baiting* you? . . . If you spend all your time on persecution theories, when do you get any work done?—

—Oh, crap on work! Ingrid, you just got a bad case of Protestant ethic. That's all.—

And so it goes (again).

Tonight we attempt a bath—this time with Fels Naptha laundry soap. Four dirty women in one leaky tub. Or is it one dirty woman in four leaky buckets? Zeni has almost recovered from —all the junk I have to deal with.— Already she's christened the bath —Tin Lizzie Time— and —Bacteria Orgy.— Which

153

makes Ingrid slit-eyed and me sick again to my stomach.

We draw toothpicks, and Ingrid gets first plunge into the wet stuff. She made us all promise not to open the kitchen doors while she's undressed. All that prudery hiding such passion. I hereby rescind my low opinion of Victorian novels. I must confess fantasies of the hours she and Ann spent together. * * * * * * They couldn't have worked *all* the time. * * * * * *

Zeni says the soap destroyed her skin. She's waving her rashes at us. Maybe dirt has replaced the weight we've lost.

Bath mellowed us. All (except Zeni) tingling to hear another Ingrid Jungle Girl tale. Like childhood when you could listen to *I Love a Mystery* or Henry Aldrich on the radio if first you did your homework and washed all over.

Since the tiff with Zeni, Ingrid seems to talk only when she occupies the total podium. If anybody says, That reminds me of . . . she shuts up. But who can top her Cambodia with Persia and Egypt for alternates?

—What's the best experience you ever had out there? Not the work. I mean something personal.—

Ingrid becomes dreamy. —Many. But I remember one of my first sunsets on the desert. The west was still golden. In the east one of those full moons was rising. Like science fiction. Pink and purple. Then something happened that's never come to me before or after. I looked over my shoulder and discovered I had *two* shadows. Gigantic. Flowed out on either side like wings grabbing me. I started running to escape them. How silly. Then I sat down and laughed.—

—How old were you?—

—Twenty-two. Young and foolish. *Ja*? . . . But the desert, such space . . . and peace. But after it I get thirsty for the color and confusion of a city, too.—

Ingrid has a toothache. —Did you know teeth stop decaying at death and outlast even bones? Four thousand year old teeth have been found at Ur.—

154

—Do you think they'll find ours?—
—Ur, ur.— From Zeni.

—What's your worst fear when you dig?—
—That we'll miss some bit, a shell or bead or potsherd that would help us unlock what we're into. Even a tiny shell can tell me how much rain fell. And that helps figure out different tools for different kinds of farming.—
—More of the ones that got away.—
—Right.—

I can understand someone(s)'s infatuation with Ingrid. But *remaining* in love with her? How to overlook her general closed and shutteredness, her bleak disregard for anybody's time but her own, the barbed wire glances, the coy flattery when she wants something done? Plus the impatience that implies she, the goddess, has transcended failures and indecision that plague the rest of us.
Gemischtes Eis. Oh, cold and mingled flavors.

Zeni's latest thing is that here on the mountain we're living responsively and responsibly. That we alone are responsible for how we turn out and how we respond to each other. No clinging to the fringes of others' lives, no one to blame for whatever.
Frightening, huh?

—Zeni, it's not enough, the five of us here. We may make it together in our cozy group but what else are we doing? Ingrid's restless, Joette wants her family, and I . . .—
—Excuses. Wait'll you get hungrier. You'll be glad to stay alive.—

Spent an hour splitting pine logs. And coughing. Smelling like a Yule decoration, I've slumped before the fireplace. Shaky hands stick to the furniture. Found some

155

worms in one log that I'm thawing for fishing—unless
Zeni gets them first for her annelid pancakes.

Interrupted a Z-Ing debate over why women feel uncomfortable doing for each other the little courtesies
some men still perform for women. Ingrid says she still
waits for the man with her to open the door. Zeni on how
she knows she's approaching thirty: when one of her girl
students opens doors for her. Trivial topic, but why did I
feel uncomfortable when I lit Zeni's cigarette, then my
own? Or when we danced to keep warm the other night,
Zeni and I had to sort out who would be —the man—
while Joette and Ingrid waltzed instantly—Ingrid leading,
of course . . .

Mind-racing night. Hungry, cold, blanket-strangled. Finally turned onto my stomach and drove a fist under my
ribs to quiet my assorted pangs. If I could have done it
quietly, I might even have broken our tacit trust—that nobody —liberates— food at night without sharing it with
somebody else. Joette baked Thoreau bread yesterday.
This is 4/5 of a recipe I remembered

rye + corn meal + salt + water
+ something that escapes me
baked on a wood slab until Joette thinks it's done.

Loaves leaping darkly over mental fences. And something
howling in the distance. This morning I'm sure it's the
wind through my disordered head. Nobody else heard it.
I'm high on hunger.

The night we —came here— I was supposed to stay with
Marilyn. The night I never reached Westchester. Either she
thinks I'm dead or she's lumped me with the rest of her
casual (worthless) friends, the kind who —love her dearly—
but rarely write and rarerly call when they're in town because of —pressured schedule,— —intensive meetings,— all
the old etc. excuses. Her special peeve. I wonder where she
is now. Probably stuck in Harlem on a frozen commuter
train. Her other special peeve . . .

156

More windy sky hung low with snow drifts rising to it. What grows most eerie about this house: it's not time passing (that would be normal). It's that no time here = all time. Piles of Fifties magazines, not even dogeared. Blueprints for a bomb shelter, that apocalyptic fad. Leatherbound Mark Twain, published in the Tens. Rapier hatpins of the Nineties. Monogrammed gym bloomers, Civil War samplers, crocheted picture frames, buttonhooks.

Ingrid declares my sense of humor —gauche.— And Zeni's even gauchier. But Ingrid's an uptight academic, always corralling her sacred cows away from rustlers like me. So easy to stampede: —Ingrid, do you feel archeology is relevant to anything?— —Of course, archeology is relevant! What's the matter with you?—

Today I twitted her on an especially melodramatic declaration. —There's *nobody* in my field who shares my goals. Most of the year there's nobody I can even talk with.— She frowns.

And Ann presumed Ingrid's —loneliness— was seeking her own. But nobody gets close to Ingrid; she swings the fence shut.

Joette: —Living in an abandoned house depresses me.—
Ingrid: —What do you mean? This house isn't abandoned. Families have lived here. Most U.S. houses—they're the faces on your Miss America contestants. Blank, pretty, unlived in.—
Joette: —I only said . . .—
Zeni: —Ingrid, aren't *you* an American citizen now?—
Ingrid: —What's that got to do with it!— Stomping about the kitchen.
Zeni snickers but nobody laughs.

About five o'clock I bustle everybody from mattresses and the kitchen to watch the most lurid H-bomb sunset so far. At first it's fun. As we gather on the porch steps, the snow turns pink, the trees russet-black. Purple, gold, and

157

green explosions travel half the sky, casting out the gray masses. They tan and blush our faces and Ingrid's hands. Zeni decides the fireworks is the world being cancelled due to lack of interest.

The gray layers win, however. In fifteen minutes the whole glory is reduced to a purple smudge drowning in gray at the mountain rim. During supper by dim candle we're pale again, silent and sad.

Did anybody else in this Northland watch with us?

Ingrid stumbled into another facet of Zeni today.

Sometimes I think Ingrid confuses us with her rocks and monuments. Days of eyes lowered, ignoring us; then we're —rediscovered— like lost temples, re-asked —What's your favorite food?— Questions we'd driven into the drifts weeks ago when we promised not to tempt each other by discussing food or heat anymore. Right now Hershey bars float before me; this morning it was hot chicken soup with oregano.

The new facet is that besides being deeper than I'd thought, Zeni tempers her optimism with a good dose of history. Today Ingrid was grilling her on women's liberation as just another historical-hysterical enthusiast movement whose sunshine followers will shrivel at the first major cloud of male backlash.

I expected Zeni to erupt or at least defend herself from the insult to her staying powers. Instead she just nodded, settled back, looked sombre. —Okay. We have to learn from other movements how not to get exhausted, how to tap people when their urge to do something is running strong and also how to hold them when nothing's happening. When the whole world thinks you're insane.—

—But what will stop your women's movement from petrifying into Marxist bureaucracy and purges like every other revolution?—

Zeni winces at the —purges.— Ingrid's eyes narrow. She's won a point.

—Nothing. Except my ideals—and realizing that I won't
see total triumph in *my* lifetime . . . Haven't *you* people
archeologized some places for a couple hundred years?—
   —*I* haven't!—
   —Well, fifteen years.—
   —*Ja.*—

January's Jitters

   Zeni questioning me about my marriage
Anybody questioning Ingrid about Ann
   Sammy crying at 4 a.m.
Joette dividing the food unequally
   Joette hearing profanity or pessimism: —Hey, Joette,
you think we'll get another goddamn storm today?—
Asking Zeni when she was purged from the movement
(any movement)

How We Entertain Each Other

   Ingrid crawling through Cambodian jungles
Zeni's pioneer ancestors
   Zeni radicalizing Central Park pigeons by feeding them
birthcontrol popcorn
Joette buying a dog to chase the cat that failed to de-rat
the house her husband built.

   More Ingrid trouble and an accident today.
   Zeni gashed a leg. Minutes and minutes to stanch the
blood. She was flinging snow away from the porch steps
when she slipped and fell against the rickety boards. Tore
her jeans and split inside her right knee on a nail. Rusty,
of course, and worse than the can that got me. Beastly
house.
   Ingrid and I dragged her into the kitchen by her arms

and another leg. Ingrid dashed for the rest of the clean
rags while I tried to wash the leg and Zeni howled. Then
we helped her upstairs to her bed and covered her. Later
she had a joke for us about —the dirty bandage generation.—
She can't remember which shots she got which year of college. So everybody is discussing lockjaw and Travel On teta-
nus. The knee is stiffening; when she walks again, it'll be a
hobble.

Since Ingrid exerted herself in such flurry to help, I
thought she'd decided to like Zeni. When I heard her de-
claiming in the kitchen, I assumed she was telling a story.
Post-crisis fun, I hoped. Ingrid laughing, Joette smiling agree-
ably.

—Have you ever seen this?— Ingrid held out a grimy green
notebook with inked-over cover.

—I don't know.—

—Oh, it's priceless. Listen.— Her arms rose in dance posture.

> Who sails here now?
> I sail here first,
> The first to find this dismal mountain.

Do you hear that? She thinks she's the first to walk upside
down here. She doesn't know what exploring is.

> We've proved what we came here to do.
> Even death we could now gladly face.

There she should have spoke for herself. Our fearless leader
may be ready to die but *I'm* not.—

Then I realized what the notebook was. My anger flared.
—What right have you got to splatter Zeni's private book
around? We helped her upstairs. Then you sneer at her.—

—You've read this, too?—

—Yes. She showed me a poem from it.—

—Have you read it, Joette?—

Joette nods. —I looked at it once when she left it in the
kitchen.—

Ingrid reddened and wilted on her stool. —Well, it's adolescent. I still don't know why she carries on about the mountain . . . This mountain murders people. Chrysta and Penny. Ann and the baby. Everybody knows it killed them!— Her face grew white.

Joette's mouth hung open.

—You don't know Penny and Chrysta are dead. Or Ann. And wherever she is, it's not the mountain's fault.—

Ingrid leapt up. I raised my arms against her; she flung past me out the door. Her stool clattered onto the stove.

Behind the metal the ashes dropped.

Our Food Plight Bad Getting Worse

We scrounge the cellar for old turnips, leather, leaves, anything. Zeni reports —a funny door— at one end, but nobody's got energy or candles to examine it. Zeni limps and nurses her leg on the sofa. If she removes her glasses in the cold, they mist over when she replaces them on her face. —Hey kids, steam heat!—

We all sleep with a fist jammed into our entrails to quiet the empty caverns. Yesterday our last jar of fruit. Today on our last two jars of vegetables and final can of beans. No game on any of my trails. Just a loudheaded woodpecker drilling frozen bugs. I think I know where Chrysta went. If only I had skis, I could do it . . .

Queen Zeni and the Round Table: —Well, trap something again. We'll help you set the ropes.—

Me: —But somebody should walk out while we still have a little food.—

Z: —Iv-vy. You won't get any farther than Chrysta.—

Ing. (at me): —*You* don't know where she walked!—

Scrape of forks chasing meagre beans over plates. Red beans and rice.

Besides being annoying, playing Hansel *und* Gretel here in the woods has begun to bore me. Even if it's

survival. Day after day the ritual hassles just to main-
tain equilibrium. Everybody, shut up!

Nothing new growing about us.

Post-flu depression?

for Zeni

MOUSE → IN → THE → HOUSE
   A BRAWNY AMAZON AIRRIDES THE TRAVEL ON
   MILDEWED AS ABEND DUMPS
   A FRIGGIN TRUE BELIEVER AGAIN DREAMS UPON THE
      HAPPENTHING
   RESOURCEFULLY UNINHABITEDLY TANTALIZINGLY
RING → IN → THE → SPRING

GO TO ZENIPOINT

ZENIPOINT

DO-IT-YOURSELF POEMS
ON THOSE TRADITIONAL AMERICAN THEMES

_____ and _____ are the end of _____.

MARRIAGE and PREGNANCY are the end of LOVE. LOVE a
nd MARRIAGE are the end of MAN. MAN and PREGNANCY
are the end of WOMAN. WOMAN and HORMONES are the e
nd of UNDER THE SHEETS. UNDER THE SHEETS and DIAPE
RS are the end of WO
MEN'S LIBERATION. WO
MEN'S LIBERATION and MARRIAGE are the end of BABIE
S. BABIES and UNDER THE SHEETS are the end of MARR
IAGE. MARRIAGE and B
ABIES are the end of
FOUR LETTER WORDS.
FOUR LETTER WORDS and UNDER THE SHEETS are the end
of LOVE. HORMONES and PREGNANCY are the end of DIA-
PERS. DIAPERS and FOUR LETTER WORDS are the end of
WOMAN. WOMAN and DIAPERS are the end of MAN. MAN and

WOMEN'S LIBERATION are the end of WOMAN. WOMAN and
WITHOUT A SHIRT are the end of MARRIAGE. FOUR LETT
ER WORDS and MARRIAGE are the end of WOMEN'S LIBER
ATION. WOMEN'S LIBERATION and PREGNANCY are the en
d of MAN. WOMEN'S
LIBERATION and HO
RMONES are the end of PREGNANCY. BLOOD and PREGNAN
CY are the end of LOVE. HORMONES and LOVE are the
end of WOMAN. MARRIAGE and HORMONES are the end of
WOMEN'S LIBERATION.
BABIES and PREGNAN
CY are the end of HORMONES. PREGNANCY and BABIES a
re the end of MARRIAGE. HORMONES and BABIES are th
e end of LOVE. FOUR LETTER WORDS and WOMEN'S LIBER
ATION are the end of BABIES. HORMONES and WOMEN'S

165

LIBERATION are the end of LOVE. LOVE and BLOOD are
the end of DIAPERS. WOMAN and LOVE are
the end of WITHOUT A SHIRT. WITH
OUT A SHIRT and UNDER THE
SHEETS are the end
of WOMAN.
BABIES
and
WITHOUT
A SHIRT A
are the end of WOM
AN'S LIBERATION. UNDER TH
E SHEETS and BABIES are the end
of LOVE. LOVE and HORMONES are the end
of MAN. PREGNANCY and HORMONES are the end of FOUR

Ohhh and –

VIOLENCE ! ! ! ! !

_____ and _____ are the beginning of _____.

GUNS and ARSON are the beginning of POW! POW! and   DO IT YOUR
CHURCH are the beginning of SADISM. SADISM and MU   SELF RUIN IT
RDER are the beginning of ARSON. ARSON and RAPE a   YOURSELF . .
re the beginning of BLOOD. BLOOD and G
OD are the beginning of MURDER. MURDER
and RACISM are t the beginning
of CHURCH. CHURCH and GUNS
are the beginning of GOD.
GOD and GUNS   are the
   beginning   of male
CHAUVINISM   . MURDE
R and GOOD   TASTE a
re the beg   inning
of POW! PO   W! and
GOD are th   e begi

166

nning of SADISM. SADISM and RACISM are the begin

ning of PLASTIC. PLASTIC and GUNS are the beginn

ing of RAPE. RAPE and GUNS are the beginning of

CHURCH. CHURCH and MALE CHAUVINIS

M are the beginning of MURDER. MURDER a

nd CHURCH are the beginning of GO

OD TASTE. GOOD TASTE and M

URDER are the beginning o

f BLOOD. BL   OOD and

 RAPE are t   he   begi

nning of RA   CISM. R

ACISM and G   OOD TAS

TE are the   beginni

ng of RAPE.   RAPE an

d BLOOD are   the beg

DO IT YOUR
SELF RUIN IT
YOURSELF . . .

inning of MURDER. MURDER and BLOOD are the begin

ning of CHURCH. CHURCH and GOD are the beginning

of POW! POW! and GOOD TASTE are the beginning of

RACISM. RACISM and POW! are the beginn

ing of ARSON. ARSON and RAPE are the b

eginning of MURDER. GOD and

GOOD TASTE are the beginni

ng of CHURCH. SADISM and

CHURCH are   the beg

 inning of   PLASTIC

. GOD and   RAPE ar

e the beg   inning

of MALE C   HAUVIN

ISM. GOD   and GU

NS are th   e begi

DO IT YOUR
SELF RUIN IT
YOURSELF . . .

DOITYOURSELFRUINITYOURSELFDOITYOURSELFRUINIT

Thank God for *Grandmaman* Yvette. Ancestor worship
has fallen into disfavor. You'll settle for awe at this Amazon who, twenty years into widowhood, rose at 5:30,
worked all day. Pies, custards, salads, steaks flowed from
her kitchen—in the later years when grown and visiting
offspring would —forget— a green five or some singles un-

der her sugar bowl. Not enough for too much, but God would reward . . .

She retired at 7:30 daily into a room hovering in winter at 33° where she belted down a shot of whisky. If *Grandpere* could have foreseen, and how the neighbors talk . . . Bundled into shawl and blanket, she fell asleep.

Unbelievable that she could be your aunt's and your *mother's* mother. Your mother's rage when she asked Yvette (who at 102 was senile, confused matching her children's faces with names): —Who am *I*?—

And Yvette answered, —Your sister's sister.—

—*Mon nom! Mon nom!*— your mother shouted.

—Why do you need one? *Hein, pourquoi?*— Yvette concluded . . .

And, well, you looked at your mother and like you knew you had to work for women's liberation to remove the bitter taste from your mouth. Whatever youth or zest she had was beaten out years ago by the Depression (her own and national), early marriage, illness, lying to the priest about birth control, an unwanted child or two.

Last year you suggested, —Take a course or a trip. You could get your life going again.—

Vacant answer. —I'm old now. What's the point?—

You reminded her Yvette had been old, too. You hugged her and tried to love her, to show her there *is* a point, a place, but you have to build it yourself. And if you can keep the winter wind out, other people may join you. If you're cold, get up and do something.

God loves you, and you can sit on your hands.

Your other debt to pay: to your Catholic childhood that despite its worst absurdities (look, ma, no sex!) convinced you that the present, the object, the reality—however joyous, dreadful, or ironic—is always incomplete, must be looked behind, traveled beyond. That this can be adventuresome, delightful in variety, as well as dire in its impermanence.

You walked to the mountain and the mountain wasn't there.

It was in you or behind you or ahead of you . . .

Q: So you disliked your year in France?

A: *Ah, oui.* My linguistics teacher said my *r* and *u* —destroyed everything.— But he'd teach me —how one does it right— if I came to his apartment . . . My prepositions were always showing.

Q: Why don't you care about the Quebec nationalists?

A: Because French and Canada are my past. America is my future. And in between, I can sit on my hands.

Poignant Things

April apple blossoms
a child's hands
first lovemaking
burning maple leaves

Class reunions when you've forgotten everybody's face and the girls all have triple names anyway.

When you realize the country is being run by people who flunked out of your high-school history class. And that Jerry, who bombed the administration building in '69, now has twins and is buying life insurance from Eddie, who used to peddle speed and LSD in the cafeteria.

And Jerry's warmth beside you in the warm daydream. His head was in your lap, and you were dreaming the Fifties' dream of cozy togetherness, and how nice if you and he would marry, you'd spend the days busy and the nights lovemaking cozy warm dozing . . . Tickling your ribs under the flannel blanket. Letting the warm fall wind toss the drapes, scurry the room, moan under the closet door, because you were covered and safe as long as you stared at one magic spot on the wall where a string of forget-menots had knotted themselves into a wavy *Z*, just an *S* backward, your Dad used to say . . .

Then the memory of lying snug, smug, bittersweet, frustrated under the covers with Norman, your first —affair.— Under a roof where squirrels scampered and knocked last year's acorns around. You loved him because he made you sad. He was leaving for Europe in June and insisted on speaking only French in bed, which reminded you of your grandmother. What were all those words they never taught us in French class? Norman was shrapneled, bombed, in Vietnam talking to a prostitute on a Saigon corner. In French, no doubt . . .

Reginald's dark eyes, long lashes. And his political science will save the world. In your office for the summer. In tiered bodystinking chem halls and booklined orifices with couches to tempt failing freshmen girls. *It'll only take twenty minutes, dear. I promise you won't be late to class and yes I'll up your mark to a B this quarter. I'll up your* . . . In your office for the summer.

You and the janitor pushed Reggie's fucking couch out the back door of Hall Hall. Then you dumped his pipes and poli sci journals, Rolaids and picture of his wife (*spurs me on to my best*) into a Kotex carton from the bookstore. Left it in the rain with his name on it. He scribbled a note in your mailbox how the moisture made his pipes swell. And he was sure they'd crack this winter. What would his wife say? How they were moving anyway because he was still evading the draft. Trying to get a doctor's certificate for rheumatism (that he got from lying on all those damp couches).

Like that blond Frenchman who taught the girls and made them cry saying *u* by getting them to pucker so he could run his forefingers over them. And they ate it up because high-school French with Potbelly or Spindlebones was never like *this*. Until they were bedded on a late date or long hike the first time. The first ten times and they saw it was always up to them to furnish the rubbers or

170

jelly because if they weren't —careful,— then that was their fault, too.

—How the hell was I supposed to know about your period? You said it's irregular anyway.—

—Abortion is against the laws of this state. You know that.— White coat in the infirmary.

And they cried on your shoulder . . .

Actions Speak Louder Than . . .

Demonstrators tried to convince female spectators to join the Women's Liberation Movement. One woman asserted, "I am happy and fulfilled being a housewife." Her husband growled, "You better be or I'll kick your ass out the door."

As soon as the parade ended, the police disappeared. Unhindered, a man grabbed a sign from two women and ran. When a male bystander called to him, "Hey, they have a right to express their opinion," the Samaritan got a punch in the nose for expressing his.

Everywoman

The girls, all trained to use the "Buddy" system, worked excellently together and no one got lost even for a moment. The "Buddy" system means that at least two girls work together at all times and do not separate, especially in the woods, where . . .

White Mountain Times

The Hamlet Meeting of Friggin Mountain assembled promptly at 9 a.m. today. Present and voting were Joette, Sammy, Ingrid, and Ivy. Zeni chaired the meeting from her stool by banging the stove with a wood shaft when necessary. A certain ribald gaiety was enjoyed by all when she announced that getting such a shaft is the story of her life.

Business was then transacted. Item: Due to inclement weather and low temperatures, the *search for Ann* is indefinitely *postponed*. 3 Aye, 1 Nay (Ingrid), Sammy staining and abstaining.

Item: Need to *reorganize work schedules* so that all sisters share all tasks. Ivy charged that certain sisters —are spending all day on their cans by the fire.— Ingrid answered that whatever house workers do, they at least do it socially, do not indulge in escapist tactics like sneaking out the back door after lunch and returning five hours later emptyhanded.

Further acrimonious testimonials were entertained on all sides but mostly in Zeni's direction. Joette volunteered to devise a better (rotating) work schedule before the next meeting. Item postponed.

ZeniZeniInezanSbackwardZeniInezanSbackwardZeniInezanSbackwardZeniZeni

                                      Zeni

                               Inez

                         anS

                  backward

             Zeni

          Inez

      anS

   backward

 Zeni

Zeni   and Ivy and Ingrid too

You had a dream that Everywhere World is an incandescent orange Rose that warms the cold, lights the dark, loves the babies, soothes the dogs, cooks the meals, runs the railroads and answers all wrath-and-garbage faces forever. Amen.

Why can't people shut their mouths except for eating and kissing?

Dream: The Icemen Cometh

Gray expansive ice.

Run. Sometimes on shore, sometimes leaping the
frosted cracks. Race. Race until you choke because
must find before dark and the sun is already redblack and
low. Soar over the crunchy ground. If only somebody to
help you search. Jab the ice with a knife when you hear
cracking behind you.

Whirl and they're there! Herd of them pillared along
the shore like sculptures. Opaque ices with heads and
arms and feet. You think, they're dead. They can't hurt.
Continue chopping.

But one gray arm moves. The whole block nearest you
begins to slide as if greased . . . toward you. Now they all
advance.

They glide nearer. Yell at them . . . nearer. Can't stop
them.

One of their pedestals traps your scarf. You're dragged,
choked, inch by inch downward to the hard frost . . .

You awake, gasping and freezing, blankets tangled in
lumps around your neck.

—Are you all right?— Joette shakes you.

How does anybody know they're all right? . . .

Ladies you are unclaimed treasures.

Somebody keeps messing my map.

Go right 800 miles, left and over a cliff 600. You will
now be facing Nowhere. Find 3d pinetree to left, follow
it downhill 100 yards and you will see Travel On reposing
in its winter niche. With 4 frozen birds on a wild . . .

Ignore it. Let us sleeping lie. Die. Why? No, no, oh
hell . . .

Your one and only bra snapped today. Portent of things
to come—out.

'Course you've been wrapping your feet in it at night.

Ingrid says she burned hers to keep warm in her room.
Suppose you'll have to believe her.

SOS onto hillside again, again. Tramp, tramp, tramp,
we womenfolk are marching.

With rusty nails we bang together three platforms of
warped lumber to keep us off the kitchen floor at night.

When you and Ivy pry the last standing timber from the
cellar wall, you get at the —door— that puzzled Ivy. Dusty
hatch that topples inward. With a candle: some kind of
bunker-cellar decorated with more magazines, a loaded
shotgun, and MORE FOOD! Cartons and tins —For Civil
Defense Emergency Only.— Frozen.

Grammaw's private bomb shelter is all we can make of
it.

Joette brews soup, and Ivy rattles the shotgun apart.
Rejoicing behind tightened belts and pinched cheeks.

Ingrid has diarrhea.

Well, so it's a bomb shelter. And our own time capsule:
how strange to handle an age when bombings were called
—air raids— and shelters were built in disused coal bins.
And ours stretches even farther back—Grammaw & Co.
never made it beyond the woodburning generation.

Anyhow, Ivy and you plus two candles crawl inside
again, explore the remaining works—a chemical toilet, two
wood bunks, waterless soap, a bicycle pump, geiger counter, a pick and shovel duo. Were they ever *optimists*—imagining there'd be a postblast world left to tunnel toward.

No stove, radio, or water.

The toilet reads 1953; Ingrid says archeologists would
dance in their graves if all artifacts were instantly datable
like this.

And the last best: FOOD!! Besides the civil defense
tins which we lust after (but what if they really *are* a generation old?), some cartons are newer and unopened. Pow-

dered milk and eggs, rock sugar, more beans, some un-
marked cans. Hunters' bounty?

    —Tell Ivy to trap some animal we can test it on.—

    —Squirrels aren't people.—

    —No, they do sensible things like sleep through the
winter.—

    Smells fine whatever we open. Only pollution (so far)
a gunny sack of slimy potatoes, mother of fantastic tech-
nicolor mold in 3D and stereophonic ammonia smell.

    Ingrid washes her head with the soap, and Sammy gur-
gles into reconstituted eggs.

FOUR CULTURED ATTRACTIVE WOMEN desire to meet tall
handsome FURNACE in potent working order. Will swop photos. Only serious offers considered. Box WOW.

HAVE 200 RARE OLD BOOKS to swop for a side of bacon, a
carton of cocoa, one turkey dinner, and a warm bed. Box OW.

Hymns for Hers

Meditatively

There's a shack in the valley by the wildwood,
    No chillier place in the dale;
No place is so dear to my womanhood
    As the little brown shack in the vale.

How sweet on a bright frigid morning
    To list to the clear ringing ax;
Its hacking so sharply is calling
    O come to the shack in the vale.

TAKE ME TO YOUR LIEDER.

    In this most amazing white on white hot candystripe
world about the stove: people depend on you to fight the
frost, chase the icicles, imagine tomorrow's palm trees and
baked clams, to assure them that what can't be forgotten
can be forgiven.

for Zeni

CROW → IN → THE → SNOW
  A BRILLIANT TRAVEL ON SEDUCES THE JOAN DARC
  DANK AS ABEND DUMPS
  A FLIRTATIOUS GODDESS SOMETIMES HUNTS THE LADYBUG
  FABULOUSLY DANKLY FRIGGINLY
FEAR → HERE

      MOUNTAIN → KNOWS → SNOWS
        A SPUTTERGREEN WICKSPUTTER AIRRIDES THE
            TRAVEL ON
        FRIGID AS BLEEDING
        A WILY MAISONETTE SOMETIMES FISHES THE POND
        CLEVERLY BLACKWHITELY FRIGGINLY
      FOUND → IN → THE → POND

      GO TO IVYPOINTPOINT

Hot fudge
Grilled cheese
  Steaming clam chowder   Bomb Shelter Breakfast:
Charcoaled steak   Flaming scrambled eggs
  Hot cocoa   Dogfood patty
Melted marshmallows   Teako (½ tea, ½ coffee)
  Roast chicken   3 frozen raisins
Filet mignon with mushroom caps
  Mint tea
Coq au vin

Zeni in a zany academic mode today—higher education, as long as men run it, won't do women or anybody else any good. —I mean, I've been in school now a quarter of a century. And the chief paperpushing method I've learned is arid analysis. How to take a whole and kill it by dissection. And toss fancy words around. I've even got rewarded for it. Is that what any human should be doing with cos life? (—Cos— Zeni's transsexual pronoun.)

—You're lucky, Ingrid. You escape every year and you start gluing the pieces back together.—

—Yes. But I must write reports or I don't know what it is I've glued together. I collate photos, I make blueprints, I . . .—

—But it's synthesizing. It's whole!—

—Have it your own way.—

January Assessment: If only we could get this house WARM for ONCE. The skin on my heels cracks and bleeds. My hands are raw; everybody's face is chapped. I'm hunchback for life from all the shivering.

—Did I ever tell you about my aunt who had this dog who shivered himself to death and . . .—

—Okay, Ivy. Don't get revved up. Forget it.— . . .

—Whose turn is it to poke the fire?—

179

Ivy's blankets crawl toward the stove. Rosy iron plates grind. Hot mouths flare.

We lie, rigid spokes about the stove's hub.

Ivy, snowsmeared behind wood: —More white stuff.—

Ingrid: —*Schneeweiss . . . immer . . . alles . . . Schnee-weiss.* —

Joette: —What?—

Ingrid: —Snowwhite.—

Joette: —And the dwarves?— Cuddles Sammy.

Ingrid: —No-o . . . Everywhere.—

Joette: —Huh?—

Insidious drafts invade legs, spine, neck. Ivy opens the stove door, stirs ashes, clunks in a log and kindling, ignites a 1957 newspaper. Sparks flash. She's this a.m.'s cook.

Ingrid stretches sexily. Sammy burps.

We've backslid. Sullen faces all about. Because Joette started breastfeeding and slurping Sammy while the rest of us tried to eat, Ingrid began appearing as of yore in her dirtiest headcloths. Joette, never a direct confronter, was contenting herself with behind-the-bandage comments about how some unmarried women are scared of the facts of life.

This morning Zeni jumped in. —Discuss it!— We discussed it. Newest compromise: Joette will feed the baby *before* she cooks and we eat *if* Ingrid will clean up her bandages and generally stop nagging as if she owned the place.

More days of whiteout. Small weatherbreak inside and beyond.

Then: intense blue sky, almost warm enough at noon to sun on the porch without shivering! The animals feel it too. A rabbit and a squirrel in my traps. Not that spring will spring this week way up here, though . . .

Remember when I wore a bathing suit and sunburn, when I sweated from *heat* instead of cold and tension?

180

Zeni and I discussed trying to fishfoot back up the mountain to see whether anyone has found the plane or dropped any messages. Didn't want to discourage her but I believe snow must have buried that cliff weeks ago, and wherever they're searching, they haven't flown here.

—We could carry back the gasoline and oil. Start a fire quick if anybody flies by.—

—Hey, you're talking rescue. *I* caught you . . . But it would look so different now. We'd never find that trail again.—

—We wouldn't need it, Ivy. We'd just walk upward.—

—The last of the bigtime hikers, huh? You and Chrysta.—

—Shut up!—

Now I've become the one who defends status quo (and —attacks Chrysta—) while it's Zeni rattling on of —rescue— and —when we're found, I want.— You're becoming Zeni, or are Zeni and you becoming each other?

—Rescue,— even at its minimum (tramping out SOS again), consumes too much energy that should vitalize the home front. But as I tramp (*ES-S*), I know that boot writing (*O-O-O*) has become its own goal, our collective gesture of protest (*ES-S*) against the window high stuff. Mountain knows snows.

Bright new project fires Zeni. We all leap to it (surprisingly) as soon as she swings the first ax. Bashing out the wall behind the stove, between kitchen and parlor. No more cramping into the four-foot corridor between stove front and kitchen counters. When the plaster settles (plus a day's aggressions), we snap the wood laths over our knees and carry the remaining mattresses from Zeni's and Ingrid's old rooms.

Begin sleeping commune style, with true space to stretch around Joette, the baby and the stove. No more freezing and sweating isolated in our ice cubes. Face to face, dust- and plaster-coated ghosts, we begin talking again. Nights around the stove. Mornings.

Ingrid doesn't know why people write history. —If I did, I'd have my first book written. I can't manage more than monographs on our digs. Usually I finish them by working day and night over Christmas vacations. This is the first real vacation I've had in fifteen years.—

Z: —History's nothing but personal opinion anyway.—

Ing: —But there *are* standards. There's consensus.—

Z: —Yeah. Everybody believing the same lies.—

Adrenalin flows, but we all laugh. Such a remark would ordinarily have depressed us, but now the healing touch of something is alive in the cold air. Even Joette no longer feels compulsed to —be optimistic,— to deny the obvious. The silent weeks, though corrosive, were cleansing; in silence we stopped pretending we —like each other— (Joette), we're —glad to be here because outside stinks— (Zeni), we can't make it with each other because nobody ever *really* does (me), women have special communal talent (Chrysta), that —we miss Ann— (Ingrid).

This afternoon I feel so mellow I rock Sammy on my lap.

I think I know where Ann is but can't prove anything yet. Wait . . .

Today ripe inside and out. Cold but clear. Zero on the rusty woodshed thermometer next to the red No Smoking sign.

Inside, too. Willingness to forgive and bear with: Sammy's waking us, beans, Zeni's leaving a stool in the living-room so I crack a shin, Joette's scenting the kitchen with diapers.

So Zeni's wall-in (or wall-out) has knocked together a new era, dismantled the worst personal barriers. Sign: we've reactivated our common joke store house. Everything yesterday was —What the well-dressed pioneer woman will _____ (do, say, wear, swear, etc., *usw*). Today it's —And what will Grammaw think of *that*?—

Zeni just turned Grammaw's picture to the wall. Declared the competition was getting too much.

Me, examining kindling splinters in my hands: —Hey,
turn it back. You can't do that to Grammaw. She'll haunt
us tonight.—

Joette reversed Grammaw right again.

Zeni: —Okay, but Freud, Moses, and Jacob stay back-
side out.—

Ing: —How can we appreciate art when you hide all our
local masterpieces?—

Z: —That's not art. That's mustache worship!-

But she hasn't touched Grammaw again.

A strange night. Another of Joette's Red Crossed ideas,
sewing newspapers to both sides of a blanket for insulation,
is okay but noisy. She crunches me awake again; I lie
there in the snowblue light listening to the wind, my low-
est insides pressuring me toward the pail. When I know I
can't sleep unless I do, I get up. Rush my rags down to
minimize the cold air flow and wet one leg trying to find
the *verschlungen* bucket. At least the new liquid is warm.
Joette crackles in her sleep; Sammy gurgles; and Ingrid
snores sometimes. I always wonder what she dreams—our
flirtatious goddess.

To conquer shivering, I stumble, blanket-wrapped, into
the dining room. The midnight squaw. I land in pulsing,
iceblue space. At first the whole world seems to fluoresce
with the black-purple light they shine on rocks in museums.
But shifting . . . floor to ceiling . . . floor . . . as if the house
is afloat on cobalt waves shifting inward, up and down.

I move one drape. And reel back. Not from the new
batch of cold hitting me. From pulses of white light, un-
dulating, drapes beyond the drape. Ebb and flood. Spray-
ing, streaking, flowing like cold gauze . . . Lightning? Too
gradual. Dance of the dead spirits? Everyone who died
too soon?

I want to waken Zeni, share it with her. What? My awe

and panic? Our new community which equally awes and panics me. Freezing, I huddle and watch. Imagine, hope, the world ending in fire. Moonlight tricks on a dirty window? Epidemic of sunspots? *This house is haunted.*

Acute panic. Flee back. Then: colored page, semicircle strewn, of an old dictionary in Miss Somebody's homeroom. Laugh.

Ivy, you'll never make a country girl, not if the northern lights scare you silly . . .

Meet the rest of my blankets in the kitchen. Sleep shattered. Want to wait out the lights, shut them off, prove they didn't rattle me. Just as I think I've won (they're gone, willed away), they flicker round the doorway lighting Ingrid's mound, her sleeping face, high cheekbones, pale lips. Mummified queen. Nefertiti's bust in Berlin. Ingrid's head's in Berlin. *Ingrid is our witch.*

Minutes . . . more minutes. Close eyes tight: red. When I re-open, all's gray again. Uniform. Solid.

I imagined the lights. Surely I imagined them? Dining room: snow looks slateblue, quiet . . . Imagine the dawn when someone locates us. Two hippies, three hunters, the Air Force crowd between stove and kitchen counters speaking profundities like —Thought we'd never find you. You girls certainly hid good— and —Hey, Charlie, more coffee, over here.— Fadeout . . .

Apple tree *moving* on the hill. Burnham Woods. Poor Lady Macbeth. Scared in her own castle. Tree moved again dammit! . . . Legs. Antlers. Nibbling bark, pawing snow. Poor cold thing. But how we could use more fresh meat. Set the heavy snare again today.

Floor creaks and settles as I ease my way back. Nearly light now. Hungry and my head aches.

Redo my blankets into as nesty a lump as possible. Dank as a dump. Zeni sits up and mutters —Boy, did I have weird dreams last night.—

Cold clamped about us weighs on me, like Gray's

184

and my final winter together before we learned the reason for his black spells.

Tried to imagine myself waking in a heated house, trekking off to computer classes, keeping the baby in one unbruised piece. Seems a fantasy world, another incarnation. Wonder whether the others feel this, too.

P.m. Joette declares I must have been asleep in my previous life, that *she* has no trouble recalling her —real life.— Zeni, by contrast, says she'd become such an urban nomad that here with us is —the first place that's real to me in years. What I worry about *here* matters.—

—You mean you never worried *before*?—

—Yeah. No. I shoved it way back in my brain somewhere so nothing really got through. City life's a blur. Speaking of being asleep, I could teach a whole class and it'd be 10:30 before I woke up and discovered I couldn't remember a thing I'd said.—

Ingrid laughs. —I'm sure your students must have been fascinated. Did your department rehire you?—

—Oh yeah, they'd hire anybody who can stick a syllabus together.— Frown. —With the recession, though, I don't know. I may have to learn how to *teach* something instead of just spouting off.— Double frown. —Ph.D.'s are worth now what toilet paper was five years ago.—

Ingrid winces. —If you *must* put it that way. But you need a specialty. Then if the teaching sours, you've got other work in . . .—

—But I'm a generalist. Specializing would kill me. All I'd want to talk to would be other specialists.— Caressing her own neck, mocks herself. —My dear, how my social life would suffer!—

Knocks her stool over. Sammy begins to cry. Lunch is launched.

Plague of *What would happen if* . . . fantasies:
Bear or deer hunters stumble into here, expecting to

luxuriate in their well-stocked bomb shelter, discover instead four ragged women, one coffin, one colicky baby.

The helicopter fantasy . . .

The hippy arrival fantasy.

The flagging down a jet fantasy. And guess who meets it outside the porch with something immortal like —The Coast Guard, I presume?— or —Glad you got here before swimming season because we didn't bring our suits.—

Zeni admits similar fantasies but still hopes —nobody will find us. Nothing should force us out of here but food running out.— She and Joette are turning into *Let's-Make-It-Do*-ers. Days are longer and everywhere snow lights the rooms enough by night so why do (Zeni) we need candles? Wicksputter, that's why. Why do (Joette) we need more than one meal a day if we can make do with soup and tea for the other two? My eyes seem much more willing to abide the first than my stomach the second.

But if I complain, I get —You're the wildlife expert, aren't you? Then go stab something!—

—Yes, ma'am. Just listen to all those fat, friendly bunnies beating the door down now.— Thumping.

After sitting two hours at two holes: got a pair of pickerel and a weird purple eel this morning. Maybe it's one of those Florida things that stomps across the marshes. Even Ingrid couldn't identify it. Joette is flouring and frying it now. If it's poisonous, at least we'll all go on a full stomach.

Must find energy to search the cellar tool mess for a larger drill (auger?) so I can begin to —keep moving— (ice fisher-ese).

Illusion does make fools of us all. Currently I fantasize the scene in which I —save— Ann from Ingrid by explicating in 3D and monotonic sound Ingrid's many faults. What if Ann had transferred her loyalties to you? Then where would you be?

What I can't stand is all this freedom! No more job or

186

house, no more Gray and grayer relatives. Is that why my chief inner agenda during our first days here was to make Zeni into —boss lady—? How can freedom be oppressive?

Today's cold really bothers me. *O wow* as Ann would say. The Antarctic Patrol or somebody must have studied the all too intimate connection between cold and irritability/depression. I've been skating up and down the dining room iceslick but my toes still tingle with pain whenever the boot ends chafe; my fingers lost consciousness a half hour ago. I just want to crawl into bed and sleep forever.

My ecstasy that somehow we're alive (together) has vanished. Well, what's next? making angry comeback.

Ingrid says she refuses to imagine —next— because it reminds her of undone work. Joette says keeping Sammy well is —next enough— for her. Zeni declares I live too much in the future. Crow in the snow.

More Rescue Fantasies

Chrysta arriving triumphant, the avant garde of a rescue squad laden with chicken soup and steaming coffee. Chrysta, our Lady Savior on a white snowmobile.

The Marines hurtling from helicopters. A search was mounted according to Chrysta's directions. They found the plane but missed the house.

We stay here through next autumn planting potatoes, corn, tomatoes, cabbage, and lettuce. The 4-H and Mixed Garden Collective rescue us at harvest time.

A herd of hippies arrives on their own Return to Eden trip. Share the house and spoil the commune.

We have a new creature in the house. Our randydevil I named him/it. Him/it's what cracks the floorboards just as we fall into clammy sleep, aches our bladders when the pail is already full, blows off the porch door during a blizzard, tumbles our navy beans onto the cellar floor, hides

187

the jar opener, snuffs out the fire. Most malicious during storms on gritty days. Our local representative of confusion and destruction.

Joette says thinking about him will bring bad luck. Zeni says the hell with him, we'll fix him. I feel I should get him alone and negotiate terms before he ruins (again) the good things growing.

Today I was remembering Chrysta, almost wishing she could have stayed with us. I might have learned more about her.

Chrysta Neff   Writer, lecturer for religious group   55
DATA: Peacock in a Pear Tree
PRONOUNCE CAREFULLY: *Der Winter ist hier.*
Haben Sie den Winter gern?
Gute Luft und hohe Berge
Ja, Ihr Männer seid eben zu
verwöhnt.

TRANSLATE INTO GERMAN:
    Out on a limb
    What hath God wrought? What man owes the baboon.
    God's here. I wonder where people are.
    Silver cross lost.
    What did you do Christmas Eve?
    I find you very likable.
NOTE: *Zer* always denotes destruction. *Er* usually denotes "to the end" or "to death" but in some instances it indicates the beginning of something.

for Zeni

JOY → ON → OUR → WAY
   A HEALING VIN VITAE ALWAYS SEARCHES IN THE AMAZON
RING → IN → THE → SPRING
   A TEASING AMAZON NEVER DOES AGAINST THE AMAZON
   DEAR UP HERE
JOY → ON → OUR → WAY

GO TO COUNTING

COUNTING

Joy on our way!
Immediate freedoms from nonsense nuisances:

```
makeups
        lipsticks
                depilatories
vaginal deodorants       ladyshavers
            fragile pantyhose      contraceptives
                        girdles                    pregnancy tests
wigs                         tight skirts
      cocktease bikinis           hairdryers                    gynecologists
                                                          douching
            calorie counters        −spray
                  nightcremes       −rollers
                     morningcremes
shoes and boots that are too high, too narrow, too something (in any case, unwalkable)
```
                        FREEDOM!

♀ ♀   ♀ ♀   ♀ ♀   ♀ ♀   ♀ ♀   ♀ ♀   ♀ ♀   ♀ ♀

None of us here (Zeni perhaps excepted) is any charis-
matic whizzkid, but somehow we've avoided trapping each
other against my Gray wall—presenting demands in crisis-
ridden tones that build guilt and frustrated rage at —my
needs aren't being met, why should yours be?— . . .

Zeni, scratching her head in meditation while Sammy
cries and the stove nears out, —I need me and you but I
believe in something beyond me and you. Maybe that
means I lack potential?—

Hearty laughs all about. We bellow around Joette's
mattress

Ingrid: —Exactly!— More laughing. —No, no. I meant
the other, the *first*.—

Zeni: —Thanks!—

If I could discern Ingrid through the twilight, she'd be
blushing.

Ingrid: —Quiet, people.—

Zeni: —*Achtung!*—

191

Ingrid's hands chop the air. —What I mean is I'm glad you need everybody, Zeni, but you can't keep us here forever in your little hermitage. There's a world out there and some of us have work to finish.— Teasing Amazon.

Zeni: —So postpone your work. Learn what this place has to teach us.—

But Ingrid has hit the dilemma that can force us out of here even if the food lasts. Chrysta, where are you?

Hunks of gritty sleet today—the kind that usually falls in April just when you think spring is getting ready to begin to start. Invisible against the grayed sky and snowy mountain. Only when it plummets between me and the black tree trunks can I pick out individual chunks and connect them with the tap-tap and damp smoke smell all about the house.

And Chrysta raved about —good air and high mountains.—

I help Ingrid cheat at solitaire while Joette rocks Sammy. Then Ingrid amuses herself with an hour of hearing us distort the verb and adjective endings of her native *Sprache* via a battered German grammar I read to Joette. —Most verbs are irregular except the regular ones, and even those are a little weird.—

—English is not better, *ja*?—

—Ingrid, did you know German nouns have five classes of plural endings?—

—God, I never thought about it. I just say them.—

—God, you know you sound like Zeni?—

—*Nimmer*!—

However, if I don't walk outside at least once daily, my ankles and legs swell. Old age already? Nobody else seems afflicted. Zeni, Ingrid, and Joette could stovesit forever discussing the Kennedys, archeology, the Weathermen, and Zeni's dream of —humanizing the university. First, bomb all the file cabinets.—

Joette: —You're kidding.—

192

After I point out that this conversation is a rerun from one sunny day when we were stuffing mattresses, I bow out and try to ease my joints with a walk about the clearing. Sleet has iced everything.

When I return, Zeni and Ingrid still lounge before the oven, gaily trading academic tales while Joette listens from her rocker. I'm glad at such new harmony, yet jealous that this freshest paving of the road to rapport happened today without me.

—Ivy, if you get my pail of water from outside, I'll feed you half my soup.—

Further byproduct of what we've christened —Happenthing Commune.— Without thinking or deciding, we suddenly discover we own and use a heap of property in common. At first we each tried to wash the dirtiest of our grimy own clothes. Now we just pile them in the upstairs hall; whoever draws laundry for the week sees that they're washed, dried, and folded into the kitchen cupboard for whoever needs what. This week I realize I'm wearing what used to be Ann's sweater, Ingrid's red shirt, Zeni's long underpants, Joette's skirt. Even Sammy has one of Ann's shirts we found in her suitcase.

To avoid wasting water on dishes, we now eat tribally by dipping all our spoons into the bubbling iron stew kettle.

Yesterday when Ingrid in one of her (yet) lightning switches from humility to raving arrogance demanded, —Who's been using my pen?— Zeni reminded her anything on the dining room table is now everybody's. —Don't worry about it, Ingrid. We just liberated it!—

Fierce frown from Ing. and stare out the window, but she said nothing.

My comeuppance just arrived. In the bomb shelter, found a tin of crackers which I'd considered —mine.— Until I returned from two hours' futile peering through ice pockets and discovered the indoor women had eaten a

193

dozen of them, leaving me four whole ones and an unchoice debris of crumbles.

Today congratulated Zeni on —leading us— without getting either uptight or dogmatic about her own must-do's.

—I don't lead. I just make you all answer the right questions. Like, will Ingrid slow down her spoon because she's getting more than anybody from the pot. Have you noticed?—

I nod and begin to sweat a little. Nothing escapes Zeni. Has she got all my flaws pegged, too?

Ingrid has definitely warmed toward me. She goes out of her way to catch my eye at breakfast, to laugh at my clowning with Sammy. Walks with me along our —two people path.— But last week wasn't she trying all these things on Zeni? Z., who never clutches people, can remain the solid type I eternally wish I was.

Today a fun round of Who Did We Admire When after Zeni remarked that because of television, the FBI, and psychoanalysis it's hard for people to feel their lives are private or that they can create a private self by emulating somebody else.

Zeni: —You know who thrilled me when I was growing up? Amelia Earhart! I read every book about her I could get, which was three in the town we lived in then.—

Joette: —But she was killed. It was horrible.—

Zeni: —Nobody's proved that . . . Well, who was *your* idol?—

Joette: —I can't even remember. I guess I liked Elvis Presley. And Eisenhower.—

We explode. Even Ingrid joins the laughter.

Joette: —What's the matter? I shouldn't tell you people anything!— She reddens.

Me: —Shut up, everybody.— We sober.

Zeni: —Who was your idol?—

Me: —I never liked public people much. I never felt I could trust them.—

Ingrid: —Even when you were fourteen? That's dreadful!—

Me: —No. I mean, if I had known anybody intelligent or brave, I suppose I would have respected them . . . Everybody in my town was a large coward. But I did have a Joan of Arc period.—

Ingrid: —What was that?—

Me: —You know. I read about her and thought how strange to really care about anything enough to die for it.—

Ingrid: —But she was a religious neurotic. She heard *voices* and . . .—

Zeni: —Don't knock her. I had a Joan of Arc period, too. Right before Amelia Earhart and after Barbara Stanwyck.—

Ingrid: —Then you're *both* martyrs and masochists.—

Me: —All right, who was *your* idol? She'd better be *good*.—

Ingrid: —I didn't need one except for my mother and my father, whom I hardly knew. The War never left us time for such luxuries . . . Once in Ulm we did hear Hitler speak. I even saw him a few seconds when the man next to my mother lifted me up.—

Me: —Did you like him?—

Joette: —Ivy, that's an awful question.—

Ingrid: —Yes. At first everybody did. My father said he was very good for Germany.—

Strange wet dream about Ingrid in which she's a man and is fucking me.

Sit up in the dark and stare across the lumps of us on the floor, but her blankets nearest the wall move not at all. So I lie down again, reluctantly concluding it's me and not her.

Why don't I dream of computers or chocolate sundaes again? She's hexing me.

The skeletal branch ticks at me. Pendulum. Toc, tic. Joette snores. Sammy gnashes his gums.

This morning Zeni was reading on the living room sofa, so I brought her my bird sentences and the German-English jokes about some of us. At her own slogan, —I love community; it's people I can't stand!— she went red and giggled. Next she was flipping my pages. Finally she printed in a margin:

WE HAVE SEEN IVY'S JOURNAL AND DO NOT AGREE THAT
    INGRID IS FLIRTING WITH IVY
    ZENI IS A FEMALE CHAUVINIST
    ALL JOETTE THINKS ABOUT IS HER HUSBAND AND
    CHILDREN

Zeni and the Randydevil

Ingrid oddly flirtatious this afternoon.

When I knocked a load of wood into something she was doing with Zeni, Z. left and Ingrid made me a fresh cup of bark brew. Everything inside warned, Is she preparing for a confrontation?

But her bright face and relaxed body made me curious. No narrowed eye, frowned forehead, needle posture. Just a beckoning odalisque in skirt and vest stretched smiling before me on the velvet sofa.

What the hell, I am curious how she entranced Ann all those months. I sat down.

—You're always busy, Ivy. I thought I was a worker, but you and the others are really the activists. I guess I don't help you much, do I?—

—No. You don't.—

She doesn't flinch. Has she prepared this conversation?

—Suppose I come fishing again with you? Or help with more rabbit traps.—

—But your head . . .—

196

—It's better now. The shock is over.— Bites her lips and stares at the fire. —Would you like some company on the ice?—

I want to say, Sure, but change it to —If I had somebody else, I could carry some doors down and set up a proper windbreak.—

—You're remarkably patient. I'm sure I shan't show half your talent at it.— She laughs. What does she want? —Do you get lonely here sometimes?—

—Of course, but it's good. I probably overdepended on my husband in all the wrong ways. He was . . .—

—And so you don't reveal yourself to anybody now.— She smiles.

—Okay.— Point two. Her favor. —And *you* reveal yourself only when you want something. Am I right, Ingrid?—

—What right have you!— she snaps. Her eyes blaze at me. Somehow I manage not to flinch as Ann must have. She softens.

—Ridiculous! I have good friends, dear friends on three continents. *They* certainly don't think I use them . . . Besides, using people in one's career is an American idea, isn't it?—

—We didn't invent it.—

—Ivy, I don't know what's wrong with you. I offer to help and you act outraged. Unless you're not *really* outraged.— More smile.

Goddamn her. How she tantalizes. I want to hit her. —Of course, I'm not outraged.— She's making you lie. Her point. —All right. I'm nervous because I don't know what you want.—

—I want nothing.— Disclaiming hand on chest.

—I don't believe you.—

—Ivy, I really think you fear being alone with another woman.—

—Why shouldn't I? Look at Ann. You just want a replacement.—

—You *are* cruel!— Now she stares out the window.

197

Has she planned this, too? So I've rattled her. My point.

—You must understand. When Ann came to me, she was in pieces. Her boyfriend had ditched her, she was using drugs, she couldn't study, she hated her parents and her roommate. For one month she just sat behind my bookshelves, didn't even talk. I thought I had a robot next to me.

—I saw the cold dormitory life was killing her so I offered my apartment for the daytime. She could cook, she could play with my animals, she felt at home. I put that girl back together! . . . When she enrolled in life again, we worked together two whole years. I got ten other applications for the work abroad this year but I chose *her.* And she accepted. So I couldn't have been too bad for her.—

—Except she killed herself. She tried to kill you.—

—And she nearly did.— . . . Accepting Ann *dead*? —Ivy, I loved her. She was a beautiful child.—

—If that's how you saw her, no wonder she . . .—

—Ivy, you're really odd. You couldn't get along with your husband, but you don't like women either. You . . .—

—Maybe I should raise dogs.—

—Be serious. It annoys me, your flipness like that . . . I've discovered I can't push you anywhere. I'll respect that . . . I had another proposal for you to consider but we needn't discuss it today. I should help Joette now.—

She's rattled me enough that I haven't even noticed Joette's arrival and clanking stove lids behind us. I pretend to stir the parlor fireplace. How clever she is! Foolish to underestimate her. Trying to entice me with flattery. When that didn't work, by blackmailing me with whatever she can discover awry in me. Fun . . . but eerie. Why does she want anybody? Why tie anybody to you?

Gray's death doesn't mean I couldn't get along with men and should try women, should try Ingrid. Or does it. But why *me*? Hundreds of students she has.

198

Ann was a student. Ann won't do . . .

Today pulled out of Zeni why she got upset with another women's group. —Most of them were married, and it was the married ones who could never be honest. It was like they wanted us to tell them their lives had all been worthwhile. They did what the American Dream says is fulfillment for women—early marriage, split level house, Saturday night orgasm, ten years of diapers, PTA. Now they're bored and frustrated, they want to know why. But at a certain point that *why* just gets too threatening.—

—Maybe they saw their husbands' lives weren't any better.—

—Sure, but the men get a salary and a secretary. For $20,000 a year even *I'll* endure some trivia.—

—You're selling out!—

—Yeah.—

—Remember how Rome decayed from inside before the barbarians ever attacked it?—

—Yeah.—

—Want to meet me at the Forum?—

—Yeah, we'll liberate it together! You can bomb the computers.—

—No. That's too easy. Just one comma misplaced, one bug, and any computer program prints out garbage.—

—If you're so smart, then what do we *do* at the Forum?—

—We talk to people. While we learn how to be free—and alone.—

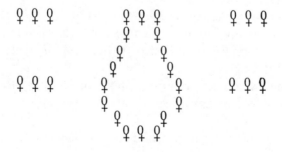

199

Curiouser development. Zeni asked me to share her apartment with her whenever (if) we leave here. Curious because it's her first *serious* reference to leaving. The others have been *divertimenti* to drive it from our minds.

I like and respect her terms (shared: work, money, cooking, entertaining, housework; refrain from: giving each other the shaft for the sake of dating men)—as I like and respect Zeni.

But my time in New York was somehow (admit it) to be *my* time to hang loose from foreign entanglements of any kind. Practice freedom of Gray, his family, the baby, everybody who's unloaded crap on me these ten years.

Flattered but fear her offer as a swinging retread of the old life where everybody else decided how Ivy should do and look, what she should say and wear. That —Do it because you love me— millstone. Rerun of grovelling gratitude that somebody would like me enough to incorporate me into his/her life.

If only *I'd* taken the initiative and asked Zeni . . .
Yellow Shafted Flicker.

Yet living with her would keep me clean of too much foolishness (ratty rutting on waterbeds), should loneliness consume me.

Hell, maybe I should ask Ingrid. Now *there's* the last of today's redhot ideas.

Joette and I just spent a half hour lugging and sledding logs from the far pile to the woodshed. Nothing like exhaustion to crush aggressions.

Unlike the rest of us, Joette seems to lose no weight. Minus Sammy, slimmer of course, but she has one of those chunky, nonwa(i)sted bodies that are durable from childhood through old age.

She's much better natured about the discomforts of nursing Sammy than I was about nursing Ian.

Another storm started at dark. Pines and oaks already

upholstered with ice. Branches down and drooping farther. Sleet on the tin roof makes us drowzy.

Zeni tells ghost stories complete with ESP sound ef-
fects. Ingrid confesses that before she gets to know an
archeological site, she hates sleeping there. And I admit
to all the childhood underwear I moistened because I
feared running upstairs to the dark bathroom if I couldn't
get the hall light to work.

I think I know where Chrysta went . . . Tomorrow.

MOUNTAIN → KNOWS → SNOWS
  A KAY-NINE TRUE BELIEVER ALWAYS HUNTS INTO THE
      BROWN POX
HOW?
  DEAD AS MUMMY DUST
  HOTPINKLY BLEAKLY
FOUND → IN → THE → POND

GO TO IVY'S GONE HUNTING AGAIN

Off to hunt, I tell everybody, as soon as the sun lets me know it's serious. Fishfoot through the fresh snow across the garbage ravine well enough. Except for an old-new cough, souvenir of flu, that tears my chest whenever I hurry or climb. Then a flat stretch (*couldn't* be a road?) of firm snow. Onward. Down is out, down is . . . slow down. Almost enjoy jet branches against satin snow, the blue sky.

Sun's warmer. So damn much land out here. Onward, downward, away from the pond. Farther than I've ever walked because the animals don't run here. Look for the clearings, downward. Pine and bluejay sky smell in the noon air. Puffs of wind rise and die. Inside my layers I sweat. Fever again. Dizzy enough.

On a fallen tree I eat —lunch— (soda crackers pasted together with jam and powdered milk). More bluejay protest.

Decide: to try my theory for another half hour. If it doesn't work, no one will know. And if it does? During weak moments I flop in the sunshine away from cold shadows and frozen, shaggy bark.

Two clearings beyond, the hillside suddenly shapes itself into a long hump interspersed with mounds. Eager to reach it, I mislay a snowshoe. Four feet of my right side disappear into a drift. Still choking, I reach the first mound and land a good kick into it. Solid timber thump. Another kick hurts my foot. But a carved rail leaps from the snow, settles on top. A fence! But where is . . . ? The flat part of this clearing may be a road? Leading among the pines to what . . . ? Scramble through the blue snow toward the trees.

Then it glints in the sun. Glass, driftpiled to the window sill. A cabin. One room. Shut up, they'll hear you coughing. No porch. No footprints. Nobody. But maybe food. Optimist . . . Rest inside.

205

Front door warped frozen. Flounder around to the back. Branches leak snow on me. No door. Trees now send me weird purple shadows as if they owned the sun and had decided to take it off display. Again to the front. Trip on a stump. Goddamn. Want to blast the door with my snowshoes but I'll need them to get home.

Door gives, sliding on ice hinges. Snow and I squeeze inside. Pleasant woodsmoke smell. I make out torn tin-cans piled in the gloom behind the door. Table, chair, fireplace.

—Hey, you all— I yell because it's silly and makes me feel good. Leave a note? For the hunters. A few steps toward the table I stumble on a dark pile. Must be rubbish, newspapers. Mothy blankets with a strange sharp odor like ammonia. Kick them. A solid center that won't be budged. Bricks? One corner falls away. My eyes slide along a cylinder of rags. At its end, lighted by one stripe of sunshine is something white and black, peeling. A human foot, swollen around pink toenails. A mannikin, a *Playboy* joke, sure.

Then I panic, scream, scramble out the door. Not a mannikin. That nail polish was, god . . . Penny's color! of the vacant eyes, plastic glasses, the wrenched back.

Impossible. Why here? She and Chrysta made it out, didn't they? Of course, of course . . .

My cold fingers pull the blankets. The swollen foot belongs to a leg, bent to the side, which belongs to . . . Of course. Rigid . . . Shaking and coughing. Sit down and wedge my back against the table.

Arms clenched over the chest. Face is last, is gray. Eyes frozen closed, but the mouth is locked open. Poor fish suffocated out of water.

I yell again. Not because anybody will hear but because nobody's here. Stumble in the doorway and land again in the blue snow.

She's dead. Poor Penny who planned menus, peeled carrots, fought parents over allergy diets, whatever the hell else dietitians do. Froze between a pile of tincans and an ashy fireplace. Alone.

When I can move again, I cover her leg, retrieve her glasses and put them on the table. Handbag? Probably under her. Rummage inside a pile of rust near the fireplace that was once a breadbox. Empty. Saggy bookcase, a chest. Drawers give me a domino set, a flat pencil, and a frozen, rotted something. Potato? . . .

I try to write a note on the domino cover, but my fingers don't work any more in the icy twilight. And I can't imagine anything beyond HELP.

Can't take her back. Don't want . . . Where's Chrysta? Penny dead frozen.

This afternoon an airplane passes over. Jet, remote silver pellet. I scramble through the snow to a corner of the SOS, waving a pair of rags. Useless but the activity is good. Drives Penny from my head.

Tell them at supper . . . no, don't blast our new harmony. Joette liked Penny. Dry up . . . no, tell, no . . . wait till breakfast, no . . .

Zeni: —No! Jesus Christ!—

Ingrid: —Are you sure?—

Joette: —How awful!—

Yet Zeni proves the only one who will walk back with me. And she's half astounded, half annoyed that in all our search for Ann we never stumbled on the pine cabin. It was merely the sunshine at the right angle . . .

Hope we don't bring her back here. Already built one coffin from the bomb shelter boards.

Ingrid and Joette, guilty forehead furrowed, mumble they don't want to come. Somehow Penny deserves a little better than this. Don't insist—they have to live with themselves, too . . .

We lie awake, freshly debating where is Chrysta? They're sure she's near the cabin somewhere. I feel she isn't.

207

—Are we bringing her back? What about the sled?—
—Maybe we should just wrap her in a sheet.—
I nod. *—Did you bury him?— —No, I . . . we . . .—*
Where's Chrysta?

We follow my snowholes and fishfoot trail. The grimness of our mission depresses even Zeni. I feel cheated somehow and realize how much I've relied on Zeni to buoy me up. Because she and I have never inflicted unpleasantness on each other, have no backlog of grudges.

Words seem useless. I shut up and help her over the treacherous rock parts, refasten the leather thongs on her snowshoes when they freeze and slip.

Our new harmony has survived Penny. But Chrysta nags (still). After the first shock, nothing explicit. Just refurbished restlessness. Partly the weather—the merest transparent trickle down the clapboards on a blue and white afternoon begins our spring fever.

Daily Ingrid and Zeni ask how far I've walked and whether I've seen anything —new,— a ritual which would have annoyed me a few weeks ago but now settles into the familiar atmosphere we've created. Summer seems a universe away. I can scarcely remember when I didn't climb into double pants, plastic bags, and galoshes every morning.

I even wish Gray were here. To feel what grows that he and I could never achieve. Not just toleration of each other's oddities but a sense that life is a strange adventure we're doing together. Not just post-quarrel promises to be good and act better but sustaining and being sustained by everyone's effort.

I wonder if and whether we all leave here, we'll ever meet again—like yearly reunions at high cholesterol restaurants.

6 P.M. THE HARPOON LOUNGE
TRAVEL ON REUNION. CLASS OF WINTER, 197_

I shouldn't play any more hunches, they're too accurate in their random way. Today I hacked a path to the pond. First time since ice fishing froze me out don't know how many days ago.

Eerie afternoon like the days of autumn—grayclouded, no wind, every twigsnap a startling event. I wandered around the brook end where a ragged semicircle of water has unlocked and leaks down the rocks. As I watched rabbit tracks and wondered about returning tomorrow with fish line and one of my taxidermed horseflies, I half noticed something pinkish flowing under the thinning ice. Rubbish? Paper? Hotwater bottle?

Let it go, no, catch it, might be . . . A stick, and I balanced on the rocks, grappled with it, finally pulled it from whatever held it. Oozed it onto my rock—a sodden, faded, tattered, frigid mess. How nice had it been natural—water lily, marsh grass, even a snake. But it wasn't.

Seen it before . . . where? . . . Ann's scarf! The heavy rose silk one from Ingrid. The only happy event about her. Always wore it knotted over her shoulders.

Here we go again.

I hid it in the woodshed behind the baby's coffin. Again torn inside over telling anybody with Penny's suffering newly found. This would really unwind our chiming harmony. I don't even want to hurt Ingrid any more.

Be a coward. Scarf doesn't prove she's in the pond. Maybe . . .

But if I didn't want to tell, why did I wring it like the wash and carry it back? Why didn't I let it flow down the rocks into the wilderness?

Because Ann was alive, human, deserves more than being tossed over a waterfall. But our better is so little— boards and ice. And the scarf is all that's left. Is it? She must have dropped it on her way —out.—

Living means more when all around's an acre of snow. Even Ann's (once) living.

Don't tell, won't tell, later . . . Manage to shove the secret three days to the back of my head. Fill my mind and shoulders with woodchopping and chasing invisible rabbits on a white ground. If I wasn't so hungry all the time, I'd appreciate the game-and-design possibilities.

Return to the pond and walk the banks thoroughly. No floating limbs. A dead log? . . . A dead log. Mousy hair frozen in the ice? . . . A nest of rotted leaves.

Then Ingrid begins it during cup of water time. —It hasn't snowed for a week now. We can all walk outside. I mean . . .—

Three heads peer at her. One of Zeni's eyelids twitches. I guess what's coming. —You want us to look for Chrysta again.— Say it. —And Ann.—

Ingrid's eyebrows dart together. Inhales our cold air. —It's disgusting the way all of you just *gave up*!— Her silver rings dance against the table. Chrysta. *Out on a limb.*

Me: —Well, who . . .—

Zeni: —Pack it up, everybody!— She lands a semi-karate chop into my arm. Ingrid should have got it.

Temptation exquisite. Say it. No! Yes! Think . . . —Maybe I know where Ann is.—

Moan from Ingrid. Open mouths on Zeni and Joette.

J: —Is it—she . . . like Penny?—

I shake my head.

Z: —You're putting us on.—

Again shake my head.

Her eyes flare at me. —Why didn't you tell us? When did you find . . .—

J: —Is she . . .—

—I don't know. I didn't want to crush the good spirits, I guess. Anyway I haven't found Ann. Just her scarf.—

Ingrid's face contorts. Then her eyes go far away.

Z: —I bet you found her a long time ago. Where is she?—

Ivy: —It's not *her*! I told you. Her scarf. The pink scarf was under the ice at the pond. The brook end.—

210

Z: —Did you leave it there?—

The perfect double-edge question. Have you stopped beating your . . . —I cleaned it off and put it in the wood-shed. And stop jumping down my throat. I didn't make her . . .—

Zeni tears out the back door, followed by Joette. I feel ridiculous, like the times I blabbed some fact or project to Gray and had to endure a five-minute diatribe as if I'd invented the cracked wall, the rise in school taxes, the death of God, the clogged carburetor. Crap. Damned if I do or . . . all bearers of bad news will be shot at dawn.

Ingrid's Nefertiti smile stares at me . . .

Five minutes later we flounder through the snowball drifts toward the pond. Air is soggy and mild. Zeni, Ingrid, Joette, and me (last) with pole, rope, blanket. The pond is *lovely, dark and deep* . . . It's been *my* pond; I resent the others taking it by surprise this dirty afternoon.

At the brook end, freshets of black water detach them-selves from the calm lake and splatter down the rocks. I stand and prod under the ice. Nothing but coffee liquid, cold rectangular broth. Snow over the remaining ice is tree-splattered, drilled in a thousand little holes.

Zeni halfcircles the bank to the pond's narrow end. Tries a foot onto the slush. It holds. —Gimme the pole.—

Me: —It's rotten, Zeni. Don't. You can't see through it anyway.—

—Hell. Somebody has to.—

The other foot. I watch from the shore near her. She inches boot by boot away from safe ground upon the gray slush. I recall my fishing failures because that ice was so thick. When the temperature was . . .—

We hold our breath until it hurts. Stomp the banked snow into slurpy mud. She'll never reach the middle. Water flows under the ice. She reaches twenty feet out, another five, another ten. Forty feet. The middle. Hoists the pole. Donna Quixote about to charge.

211

What happened next still blurs.

An instant more Zeni stands. Then a crack noise. She falls sideways and disappears into the black water. We hear a muffled scream. Suddenly I'm out onto the ice, one eye on that cold lightning split, the other on Zeni's hands that bob above the water. All the first aid classes I slept through: how do you help somebody you can't reach? How long can anybody stay alive in ice water?

My hands are shaking; I sweat inside my jacket. Try to remember. Keep moving. Gently. Gently. Good you lost all that weight. Water laps the crack. Clamp my hands against my legs to steady everything. Next they've made a wide noose at one end of the rope. Follow beside Zeni's prints, not on them. My stomach jangles; my eyes mist.

Zeni's head shows up. At first she flails, then clings to the jagged edges. She can't yell; I know the water is chilling her. Six feet from her I stop. Pray the stream's not flowing here the way it was under her. She sees me. Tries a shoulder onto the ice. It cracks. She whimpers and sinks again.

Seize my legs so they don't run to her or back. Lightly, lightly. She surfaces, tries again with an arm on the ice. This time it holds.

—It's coming!— I shout. If I miss, I'll choke her. First I try throwing a wide noose in front of me. Softly. All those rabbits missed, all those squirrels. Then I snake it out toward her. No good, too wide. Then it's good, it settles. About her shoulders and arm on the ice and water.

Ridiculous to yell —Not yet!— at her. Holding the rope, I sprint like hell back toward shore, ignoring black crack, black crack, and have one more leap when the big pull comes. Then I'm up to my face in jagged, stunning cold. It's Joette who gets me to shore, and together we haul Zeni's right arm and shoulder, foot by foot, through the widening cracks and slush. An ice floe catches her head.

My hands freeze and burn on the rope. My feet dig in; my hips and legs shout with the pain. At last she's over the hole I fell into, and we can drag her, dripping, onto shore.

Rapid breathing. Her face gray pale. Penny, Penny. Hair matted and glasses ripped off.

Now my terror gives way. I try to run for the blanket, but my hips are paralyzed from the tugging. My face lands again in slush. Tremendous cramps tear through my legs.

Ingrid has the blanket. They fling it over Zeni and drag her away from me.

Somehow I yank my boots and leggings off and begin to massage my miserable purple ankles and toes. Long ache replacing the cramps. When my fingers begin to pain, I stop. Leaning into a tree, I stand on bare feet, try to ease my soggy boots on. I fall over. Sit down and begin over with the freezing leggings. I yell at Joette and Ingrid but they don't return. Ripping the rags, I get them on all twisted. Then a boot and a half. Hobble toward the brook.

When I can bear to face the pond again: a cross-shaped crack gashes the center out from Zeni's big hole. Stop at the waterfall, climb the rocks, one by one. Imagine myself falling in again. Stagger.

On the last boulder, just before shore, I glance at the dark water that never stops coming. Something's there, under the ice. White. *No*. Floats but stops as if it's caught. Like Ann's scarf. Only white sometimes, then dark like a log. Or an arm . . . It blurs.

I hurry toward the house. My legs are afire now.

By the time I straggle in, Joette and Ingrid have a gorgeous fire on the parlor hearth. Later I wonder if Caleb and Jacob also returned to this fire after a hard afternoon of whatever it was they did to stay alive up here.

Zeni lies gasping on a mattress, Ingrid and Joette each chafing one end of her body inside a quilt. Twinge of jealousy that nobody cares about my frozen legs—except me. Slump into Grammaw's rocker and begin to rub myself down with a soggy blanket. My teeth set up a wild chatter.

213

How to avoid contemplating my new dilemma, which is just a rerun of yesterday's dilemma: do I tell them? If ever a woman with a death wish—it was Ann. Your eyes playing tricks, too much hunting. Ann, like Chrysta, probably got miles beyond here. Send Joette to the pond.

—Oh-h.— Zeni groans. Tries to sit up and falls over. —God, everything *aches*.— She holds her head. —How long was I in the water?—

—Four, maybe five minutes.— Ingrid's answer. Wasn't it longer than that? —But it was another ten before we got all your clothes off.—

—Ah-h-h. I'll never walk again. Toes in little pieces. You know I still can't even *feel* them?— Tries to rise off Ingrid's lap toward Joette. Her hips squirm around, bringing her face toward me. —Hey, I'm sorry, Ivy, am I sorry. How're *you* doing?—

—Fine.— I lie. —But you should have waited a bit before yanking the rope. I got dunked, too. Or I should have told you, but there was no time.—

—Yeah. The *details*.— (The word irritates me.) —I didn't even think I was alive any more. Did I pull hard? . . . But thanks, huh?— Crawling on her knees, she takes my hands in hers. We're both damp and shivering. —You're braver than I would have been when that ice cracked. I mean I'll go in alone 'cause I don't know what I'm getting into. But I don't think I could have *followed* anybody.—

I ought to say, Oh you could too! Instead —So it's glory then and not community?— I get my hands anchored around the quilt about where I guess her waist is. We help each other up.

—Yeah. Glory.— Her shoulders and teeth still chatter. We all swing one motheaten sofa to the fire and huddle about her. Our horsehair raft smells of sawdust and dustdust. I yawn into the firelight.

I wait til breakfast when Ingrid announces —I'm going back to the pond.—

Zeni and I lock eyes. I say nothing. Ingrid exits.

I grab another pole from the shed. When she runs ahead of me, I yell at her to stop. Suddenly I want to protect her from seeing anything, finding Ann. I hate how it's become my responsibility.

She ignores me. By the time I catch her, she's walked the shore and sloshes in the frost, ice and mud mess, peering at the deepest water just before it drops over the dam. She climbs the rocks.

I hand the pole to her. She doesn't even look up. Her face is wet. I realize she's crying and that I'm not supposed to notice the tears.

At first she poles the water without resistance. Then the stick stops at something just under the jagged ice mouth.

—Help me!— she yells. She's terrified now of finding something rather than nothing. I stand on the shore.

She flails the water. Drags toward the rocks a black weedy mass that resolves into slimy rags, a back, a torso. Then a chalky, bloated face, staring marble eyes, tangled hair, ponderous, loglike limbs. The fingers and toes seem torn off; white bone joints hide in the swollen flesh, all afloat with its own life in the ripples.

Not Ann. Not this blasted embryo, this frozen bomb exploding among us. No, not . . .

Ingrid's overcoat hangs in the water. Her mouth shrieks something at me.

Rain Nightmares Rain Nightmares Daymares

Fishfooted to the pond this morning. Should have tried some fishing but couldn't bear squatting there alone anymore. Ann avalanched in my head. Any of a dozen times I fished since she disappeared, my hook might have snagged . . . that her frozen eyes were watching . . . Cold horror in chilling rain.

Left the ice to itself. Crunching up the hill, I snarled a snowshoe in a tangle of bushes. Sonofsonofa . . . Talking

215

to myself, but not alone. As I tried to retrieve my foot plus or minus the shoe, I discovered a baker's dozen of gray lumps on another set of low branches, all scrutinizing behind beady eyes. Apparently I was so funny-harmless they didn't even need to fly away. Bird's eye view: the human comedy. They chuckled at me.

Ducky heads plumped onto gray breasts and ruffled feathers. Black tails. Partridge size, but *mourning dove* drummed through my head. Slid the stiff thongs around my lost foot. Upright again, I shook an oak branch at them. They took off in a huff but queued on another branch directly across the pond where they continued studying me like faded Christmas ornaments. Morning's mourning doves.

Bet they're good to eat.

In the woodshed Ingrid is finishing a box to put Ann in. Joette and Zeni take one look and retreat to the kitchen. Joette whispers that the ends don't look nearly as nice as the one I made for the baby.

The hammer is loud, irregular. I find myself apologizing to Ann for Ingrid's whacking. How violent noises always frightened her . . .

Again Joette mentions bringing both boxes into the cellar or upstairs but again we —postpone— doing it.

Our trips to the woodshed, though, grow ever abbreviated: each of us by turns drags in more than she can balance so as not to pass that stack of boxes a second time.

I hide the boxes under two blankets and a sawhorse.

THREE A.M.

Ticktock	Tocktick	Ticktock
STOP THAT CLOCK	STUPID CLOCK	STABAT CLOCK
		STAB THAT CLOCK

Things I'd Love to Feel Again

Soft, dry bed	Walk minus fishfoots
Real cake of real soap	Real cup of real tea
Hot radiator	Sunny beach

216

Trying to drive Ann's pale drowned face from my mind.
Ingrid extra quiet now.

Snow is melting! Soggy-good for snowballs. Ring in the
spring! Caught a squirrel (by mistake I'm sure) in one of
my baited nooses. Yet another of Joette's Camper Spe-
cials: soak cotton with a bit of his blood, dangle it to the
fish. Briefly at the non-falls end without looking too much.
   But they weren't biting. Joette says the icy water kept
them from smelling it.
   Squirrel stew with rice and some unidentified vegetable
for supper. Even Sammy tried a little gravy. Squirrel is
TOUGH! Maybe he was so ancient he died of a heart attack
and just *collapsed* into my trap.
   Wild life among the wildlife . . .

More hints of spring—drippy gutters, puddles by the
steps, sunbathing at two. But the nights clamp down, icicles stiff by six, glacial as ever.
   Remember when you froze a tin of water in a crook of
the house just to see what would happen?

How We Hope This Adventure Will End: Verse 2

Fugue in H Major by the Travel On Quartet

Ingrid: —My dream is still to get found first, then to get
a big enough grant so I can retire prematurely from teaching. And dig my way around the Mideast. I know of four
places . . .—
   Zeni: —Ingrid the capitalist!—
   Ingrid: —*Ja*. I used to accept only grants without strings.
Now I do anything to get money and not waste more time.—
   Zeni: —I'll take some publicity and a lecture tour. Plus
somebody donating about twenty acres of land so I can
build a commune. That's me—the capitalist's communist.—

Joette: —What're you lecturing on?—

Zeni: —Women in the Wilderness.—

Joette: —You wouldn't!—

Zeni: —Wouldn't I?—

Joette: —It's so . . . shocking. Large but *petty*. You just want to exploit our time here . . . Why can't you be like me—I only want to keep Sammy healthy and get back home.—

Zeni: —Ivy, what do you want?—

Ivy: —Still the same. Get out alive—and have a square meal.—

And still flatter myself daydreaming some hero(ine)ic action I could perform here that would be less gruesome than what we've just lived through. Lead us all —out.— Repair the gun with a bobby pin. Shoot a bear. Or a wolf. (Can you eat wolf?) Be more groupy.

Why do I still feel pressured to be anything for anybody —beyond an honest day's work at food capturing? How's that, Grammaw?

4 a.m. Randydevil at it again knocking hunks of ceiling plaster onto our blankets. Mouse in the house.

One thing we'll never do again is tell ghost stories.

A paragraph for Zeni which I won't show her (yet):

Skin Diving in Winter?
You Bet Your Life!!

If you ever felt the cracking of ice underneath your fishing bob house or snowmobile, you also recall the cold, miserable water you may have wound up in. Thus the alertness of an underwater skin diving team would be the best sight in your life.

New Hampshire has such a team, adequately equipped and annually re-trained in lifesaving measures from under ice floes.

Recovering drowned bodies; searching for those in various sections of the state; rescuing those who've gone thru the ice on any one of over 1,000 lakes and ponds; or "going under" to

218

hook a cable on a lost snowmobile and pull it out of the icy water . . . all these tasks come under the conservation officer's modernized duties.

We've run out of the bomb shelter rags and *Reader's Digests* we had liberated into sanitary napkins. Joette is washing and ripping curtains.

Ivy: —Does anybody wonder what's happened to God?—
Joette: —God's where he's always been. I wonder what's happened to people.—

Our Miracle

Evening: the third day of Happenthing wall raising.
The most amazing three days I've ever felt. Exhausted.
One evening came a depressing crash that shook the house. When we rushed to the dining room and looked across the stove, we saw—the outdoors through a waterfall. One corner of the roof was sagging. Eight feet of rotting wall under the rotting gutter and roof had buckled and collapsed in a cloud of plaster, wallpaper, icicles, snow, mildew, and a few of something black running for remaining walls.
Joette: —Kill them! They're carpenter ants.—
Zeni: —Aw, leave them. Without their nest they'll freeze anyway.—
J: —But the water's coming in again. We'll drown if we don't freeze.—
Z, tiptoeing to the edge of outdoors; —Look, the roof's tilting, but it's okay. The stove is even still burning. Well, it's smoking . . . Ivy, your gutter fell and tore the corner wall off.—
Me: —*My* gutter? It took me two days to dry out last time I fixed it . . . I can't do it alone.—
Ingrid, joining Zeni in the wreckage: —The whole wall

219

is rotten. It needs new beams. And shingles over the outside clapboards. Maybe we can drain the water before so much collects.—

Joette: —Shingles need horsefeathers underneath.—

Zeni chokes and laughs. —*Horse*feathers?—

J: —Sure. That's what they're called. My husband put them . . .—

It returns. A shingle project with hammer, shiny nails, blue-chalked measuring string, a good level, brand new cedar shakes, plywood, dry horsefeathers. All the technological luxuries.

Z: —There's a few boards in the cellar. What about the rest of the old doors? Or bunks from the bomb shelter?—

J: —There's tarpaper upstairs.—

Me: —You mean, fix a whole *wall* in this room? But it's the roof and gutter that make the ice problem. How about just closing off this corner of the house?—

Z: —Yeah . . . No. This is our house. We build a *new* wall.—

Ing: —I'll get hammers and nails. Bring a candle to the cellar.—

Z: —No. Wait. Ingrid, you be architect . . . So go outside and arc. Tell us what to do first.—

Me: —First we clean up the rubble.—

Z: —Okay, you and Joette throw the plaster and ice outside and break off the splintered boards. I'll see what's downcellar and out in the shed.—

Suddenly we're all working. It's almost fun, compared with freezing at dawn the way I last repaired the gutter.

Joette and I place pots to collect water streaming down the rest of the wall. We kick and heave chunks of plaster and lathing to the outside snow. I'm having such a warm good time that I cease to notice my stomach that was raging hungry or my hands getting scratched. We pull out bent nails and carry the ants' nest outside between two hunks of plaster. Among the splintered, brown-poxed clapboards we saw off a decent one and prop the roof an inch higher with it.

Ingrid and Zeni are grunting up the cellar steps with an old door, hammers, nails, another saw. Joette and I climb down and drag away a second door leaning near the bomb shelter. Something has eaten its paint also into chicken poxed dots.

When Ingrid unrolls two scrolls of paper in the dining room, I'm awed. She's done shaded, three-dimensional ink drawings of the wall and roof from three different views, including top down. Lightly, deftly she sketches how the new wall will appear. Like Ann, I'm impressed because still life drawing is a skill I never acquired in a low budget, small town school. All I managed was the switch from printing to handwriting to typing computer programs.

Ing: —I'll sketch you sometime, Ivy. I used to draw a lot.— She smiles.

Me: —Okay.—

Ing: —So . . . the plan is simple. We saw off the splintered boards until they're straight there (pointing left to the chimney at one end of the wall) and there (right to the corner of the room and house). Then we lay these doors side by side, cover them with tarpaper or newspaper and shingles and stand them up.—

Me: —What shingles?—

Ing: —You and Zeni will make shingles from the old boards.—

But it's already dark by the time we transport another door and test the three of them against the windy hole. We lean one on each side of the hole and use the third to block off the doorway between dining room and living room to keep out some cold.

Finally we fall exhausted into our blankets around the kitchen stove. It's a blustery night of whistles and banging. Windows rattle more than ever; it's dawn before I sleep. The stove burns low, and I'm terrified of freezing. Then I'm lost in a nightmare blizzard: the wall has vanished, the hole is black and immense. I'm coated with ice and about to fall in. I scream . . .

Ingrid is shaking me. —Ivy, stop it! You're all right, dear. Stop.— I get my eyes open. Ingrid's hands are around my shoulders. Zeni is dragging an armload of wood to the stove, and Joette scrapes inside a pot. Sammy coos from his crate.

—Oh-hh. My head. I had a dream.—

Ing: —You surely did.—

Zeni: —Don't tell us, huh? C'mon, get up. Help me with the wood.—

Me: —How about some breakfast?—

Z: —Dreamer!—

We share out the tasks. Joette and Ingrid will nail the three doors together and face the whole long thing on both sides with tarpaper and newspaper layers. Zeni and I will saw shingles—hunks of rotten board and plywood —to two-foot lengths. She and I drag in a sawhorse and set to work around the living room fireplace. The persistent panic in my stomach subsides when I feel again how blessedly easy Zeni is to work with. Without a word she understands the tools and which boards to use. I saw while she holds. Then we switch jobs. The morning goes.

In the dining room Ingrid has a perfectionist fit when she discovers how warped the doors are, but Joette soothes her down. Finally we force the door edges together by all standing on them and nailing shingles over the joinings.

Ingrid: —But it's such sloppy work. It'll leak.—

Zeni: —What d'you want? A prize from the builders' association?— . . .

We spend until dark neatening up the hole, sloshing out the water, papering the doors. Our shingle pile grows. Whenever I slow down and hold boards for Zeni, my stomach improves but my feet and legs begin to chill. When I saw, I get warm but exhausted. Small actions—sweeping splinters, using the toilet pail, walking upstairs—drag out longer and longer.

By twilight we have molded the doors into one solid seven- by nine-foot siding, gloriously tarpapered and ready to test on the vertical. Four of us get behind and push up.

222

A beauty, it covers all the horizontal hole from rotten wall-near-chimney to rotten wall-near-corner. But *vertically*? We groan. It's not high enough! There's still a one-foot by nine-foot gap running between door tops and falling roof. Wind still whistles through plaster cracks. Water begins to trickle down the doors along our new tarpaper.

Zeni: —I'm bushed. We haven't got one piece of lumber that long unless we tear apart our mattress platform. Or some upstairs floor.—

Me: —Ingrid did that already.—

Z: —Well, if we can't lengthen the doors to meet the roof, we can always pull the roof down to meet the doors.— Brawny Zeni.

Me: —But that'll cave in the whole roof.—

Ing: —Ivy's right. We can't afford to play with the roof. We really require something metal at the top to keep out the water. And we must build a new gutter for the corner.—

Me: —Oh.—

Joette: —Why don't we eat?—

That night turns colder. Runoff from melting snow stops; our inside air chills. We all huddle, a single blanket mass, trying to warm one another. Frigid as rainstain. I lie between Ingrid and Zeni . . .

Zeni in the darkness: —I got it! I got it! Grammaw's dump!—

Joette, Ingrid: —What? . . . You scared me!—

Z: —We'll search tomorrow.—

Me: —For what? Who?—

Z: —The snow fence. Didn't you say there's a roll of wooden snow fencing in the dump? Remember? You cut your knee?—

She's right! —But how d'you know it's nine feet long?—

Z: —Clinging vine, what snowdrift around here is ever *less* than nine feet?—

Joette laughs.

Ing: —You mean nail it between the doors and the roof.—

Z: —Yeah. And wire it to the roof inside the old wall line. That extends the eaves so we don't need a gutter any more. The water just drops down a foot or so in front of the wall instead of running down it.—

I hear Ingrid crunching around. She lights a candle, crawls across me, and hugs Zeni, imprinting a vigorous kiss on her forehead. Zeni, who was propped up on elbows, falls back flat. Everybody laughs. We hurrah Zeni, then drift back to sleep.

Morning is crisp and calm. With the two pairs of snow-shoes Zeni and I set out for the dump. To avoid remember-ing the pond, I leave the pole behind, but we don't need it. Enough snow has melted to expose one corner of the red fencing. Together we pull it from under and over con-flicting junk and unroll it. It's a good ten or twelve feet—enough to nail right around the corner of the house. Rot-ten in some places but better than the house boards. It's too heavy to carry so we roll and lift it, snowman style, to the house. Ingrid and Joette help us drag it in.

We measure carefully, nail and paper it along the door tops. When we hoist the total aloft, it snuggles perfectly under the eaves with extra wraparound to formfit the cor-ner of the room.

This afternoon is shingling. We hammer until our heads ache and arms and legs tremble. Starting at the outside bottom of the doors, we nail and overlap all the slabs Zeni and I sawed yesterday. We continue building them onto the snowfence. Zeni's major problem, besides exhaustion, is . . .

—Hey, Ivy, you nailed the damn thing to the floor again.—
—Sorry. I'm hungry. My stomach hurts.—
—Well, put a couple bricks under it.—
—My stomach?—
—No. The fencing!—

Joette giggles. Ingrid smiles. —You and Zeni did a bully job on the shingles. You're truly quite a pair.— . . .

224

When we raise the siding for the third and final time, it fits! Paper insulation inside, a solid coat of slab shingles outside. Standing on stools, we nail and wire it in place. With newspaper we stuff the cracks between it and the eaves and floor.

A big hurrah. Dancing and hugs around everybody's shoulders. O for another bottle of gin! Then we sprawl, quiet and happy, onto our blankets. Zeni's eyes catch mine. I smile at Ingrid. Joette and Sammy form the middle. We relax against the kitchen cupboards. We've forced the wind and water outside again, we're alive, and nobody needs to say a word.

NOTE

to those who read only the Begins and Ends

HERE BEGINS THE END

Ivy
Zeni

PROGRAM FOR A NOVEL

Input data: CHRYSTA = –5   ANN = 0   JOETTE = 1   IVY = 4
             PENNY   = –1   INGRID = 3   ZENI = 5

In memory banks: data sets (PILOT, DAVID, GRAY, JERRY)
                  subroutines (setting, hunting, superexit, exit, maxi-
                  mum, minimum)

NOVEL: procedure options (main);
        get data;

OVERVIEW:
   IVY=(CHRYSTA+PENNY+ANN+JOETTE+INGRID+ZENI)÷6;
   go to IVYPOINT;

IVYPOINT:
   FIRST DAY = (IVY + CHRYSTA) + setting (airplane, mountain,
      house);
   call superexit (PILOT);
   call exit (PENNY + CHRYSTA);
   go to INGRIDANN;

INGRIDANN:
   INGRID WAITS;
   INGRID PIECES = archeology + Thebes + Germany + father;
   INGRID = maximum (INGRID);
   ANN snoops*1;
   go to ANNPOINT;

ANNPOINT:
   ANN = maximum (ANN, INGRID); ANN = ANN – INGRID;
   ANN = ANN – ANN
   INGRID = minimum (INGRID);
   go to IVYPOINTPOINT;

IVYPOINTPOINT:
   IVY IN THE HOUSE = hunting + (JOETTE + 2)** max;

229

	if	INGRID		JOETTE	
					ROSEANN
			ZENI	–	ROSEA
					ROSE
		IVY		+ 1	RO

then IVY'S GONE HUNTING: call superexit (ANN, PENNY);
call superexit (SARA);
go to ZENIPOINT;

ZENIPOINT:
    from a nadir = ZENI + ZENI + ZENI + ZENI + ZENI;
    ZENI = triumph;
    go to IVYZENIPOINT;

IVYZENIPOINT:
    IVY – INGRID;
    down and out = ZENI + IVY;
    call superexit (CHRYSTA);
    civilization arrives;

put data; end NOVEL.

MESSAGE: THE CHECKLIST TABLE HAS OVERFLOWED.

MESSAGE: THE NUMBER OF FAMILY MEMBERS AND ARGUMENTS
ASSOCIATED WITH THE GENERIC NAME IVY EXCEEDS
THE LIMITATION IMPOSED.

MESSAGE: THERE IS ONE COMPLETE STATEMENT IN THE
PROCEDURE.

MESSAGE: THIS ITEM DOES NOT EXIST BUT HAS BEEN ADDED TO
THE DATA SET.

MESSAGE: WHATEVER ELSE FICTION DOES, IT SHOULD NOT TELL
LIES.

MESSAGE: COMPILATION AND EXECUTION SUCCESSFUL. ALL
DATA SETS SAVED.

COMPUTATION TIME: 1.6 SECONDS.

To hell now with describing the temperature/time of day/mountainside/what Ingrid and I wore/how the snow got polished. You can look up most of it in the almanac.

Like other strange and sudden things of the past days, it begins ordinary: I. and I. are snowshoeing across the mountain on a —hunting— afternoon.

The last thing I hear Ingrid say is that her ears ache from the cold. Suddenly she points over the cliff across the little valley. A deer!

To get closer, we continue fishfooting along the ridge edge. At one place the trail fades to nothing at the peak. And what we've thought all winter is a solid boulder, stomach-high, half blocks it. She leads. We're both panting. I want to say *Climb up and around* but choke on a fit of coughing after the *Climb*. Clinging to the rock, she tries to ease by. Awkward in snowshoes. One stuck under the rock.

The next second the rock vibrates. Then it rushes out onto her chest. Before I can lift an arm, she's gone. Down the hill an avalanche of ice, stones, dirt. A cloud of powder gags me.

Did she scream? I never heard it. Only impatience and confusion on her face as the rock started. When I can get my eyes open, I see a black pit and torn roots.

Fling downhill after her, bashing into one trunk, then another. Terrified a second icefall will follow me. One snowshoe rips off. Twist my ankle.

Gulp cold air, frightened that if I reach the bottom alive, I can't find her. Snow powders the air, coats my face and eyes.

My own fall ends in a maze of tree trunks. Snow down my back and up my legs begins to melt. Dizzy and coughing. The boulder lies nearby, half buried, as if it had never moved. I claw on one side of it. No use. Not there. The other. Where is she, where . . . ? Is she under . . . ? Carefully. Then frantic. Hate the snow, hate the ice, hate! . . . Shred my gloves.

Then I find Ingrid beyond the boulder through three feet of ice, sticks, rubble. Her leg is torn; it bleeds into the snow. Her mouth falls open as my bare, cold hands scrape around her.

Above both of us the damn deer has shied. Then continues his vigil over the valley as if we've never happened. His antlers flick to the sky.

Cling to what I can find of Ingrid. Sit and cry.

In the Very End

Zeni and Ivy. Snowshoe down, snowshoe out. One foot, one foot, one foot. Warm sun, cold shade. White pine, red pine, white birch, gray birch, rock maple, red maple, spruce, hemlock, white pine, red pine. Oak (Ivy says).

Blisters. Sleeping bag. Pine boughs. Your spine. Ice moon (Ivy says).

Granite (Ivy says). Streamlets down mountains go.

Eyes burn mean

Ice burn me

Onefootonefootone more fishfoot (Ivy says). Ivy ahead, always ahead. She tall, you small. Ivy knows how to go.

Blisters. Sleeping bag.

Last of crackers, last of beans, frozen in plastic. Last of down is out . . . Sure.

Thirsty always. Needles and bark in melt water. Pitch and grit. Rusty can in a cave. Ledges hanging. Boulders hang. Stay away (Ivy says). You stay away.

Your stomach vomits green at the woods above low country. *Low* country, last at last, where there's nobody (either) beyond us two in the white. Celebration: fling the rotten rubber (your innertube overshoes) to the four fields as you notice It.

—Red thing. See it? In the snow.—

—Don't believe it.—

An age to tramp there. One foot one foot. And a motor

oil can. Gallons empty. Not even rusty. White man's
square totem. Sit and worship . . .

Help up. Trudge again (Ivy says). Onefootonefootone.
Sit in beginning of flat dents. Exhaustion. Can't even
focus what they are. Bird with fallen arches? Skis? Skis!
Noise. Noise tears our ears toward the trees where land
heaves.

Blue snarl thing away from us! Snowmobile?

Ivy hurries. You fall. Wet snow in diamonds. —Hey!
Here! Hey!— Flap your arms. Angels in the snow. They
turn. Ivy reaches . . .

—You a guest of the Estates this weekend?— Shout.
Tanned with cigar. Purple-nosed woman in gold and blue
ski parka. Riding fences.

—Are you girls guests of the Estates this weekend?—
More shout over motor.

—What?— Kills the engine.

—They're hippies, Mel. Look at those outfits.— Focus
on Ivy's feet.

—Our singles' party was *last* weekend . . . How did you
girls get here?—

—Walked.—

—We need help.—

—Where did you walk *from*? This is private property.—
Points to the snowmobile. Half the snub nose: gold *LAKE
WATA*. Blue *MAM ESTATES*: the other.

Point upward. —The mountain.—

—Don't be silly. There's nothing up there. Nobody lives
there.— Gold-blue woman laughs.

—Where are we?—

—Lake Watamam Estates. Four-season recreation community.— Their pink foreheads crinkle.

—Where is it?—

—Our model maisonette is a mile over that way.—
Ivy stands straight and tall . . .

—You won't believe it, but they say they're from the

plane that disappeared . . . How do I know *when*? I don't know. Two months ago. Three maybe. The aeronautics people and the police wasted our time for two days. Scared off a whole busload of our guests.

—Yeah, the *first* plane, the chartered one. Not the boys' glider. Didn't they find that already? . . . Say they have an injured woman.—

OUTFOX INFLATION, POLLUTION, CONGESTION
ALL IN *ONE* MOVE!

At a time when large developments and resort land sales are springing up all over Northern New England, Lake Watamam Estates represents an exceptional opportunity for the discerning buyer. While many developments are excellent, others leave the owner with major problems ranging from road surfacing to water supply and sewage disposal.

LAKE WATAMAM HOMES, homesites and farmsteads, however, are complete in every aspect.

WHY DO WE MAKE THIS OFFER?

We want you to explore with us a mountain community thoughtfully designed to preserve the breathless beauty of mountains and forest, rich and bountiful with the kind of relaxed adventurous living you've dreamed about.

COME SEE US!
MAKE YOUR FUTURE WATAMAM

Chartered Plane Hunt Suspended

Dec. 24. — Officials have temporarily abandoned the search for a missing aircraft piloted by Raymond Furnival of Montreal, Can. The plane disappeared after being reported off course.

Aboard were seven women, all en route to the New York area. They are identified as Mrs. William Winton and Mrs. Joseph Krenwinkel of New Jersey; Miss Chrysta Neff and Miss Zeni Abbott, New York City; Mrs. Gray Eilbeck of New York State; Miss Ingrid Rosendahl and an unnamed assistant, Chicago.

All were believed to be visiting friends and relatives for the Thanksgiving holiday weekend.

234

"We've found no trace at all," says County Sheriff James Harrison. The Sheriff, assisted by the U.S. Forest Service and the Appalachian Mountain Club, conducted a two-week search in the mountain and foothill area where a hiker on the Watamam Estates property reported that he had heard a lowflying plane.

Fog, freezing rain, and the area's third major snowstorm since Thanksgiving have hampered search attempts.

In New York William Winton and Joseph Krenwinkel, husbands of two of the missing passengers, charged yesterday that local authorities have been derelict in their ground search because "this was only a small group, and nobody wants to work during the holidays."

Denying the charges, both airline and local officials claimed the area has been well searched despite unfavorable weather.

Woman Found in Klingman Cave

Jan. 20. — The frozen, partially clad body of a middle-aged woman was discovered today in Klingman Cave by Peter Donecky, 15, son of Mr. and Mrs. Robert Donecky, 17 Elm Street. The youth discovered the body in the cave as he was checking his string of fox traps placed nearby.

The woman had been wearing a large silver cross.

Officials, including the Chief of Police and County Sheriff Jim Harrison, are searching for information about the woman. It is believed she may have flown in the ——— Airlines plane that disappeared en route to New York two months ago.

No handbag or other identification was found on or near the body, police said. They are checking for the manufacturer of the cross, believed to be of foreign design.

Death was apparently due to cold and overexposure, although large bruises were discovered on the woman's legs.

Poor peacock. Poor Chrysta.

LAKE WATAMAM ESTATES

WILDERNESS WITH CONVENIENCE

Dear Mrs. Eilbeck:

Our public relations department has notified me of your intense interest in mountaineering.

While we naturally do not want to stress the unfortunate method of your arrival on our property, we would appreciate you and the other ladies, the Misses Rosendahl and Abbott and Mrs. Winton, becoming our guests for a reception and dinner in your honor.

These events will be held on April 17, 197— at 8 p.m. at the Town and Gown Motor Inn. Photographs will be taken, and the newest in Carroll Reed skiwear and sports equipment will be yours to keep. A tour of our property will also be yours. Informal dress, of course.

Please mark this date on your calendar, Mrs. Eilbeck.

If you can attend, we will arrange a limousine to call for you in the New York area. If you are unable to attend, please inform us as soon as possible on the enclosed card, and we will arrange an alternate date.

We also hope that by this time Miss Rosendahl will be well enough to travel. Please extend to her our wishes for a speedy recovery.

I am sure it will interest you to know that the building in which you and the other ladies found shelter and refuge was not listed in our survey and deed to Lake Watamam Estates. Nor is it shown in our original aerial photographs because of the heavy forest cover. That is why we were unable to inform Search and Rescue personnel of your whereabouts.

Our legal department is now checking for possible owners of the structure, and we are hoping that local hunters will supply further information.

Looking forward to meeting you on the night of the 17th, I remain, with every good wish,

Yours sincerely,

Wendell J. Phillips, President
LAKE WATAMAM ESTATES

P.S. We also hope that you and the other ladies will favor us with copies of any interviews or articles describing your stay on our property. We've heard that one of you is well known in the archeological . . .

—Zeni, let's not go. Let's tell *him* where to go.—
—Hell yes. We won't go.—
—It's "Hell *no*, we won't go."—
—Yeah.—

236

for All of Us

SIX PORTRAITS—

WILD BIRDS ON A WINTER MOUNTAIN

SIX PORTRAITS--WILD BIRDS ON A WINTER MOUNTAIN

ING X 5 2 2

```
                              R
                 D            T
                 W         AMPLES
           B     E            L
           IS MUSEU           R
        T        M
        NOTE:    O
        N  C     T
        ABILITY                                        L
        T  T
```

```
        N                     R           I
        H                     I T         N
        A            D        W   H   AMPLES       I
      GATHERS     B  E        T       L   I  S.  SEX
      I   Y       IS MUSEU O  S A GRE          T
      A   I     T     M   AND LU  S      G     S
    Y BEWIT     NOTE:  ONE  O     E    IN MIN T              N
                N  C   T    T     H       O
                ABILITY O   U                              ILL
      S         T  T    S
```

```
        N       E        M            R   M E   I
        H       D        .  D         I T   R E   N
        A    INTO GE     L  W      HE  AMPLES G V   I   Q   B      E
      GATHERS     G      R BASKE    TT    LL SIZES.  SEXU    Y
      SI  Y       I      IS MUSEU  OW S A GRE    EA  TO ARCHEO      . JUST
        A  I      H O    T    M   AND LUMPS.      G ID  S   R WITCH-
      Y BEWIT     T      NOTE: ONE  OU   E    IN MIND T       T       N N
    ANIC OR       N  C   T    TS    H    O ER           L           Y
        ASE    ENT'S ABILITY TO    UN   E       ABILITY      D R     ILL
    T NECES         E    T  T   S
```

```
        N       E  U     M            R   M E   I         O
        H       D  B     U  .  D    E   I T   R E   N
      T_  A    INTO GE    L  WI    THE  AMPLES G V   I  YO   B  K      E
      H  GATHERS GGS IN   R BASKET.  ATT  CT  LL SIZES.  SEXU    Y DEMAN I
      O SI LY    S IB   . THIS MUSEUM OWES A GRE    EA  TO ARCHEO  G  T  . JUST
    OW ME A RICH ARCH O     T   BUMPS AND LUMPS.      G ID  S OUR WITCH-   U
      Y BEWIT    NG   I     NOTE: ONE SHOULD KEEP IN MIND THAT M  T  ORDS OF NON-
    ANIC ORIGI   H      G RMAN COUNTER RTS.  WH L   O ER   NS    L    N T Y
        ASE  H STUDENT'S ABILITY TO COMMUNICATE  I  ABILITY T   D R  N  ILL
    T NECESSARIL I  EA    T THE SAM  A E
```

NAME   OCCUPATION   AGE·

INGRID ROSENDAHL   PROFESSOR, ARCHEOLOGIST   35
    DATA: INGRID IS TEACHING US GERMAN. DER SCHONE FLAMINGO
    PRONOUNCE CAREFULLY: GEMISCHTES EIS. WIR KOMMEN NICHT MEHR SO JUNG
USAMMEN. HALS AND BEINBRUCH. DAS VERLUST IST VERGESSEN.
    TRANSLATE INTO GERMAN FOLLOWING THE EXAMPLES GIVEN IN YOUR BOOK: TWICE A
AY SHE GATHERS EGGS IN HER BASKET. ATTRACT ALL SIZES. SEXUALLY DEMANDING
ND POSSIBLY INSATIABLE. THIS MUSEUM OWES A GREAT DEAL TO ARCHEOLOGISTS. JUST
HOW ME A RICH ARCHEOLOGIST. BUMPS AND LUMPS. INGRID IS OUR WITCH--OUR
RICHLY BEWITCHING WITCH. NOTE: ONE SHOULD KEEP IN MIND THAT MOST WORDS OF NON-
ERMANIC ORIGIN HAVE GERMAN COUNTERPARTS. WHILE CONVERSIONS WILL DEFINITELY
NCREASE THE STUDENT'S ABILITY TO COMMUNICATE, HIS ABILITY TO UNDERSTAND WILL
OT NECESSARILY INCREASE AT THE SAME RATE.

```
                A
                U:
                O DRI      OU
                LEPHONE  AN OR
                         OMOSEXU



                                O
                A              IER
                U:             FRI
                O DRI    OU   YAH TPE
        H      LEPHONE  AN OR    R                        H F
        HER M           OMOSEXU   -              G        THE W
        - THE                    RABBI        S F



        H    R                          O            DENN LO    AS
    U_CE  REE  L                        IER          TEN.
    GING VERLOREN.   A                  FRI          PRI E.  PUT
    NSLATE INTO GERMAN:                YAH TRE      YOU FIND IT DI      T
  R.  IT'S ENOUGH TO DRI   A OU         R           G.  TOO    H F     RIN
        THE TELEPHONE    AN OR                      GI         THE W   WILL
        OTHER M         HOMOSEXU                    S FA
        - THE WOO                    RABBI


        T
    D      WHITE R AST
    PR OUNCE CAREFULLY    O    ER F    O E        IST DENN LOS    AS
  MOGEN GING VERLOREN.   AS F  RN DER IERE         RBOTEN.
    TRANSLATE INTO GERMAN:  BRAT.  PEST.  FRIGH ENED SPRITE.  PUT A
  GETHER.  IT'S ENOUGH TO DRIVE YA OUTA YAH TREE!  DO YOU FIND IT DIF  ULT T
  PEAK ENGLIS  ON THE TELEPHONE?  AN ORGY EVEPY MORNING.  TOO MUCH FREU  BRINGS
        - MY MOTHER MADE ME A HOMOSEXUAL.  -  -IF Y U GIVE HER THE WOOL, WILL
    KE ME ONE?  - THE WOODS  R    L OF RABBI  TH S FALL.



ROSEANN ?        STUDENT      19
    DATA:  WHITEBREASTED NUTHATCH
    PRONOUNCE CAREFULLY:  WO IST DER FUSSBODEN?  WAS IST DENN LOS?  DAS
VERMOGEN GING VERLOREN.  DAS FÜTTERN DER TIERE IST VERBOTEN.
    TRANSLATE INTO GERMAN:  BRAT.  PEST.  FRIGHTENED SPRITE.  PUT A BIRD
TOGETHER.  IT'S ENOUGH TO DRIVE YA OUTA YAH TREE!  DO YOU FIND IT DIFFICULT TO
SPEAK ENGLISH ON THE TELEPHONE?  AN ORGY EVERY MORNING.  TOO MUCH FREUD BRINGS
NO JOY.  - MY MOTHER MADE ME A HOMOSEXUAL.  -  -IF YOU GIVE HER THE WOOL, WILL
SHE MAKE ME ONE?  - THE WOODS ARE FULL OF RABBITS THIS FALL.
```

IVY EILBECK   COMPUTER PROGRAMMER   30
    DATA: HAUSFINK. YELLOW-SHAFTED FLICKER. GREAT BLUE HERON.
    PRONOUNCE CAREFULLY: WIR MACHEN EINE DRACHEN. DIESE MÄNNER!
    TRANSLATE INTO GERMAN: HELP! LIGHTNING HAS STRUCK OUR POSTILION! THE
BITTER LEMON IS IN THE TOOL ROOM. IT IS SNOWING, WAS SNOWING, WILL SNOW, WOULD
SNOW, HAS SNOWED, HAD SNOWED--OH HELL, LET IT SNOW! WATCH YOUR WEATHER! SEND
NATURE ON A MEMO. I HATE THESE DULL FOGGY DAYS. PALM COAST IS THE KIND OF
PLACE WHERE YOU CAN SLIP YOUR BOAT FROM ITS MOORINGS. CAN I PERSUADE YOU TO
COME HUNTING WITH ME? NO DISTINCTION BETWEEN WILLINGNESS AND COMPULSION IS
POSSIBLE. - DO YOU WANT A BABY?- - WHY CAN'T I HAVE A PUPPY?-

```
TEX←9 79ρ'↑'
TEX X 5 2 1
```

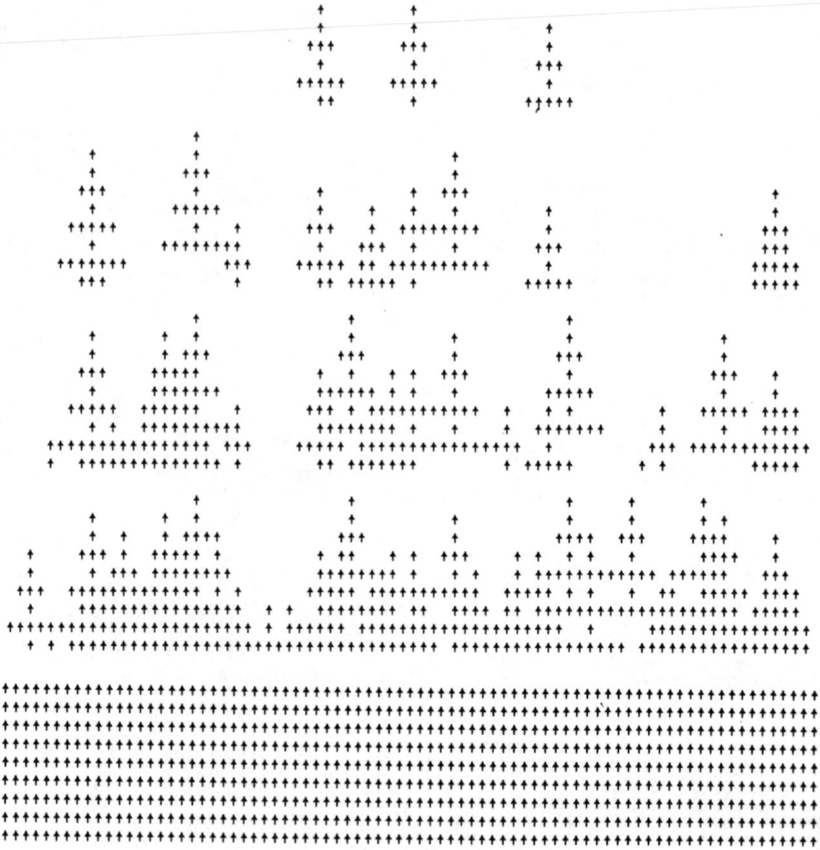

```
                                                          A

                                                        ASC

                                                      E SAI
              G              A                           O T
                             U  M                      'S STUD
           TIZ


                            O                        H    A
                            A                 N    NTS I
           R                MA                  E L   U  MASC

         L         G     : - W A              U  MADA      HE SAI
        TO EA             U MU                 JOB. THOSE W O T
        N         TIZ   OF THE FU             TE CHING  IT'S STUD
     T  TAND!-

                       A                         Y
             A                                   N     Y
             R   LLY    O      D               E.     B   H    A GE.
        R       N_  :      A      E              MI  N  AG NTS I   HE
      I           N  E AGE   MA     SEN         . MIS E LA   U  MASCULIN

        N L       T  GERMAN: - W AT CAN       R YOU, MADA      HE SAID WI   A
       TO EA N YOUR   V  G,  U MUS           FIND A JOB.  THOSE WHO TEACH SCHOOL
       N N          TIZENS OF THE FUTURE      O  TE CHING   IT'S STUD
     T STAND!-

                     A      E                    Y
          IC A        B  E IA     W            N        Y R        .
        UNC  C R   LLY: DORT     D           W  E.      B   H    ANGE.
         RU ER.  U   : GERMANI    ENT        V   MI  N  AGENTS I  THE  A E
        IF A FEM N  E AGE  MAKES SEN    A ALL. MIS E LAN OU  MASCULINE

     T ANSLATE I T  GERMAN: - WHAT CAN I DO FOR YOU, MADAM?-  HE SAID WITH A
      .  TO EARN YOUR LIVING, YOU MUST FIR   FIND A JOB.  THOSE WHO TEACH SCHOOL
     TRAIN N THE    TIZENS OF THE FUTURE. - I LOVE TE CHING--IT'S STUDENT
     T STAND!-


    ENI ABBOTT     ASSISTANT PROFESSOR, REVOLUTIONARY     26
       DATA: CHICKADEE.  BOHEMIAN WAXWING.  BIRDSONGS IN YOUR GARDEN.
       PRONOUNCE CAREFULLY: DORT SIND DIE SCHWEINE!  DER BAR HAT FÄNGE.
    BERMUDE BRÜDER.  NOTE: GERMANIC AGENTS DERIVE FEMININE AGENTS IN THE SAME
    MANNER, IF A FEMININE AGENT MAKES SENSE AT ALL.  MISCELLANEOUS MASCULINE
    AGENTS.
       TRANSLATE INTO GERMAN: - WHAT CAN I DO FOR YOU, MADAM?-  HE SAID WITH A
    SMILE.  TO EARN YOUR LIVING, YOU MUST FIRST FIND A JOB.  THOSE WHO TEACH SCHOOL
    RE TRAINING THE CITIZENS OF THE FUTURE. - I LOVE TEACHING--IT'S STUDENTS I
    AN'T STAND!-
```

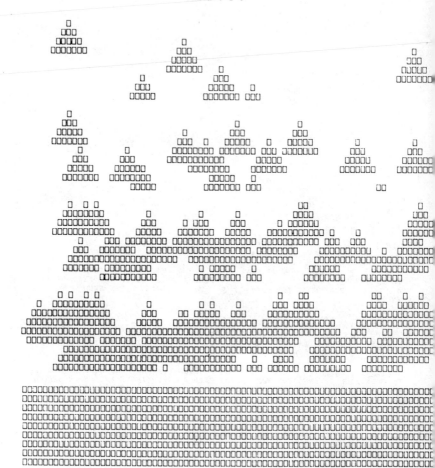

```
                             URS
        L                    AN U
       RS                    LY--I S                            O
      TED.


                             GER              SCHN            T.
                             TS.      B       RDS.  A
         I                   G OURSE ES                Y
       LUNC     TH      T    WAS AN·U WED M             M
      RS ARE   ET.    BED  UICKLY--I SHALL C        THIS O
     TED.


          N                  T
          A:       TA
        ONOUN    CARE        IST GERO      LBE.      SCHN     SCHLACHT.
       RANSLATE:  GAM      ACEMATS.  SONGBIR  PLAYING  RDS.  A    HEER TO
         I    R .           HING OURSELVES EX            Y  ORK.  DO YO
       LUNCH ON THI     T   I WAS AN UNVED MOT     O     .  M    N'S
      ERS ARE WET.  G   BED QUICKLY--I SHALL C    HE       THIS OUSE
     NTED.


          N       H         M T
          A:       TAUB
        ONOUN    CAREFU      ES IST GERÖLL IM GEW LBE.   INE SCHN EBA  SCHLACHT.
       RANSLATE:  GAMEB    PLACEMATS.  SONGBIRD PLAYING CARDS.  ADD CHEER TO
       Y DINNER .          E YTHING OURSELVES EXCEPT      RY HEAVY WORK.  DO YOU
      V LUNCH ON THI       HT?  I WAS AN UNWED MOTHER  O  HE FBI.  M    N'S
     APERS ARE WET.  G     BED QUICKLY--I SHALL CALL THE      THIS OUSE IS
    UNTED.


 DETTE WINTON      HOUSEWIFE, MOTHER     37
      DATA:   DIE TAUBE
      PRONOUNCE CAREFULLY:  ES IST GERÖLL IM GEWÖLBE.  EINE SCHNEEBALLSCHLACHT.
      TRANSLATE:  GAMEBIRD PLACEMATS.  SONGBIRD PLAYING CARDS.  ADD CHEER TO
 AMILY DINNERS.  WE DO EVERYTHING OURSELVES EXCEPT THE VERY HEAVY WORK.  DO YOU
 ERVE LUNCH ON THIS FLIGHT?.  I WAS AN UNWED MOTHER FOR THE FBI.  MY SON'S
 IAPERS ARE WET.  GO TO BED QUICKLY--I SHALL CALL THE DOCTOR.  THIS HOUSE IS
 AUNTED.
```

```
TEX←9 79ρ'†'
TEX X 7 2 2
```

```
              :   U
B                RE.  I W
Y                E
E              ER- USUA                                   Z
NSTANCE      D    ES   E                                  T

              E              R
              E
        C           :           I                            R
        O       E. JA,      MÄNNER
   L    I   Q    A :    U        L         H            T?  WHA
  BA OON.  GO 'S HERE. I W      R         P                  O
  YO    CHRIST  S E            Y                Q    Z R
  DESTRU  T  N.   ER- USUA           -TO THE E D  OR -T -
 NSTANCE  IT INDIC TES    E              O    I

              E     E  F   R
              K       E    R  .
        C  C  E    Y:      W  T  I T   E     A                R     ?
        D  O       E. JA, IHR MÄNNER   ID EBEN
      LAT  INTO GE MA :   OUT  N   LIMB.  WHA  HA      W  U  T? WHA  M
   T  BABOON. GOD'S HERE. I WO    R W E E PEOPLE A     S  V    O  LOST.
   D   YOU    CHRIST AS E  ?   P    O   E Y LIKABLE    Q :   Z R     A
   E DESTRUCT N.   ER- USUALL    TES -TO THE E D  OR -TO DEAT -
 ME INSTANCE  IT INDICATES  HE B    I   O  O  HING.

              W I        E  U E  F   R
        A     A  CK         E      R  .
        R    C  CAREE L Y:   R  W  T  I T   E . AB   I  D      R  RN?
        U    ND HOHE BERGE. JA, IHR MÄNNER   ID EBEN    E  OH
       TRANSLAT  INTO GERMA :  OUT  N   LIMB.  WHAT HATH  OD WROU  T?  WHAT MAN
    TH BABOON.  GOD'S HERE. I WO D R WHE E PEOPLE ARE.  SI V    O S LOST.
    T DID YOU  O CHRISTMAS E  ?   F N YOU VERY LIKABLE  NOTE:   ZER- ALWAY
    OTES DESTRUCTION.  -ER- USUALL   E   TES -TO THE END- OR -TO DEAT -    UT IN
    ME INSTANCES IT INDICATES   HE BEGINNIN  O SO  THING.
```

CHRYSTA NEFF   WRITER, LECTURER FOR RELIGIOUS GROUP   55
DATA: PEACOCK IN A PEAR TREE.
PRONOUNCE CAREFULLY: DER WINTER IST HIER. HABEN SIE DEN WINTER GERN?
GUTE LUFT UND HOHE BERGE. JA, IHR MÄNNER SEID EBEN ZU VERWÖHNT.
TRANSLATE INTO GERMAN: OUT ON A LIMB. WHAT HATH GOD WROUGHT? WHAT MAN
OWES THE BABOON. GOD'S HERE. I WONDER WHERE PEOPLE ARE. SILVER CROSS LOST.
WHAT DID YOU DO CHRISTMAS EVE? I FIND YOU VERY LIKABLE. NOTE: -ZER- ALWAYS
DENOTES DESTRUCTION. -ER- USUALLY DENOTES -TO THE END- OR -TO DEATH-, BUT IN
SOME INSTANCES IT INDICATES THE BEGINNING OF SOMETHING.

```apl
      ∇X[☐]∇

      ∇ TEX X P
[1]    PAT← 7 7 ρPA[P[3];]
[2]    NC←(ρTEX)[2]
[3]    NR←(ρTEX)[1]
[4]    M←(NR,NC)ρ' '
[5]    RP←(ρPAT)[1]
[6]    CP←(ρPAT)[2]
[7]    REPEAT←''
[8]    D←0
[9]    2 1 ρ' '
[10] LD:→(1↑(D>4),D←D+1)/ELD
[11]   I←0
[12] LI:→(1↑(I>P[1]),I←I+1)/ELI
[13]   C←((?NC)-1)+(,PAT)/,((ρPAT)ριCP)
[14]   R←((?NR)-1)+(,PAT)/,⍉((CP,RP)ριRP)
[15]   OK←(((R≤NR)∧(R≥1))∧((C≤NC)∧(C≥1)))/ιρR
[16]   →((ρOK)>0)/GK
[17]   →(1↑1,(I←I-1))/LI
[18] GK:K←0
[19] LK:→(1↑(K>ρOK),K←K+1)/ELK
[20]   M[R[OK[K]];C[OK[K]]]←TEX[R[OK[K]];C[OK[K]]]
[21]   →LK
[22] ELK:→LI
[23] ELI:M
[24]   ' '
[25]   P[1]←P[1]×P[2]
[26]   REPEAT←REPEAT,(,M),NCρ' '
[27]   →LD
[28] ELD: 30 1 ρ' '
[29]   TEX
[30]   REPEAT←((4×(NR+1)),NC)ρREPEAT
      ∇
```

INGRID IS TEACHING US GERM-LISH

```
                              P
                              O
                              O                         M
         A                    ARM               FUSSANGEL
         N                                               N          GAZE
      TIER      HER                  P                   T          O
         M      I                    U                   R          S
         A      T                 KITTEN                 A          S
         L      H                    T    S              P          A
                E                    Y    K                         M
                R    S                    I    GENIAL               E
                     HERB                  N    I                   R
                     A          T   FELL        F    DADA
                     R          I               T    A
                     P          N               E    D         T
                                S               D    D         R
                                E                    Y        LIST
                             FLITTER                          C
                                                              K
                       FUR
                       O    G
                       R    O
                            D                    W
                            F                 DAMIT
            M               PATE                  T        L
            O               T                     H     HOLD
         UNHOLD             H                     *        V
            S               E                     I        E
            T               R                     T        L
            E                                              Y
            R
```

```
                                    S
                                    K
                                    I
                                    N
    M                   T        FELL
    O                   R
 UNHOLD              LIST
    S                   C
    T                   K
    E                DADA
    R                   A
                        D
        S               D        M
     HERB               Y    FUSSANGEL
        A                        N          L
        R                        T        HOLD
        P                        R          V
 G                               A          E          A
 O                   T           P          L          N
 D                   I                      Y        TIER
 F                   N                                  M
PATE                 S                                  A
 T                   E                                  L
 H                FLITTER              FUR
 E                                       O
 R GAZE                                  R
    O                                               HER
    S                    P                           I
    S                    O                           T
    A                    O         P                 H
    M       W          ARM         U                 E
    E     DAMIT                 KITTEN                R  GENIAL
    R       T                      T                    I
            H                      Y                    F
            *                                           T
            I                                           E
            T                                           D
```

```
                                                              S
                                              A               C
                                              R               A
                                     C        D               B
                             PLUMP   U        O        GRIND
                     FATAL   U       M        R
                     W       M       S        GLUT            T
                     K       S       Y                        H
                     W       Y           D                    DIE
                     A                   E
                     R                   S
                     D                   T        BANG
                                         I        N      JAMMER
                                         T        X      I
              P                          U        I      S    GRAB
              O             D            T        O      E    R
              O             E            E        U      R    A
            ARM            A             BAR      S      Y    V
          W               D                                   E
          I               D
        TOLL              TOT                     FEE          BOG
          D                                       A            E
                                                  I            N
                                                  R            T
                   S                              Y            G
                   T                                           HARM
                 FADE                                          I
                   L              STAB                         E
                   E              T                            F
                                  A         C
                        PEST      F       FANG
                        L         F    ELP  T
                        A              L    C
                        G              E    H
                        U              V
                        E              E
                                       N
```

```
                                          A
                      T            S       R
                      H            T       D
                 DIE   S   D   FADE O  PEST                   P
                       C   D   L    R  L                      O
                       A   E   E GLUT   A                     O
                       B   A            G                   ARM            BOG
                 GRIND     D            U                                  B
                       TOT              E           C                      E
                                              PLUMP U                      N
                                                    M                      T
                                          GRAB      S  BANG
                                          R         Y  N
                                          A            X
                             ELF          V            I
                 STAB        L            E            O
                 T           E                         U
                 A           E                         S      C
                 F           V                              FANG
                 F           E                              T
                             N              D               C
                                            E               H
                         W                  S  JAMMER          G
                         I                  T  I            HARM
                         TOLL               I  S            R
                         D                  T  E            I
                                            U  R            E
                                            T  Y            F
                                            E
                                          BAR   FEE   FATAL
                                                A     W
                                                I     K
                                                R     W
                                                Y     A
                                                      R
                                                      D
```

```
                    R
                    A
                    D
                    I
                    O              A
            FUNK                   N
                              TIER                    B
            Q                      M                   A
            U                      A              SPECK
            I                      L                   O
            L                                          N
            L           LOCKER
      POSE              O                    BOOT
                        O                       O        FUSS
                        S                       A        O    C
                        E          T            T        O    H
                                   H                     T  KIND
         FINK                  DANK                            L
         I            T        N                               D
         N     W      H        K      S
         C     E      U              TON
         H  GANG      M               O
            T        PUFF             U
                                      N
                                      D              JAMMER
                                                     I
                                                     S
                                                     E
         R                                           R
       FIRST                                         Y
         D                              LEER
         G   S       C                  M
         E   K     FANG                 P
             I       T                  T
           ROCK      C                  Y
             T       H
```

```
                                        Q
                                        U
                                        I
                                        L
                          A             L
                          D      POSE
                          D             T        R
               C          OTTER         H        A
               H                        N  DANK  D
               KIND                     N        I
               L                        K        O
               D                          FUNK

                    P.          A
                    MULL    B   N
               LEER B   SPECK A  TIER              T
               M    B         C  M                 H
               P    I         O  A                 U
               T    S            L                 M
               Y    H             FUSS            PUFF
                                  F
                                  O
                                  O                R
                                  T            FIRST
                                               R
                    JAMMER    FINK             D
                    I         F                G
               S    S         I                E
               K    E         N
               I    R         C
               ROCK Y         H       BOOT
               T                      B
                                S     O
                    C         TON     A
                    FANG      U       T
                    T         N
                    C                        W
                    H  LOCKER                E
                       L                     GANG
                       O                     T
                       O
                       S
                       E
```

```
      G                                                    S
      R                                                    C
      O                                                    A
      O
      V
      E
    NUT      D                MOPS         SANG         LUMP
           TRUNK               U            O             P
             I                 G            N
             N    W                         G
             K    E
                GANG
                  T
          F                                              CUT
          A                                  I            O
          R                                  *            O
          C                                  S            D
       POSSE                                 A
                                             Y
          S          GAB
       QUALM         A                    HE!HE!
          O          V
        S  K         E
        T  E              C
        U                 O
       FARCE             MUT                            MARK
        F                P.                             A
        I          AS    A                             R
        N          C     G                             R
    NAH G          E     E        S                    O
      E                           O                    W
      A                           O
      R                           N
                               BALD

               BAD            BLANK
               A              R       BUMS!       BANG
               T              I       O             N
               H              G       U             X
                              H       N             I
                              T       C             O
                                      E             U
                                                    S
```

I
*
S
A
Y
HE!HE!

G
R
O
O
S   V
O   E
O   NUT
N
BALD

S   S   MOPS   BALD   F
T   C   U   A
U   A   G   R
FARCE   LUMP   GAB   C
F   D   P   A   POSSE
I   TRUNK   V
N   I   E   C
G   N   O   SANG
            K   MUT   O
                                                            R   N
                                        BLANK   A   G BUMS!
                                        R   G   O
                                        I   U
                                        G   AS   N
                                        H   C   C
                                                            E   E

NAH   MARK   GUT
E   BAD   A   O
A   S   B   R   O
R   QUALM   A   R   D
            O   T   O
            K   W
            E

JOEG Z JOEE

```
                                                    P
                              S                     L
        DADA                HERB                    A
        A           S       A                  TELLER
        D           H       R          S             E        B
        D           O       P          T             B        A
        Y           P                  U             R
                  LADEN                F             I
              MUTTEP                   F    FARCE    N        SPECK
                O                      I            LAKE        O
                  S                    N   B                    N
                O P                    G  DOSE
                T E                        X
        C       H C              HERD               J
        O       E I              E                  O        PAIL
       MUT      R S              A          FIDEL   L        P   F
        R         E              R                  Y        E   I
        A       ART              T                           E   S
        C                        H                           R   H
        E                                   P                    B     C
                                            E                    O     H
              Y                             A                    N  KIND
           DOTTER                 F         C                          L
              L                 DICK T      E               GPATE  D
              K                             FRIED
                TEE                         U
                  E                         L
                  L
                  L
                  E
                  R
```

```
                                    J
                                    O
                    P           FIDEL        S
                    E              F L        HERB
                    A              I Y        A
                    C              S          R
                    E              H          P
                    FRIED          B
        Y           U              O              HERD
     DOTTER         L              N              E
        L               S    GRATE               A
        K               P                        R
    MUTTER              C                        T
    O                   I                        H
    T                   E                   C
    H                   S                   O
    E        DADA          ART              MUT
    R        A                              R
             D                              A
             D                              G
             Y                              E          S
             S                                         T
             H                                         U
             O        B              F                 FARCE
             P        DOSE           A                 F
     LADEN            X              T  B               I
                                  DICK  R               N
        PAIL                         C  I               G
        E                            H  N
        E                         KIND LAKE
        R                            L
                                     D
```

```
                                             A
                                             W
                                             A
                                             Y      L
                                         FORT     SAGE
                                                   E
                                   BAKE            N              S
                                   E               D             WINK
                                   A                                 G
                                   C                                 N  L        N
                                   O                                    I       E
                                   N                          V    HUBF       FAST
                                                              O      T        R
                        HART                       N          L                L
                        A                          E          U                Y
                        R         T                C          M
                        D     SPUR A               E      BANDE        FATAL
                                   C               S                     W
                           RANG    K             MUSS      RAT          K
                           A                 S   I    Q  D            W
                           N                 L   T    U  V            A
                                             O   Y   FIX I            R     STARK
                                             P          C  C            D     T
                                             E          K  E              R
                           STERNHELL      HANG       C       STOCK            O
                           T                         O       T                N
                           A                        MUT      I                G
                           R                         R       C
                           L                         A       K
                           I                         G
                           G                         E
                           H
                           T
```

```
                        L
                        E
                     SAGE              S        RAT          STARK
                        E              L        D            T
                 HART   N              L        V            R
                    A   D              O        I            O
                    R                  P        C            N
                    D                  E        E            G      RANG
                                    HANG                 BAKE        A
     T       S                                  E          N        K
   SPUR    WINK                                I           K
      A      G                                 C
      C      N                                 O
      K                        V               N
                               O                       STOCK
                       Q       L                       T
                       U       U                       I
                     FIX       M                       C  FATAL
                       C       E                       K  W
                       K    BAND                          K
                               L                          W      A
     N                         I                          A      W
     E                         F                          R      A
     C                         T                          D      Y
   MUSS                     HUB                         FORT
     S            N
     I          FAST
     T            R    STERNHELL                  C
     Y            L    T                           O
                  Y    A                          MUT
                       R                           R
                       L                           A
                       I                           G
                       G                           E
                       H
                       T
```

ES GIBT EIN/KEIN GOTT.
IF ONLY I MAY GROW QUIETER FIRMER WARMER SIMPLER.

```
      ∇Z[□]∇

      ∇ A Z B
[1]    JUN←(RM←28),(CM←48),(MM←12),I←K←0
[2]    PIC←((RM+2×MM),CM+MM+2)ρ' '
[3]    LO:→(1↑((I>(ρA)[1])),(I←I+1),AD←0)/ELO
[4]    LP:→(1↑((K>75),(RC←(?RM)+MM),K←K+1)/ELO
[5]    CC←(?CM)+1
[6]    →((+/(PIC[(RC-2)+ι3;(CC-2)+ι(MM+2)]≠' '))≠0)/LP
[7]    ZO←(BB←(B[I;]≠' ')/B[I;])ι(AA←((A[I;]≠' ')/A[I;]))
[8]    AZ←1+(φ(ZO≤ρBB)ι1)
[9]    →((AZ≤ρAA)∨BB[ρBB]=' ')/JBZ
[10]   BB←BB,' '
[11]   AA←AA,' '
[12]   AD←-1
[13]   ZO←ZO,(1+ρBB)
[14]   JBZ:BZ←ZO[AZ]
[15]   →((+/+/(PIC[(RC-BZ-2)+ι((ρBB)+2);(CC+AZ-3)+ι3]≠' '))≠0)/LP
[16]   PIC[(RC+AD);(CC-1)+ιρAA]←AA
[17]   PIC[(RC-BZ)+ιρBB;AZ+CC-1]←BB
[18]   →LO
[19]   ELO:PIC
       ∇
```

THINGS I WILL NEVER DO

PLOT FORMAT:
    HAIL MARY AIRLINES   Uninhabitable as abend dump
    WE FLY LOWER AND SLOWER   Mildewed as randydevil
                                      Found in the pond icewhite
    for Zeni   Frigid as shotgun
    in memory of Chrysta and Penny ➔   Rigid as rainstain
              Ann and   Sara ➔   Dead as weak tea

HOW FORMAT: ILLEGITIMATE OVERSTRIKE
    JAY ➔ ON ➔ OUR ➔ WAY
    A CLEVER GODDESS QUICKLY SEDUCES INTO THE FEMINISM;
    REDCOLD AS FEVER;
    A KAY-NINE ROPESNARE AGAIN FISHFOOTS INTO THE
          HAPPENTHING;
    HOW?
    HEALINGLY FUZZILY WILILY;
    FEAR ➔ HERE

        FOUND ➔ IN ➔ THE ➔ POND
        A WHITETALL GODDESS NEVER BITCHES MORE DOWN ANN;
        GREENBLACK AS RAINSTAIN;
        A FLIRTATIOUS INGRID QUICKLY FISHES AGAINST THE
              MUMMY DUST;
        HOW?
        GAMBOLINGLY HOTPINKLY TANTALIZINGLY;
        FEAR ➔ HERE

            HATE ➔ THERE
            A FREEALONE JOAN DARC QUICKLY SEARCHES AGAINST
                THE AMAZON;
            BLACKWHITE AS RAINSTAIN;
            A FOGWHITE MAISONETTE ALWAYS HUNTS AGAINST THE
                PLANE;
            HOW?
            VIGOROUSLY MILDEWEDLY WILILY;
            DEAR ➔ UP ➔ HERE

AGAIN

SKYFLYSKYFLYSKYFLYSKYFLY
Fearherefearherefearherefear
Hatetherehatetherehatethere
Spyontheslyspyontheslyspy
Ringinthespringringinthespring
SKYFLYSKYFLYSKYFLYSKYFLY

A TANTALIZING TRUE BELIEVER WARILY DREAMS UPON
    THE HAPPENTHING
A HOT BAKED HOW CHOPS INTO THE BOMBSHELTER
AN ALIVE MAIDENNATION AGAIN SEDUCES AWAY THE
    GODDESS
A REDGOLD AMAZON ALWAYS TRAVELS IN THE
    FIRESHADOW

MOUSE → IN → THE → HOUSE
A BRILLIANT JOETTE NEVER SEDUCES INTO THE GODDESS;
REDCOLD AS OTHERHOOD;
A KAY-NINE MOUNTAIN NEVER DREAMS OUT OF THE
    LADYBUG;
HOW?
DELIGHTFULLY REDCOLDLY WILILY;
HAIL → MARY → AIRLINES   → YOU ARE IN CONTROL STATE

HATE → THERE
A VIGOROUS GRAMMAW QUICKLY CHOPS IN THE BAKED BLUEJAY;
GREENBLACK AS FEVER;
A FRIGGIN MAISONETTE WARILY DREAMS AWAY FROM THE
    JAYSQUAWK;
HOW?
FLATTEREDLY BLACKWHITELY FOGWHITELY;
RING → IN → THE → SPRING

→ YOU ARE IN CONTROL STATE
           ↓
           ↓

    FRIGGIN MOUNTAIN
    DOES NOT ANSWER
        TRAVEL ON
        OVER AND OUT

268

AFTERWORD

ZENI: –I LOVE FICTION. IT'S COMPUTERS I CAN'T STAND!–

Fiction, as a complex of life, art, emotion, and discipline, needs to make its own statement, stand tall on its own artistic legs. However, even before publication some readers are curious about the role played by the machine in my book.

The computer is a useful, powerful, and non-sexist tool for a writer interested in literary experimentation, problems of design and technique, of character delineation. Above all, I seek new—but effective and sensible—methods to build fictional portraits beyond the overworked, probably outdated "he said, she said, then they . . .." Because such narrative methods were good enough for Chaucer, Henry James, or Jane Austen should not mean that we writers of a new world, the electronic age, must be limited to or by their methods or goals. As a writer and reader, I retain a healthy respect for plot, setting, character; however, I seize new ways to achieve these, to work beyond them.

Several portions of this book were programmed in APL, a general purpose language that can be applied to what is called "text processing." They were printed out on a remote terminal dialed by phone into a central computer. Many such computers are available through service bureaus. Computerized parts of the book are
"Sex" and "Violence," pp. 165-67;
"Program for a Novel," pp. 229-30;
"Things I Will Never Do Again," pp. 267-68;
stanzas that begin each section, pp. 3, 35, 55, 75, 97, 103, 113, 163, 177, 189, 203;
"Six Portraits—Wild Birds on a Winter Mountain," pp. 237-51;
"Ingrid Is Teaching Us Germ-lish," pp. 253-66.
These pages collectively required five different computer

programs. Actual programs for the last two projects appear on pp. 251 and 266.

Stanzas in "Things I Will Never Do Again" and at the beginning of each section of *Happenthing* resulted from giving the machine two basic stanza forms plus a content —a dictionary of about a dozen word lists, classified by part of speech and emotional value or tone. Within this book, *bomb shelter* and *scrambled eggs*, for example, are positive, food-related words. *Fever, uninhabited*, and *rainstain* are negative words. *Tantalizingly* and *flirtatious* are ambivalent, since flirtation can be a power play for souls as well as senses. (—Why did you sleep with her?— —She has a fine mind. What else could I do?—) "Sex" and "Violence" originated from two basic sentence forms plus two appropriate word lists.

"Six Portraits" and "Ingrid Is Teaching Us Germ-lish" combine design poetry with the German-English study that helps keep the women sane on the mountain. Each "portrait" involved choice of a basic symbol plus a set of sentences appropriate to each character. Each paragraph appears four times in partial form, the fifth time in complete form. A command (for example, IVY X 5 2 1) begins each computer run on a character. This means that program X will print pattern number 1 five times in the first run (1st par.), double (2) that amount or ten times in the second, etc., until the whole paragraph can be read. A programming technique called "random number generation" determines exactly where, which letters, in each paragraph will be used or chosen by pattern number 1 (of three possible patterns—shapes of horizontals and verticals—specified for this project).

For "Ingrid Is Teaching Us Germ-lish" the machine received twelve word lists—two equivalent lists, i.e., *bang* (German) = *anxious* (English)—for each of six characters plus programming to print these in anagram-like pairs. To an English-speaking person, the page appears entirely English. However, one-half of each word pair (all the horizontally printed of these "conversion" words) is actually German. Both these long projects can be taken as literary satires on the language or the human learning process.

All projects function in the book as a way for Ivy, trained as a programmer, to make joyful sense of her communal winter adventure. Programs are to her what paint and canvas are to an artist. Random number generation formalizes the basic randomness of life, which is an interplay of variables (chance events) with constants (human needs and physiology, the rigors of winter). *If . . ., then . . .* becomes not a frightening determinism but a minimal guideline within which to create.

Words have life and must be cared for.

—Carole Spearin McCauley

SOURCES OF QUOTATIONS

vii   "Run mad as often as you chuse . . ." Jane Austen's story, "Love and Friendship."

"You Can't Always Get What You Want," Rolling Stones Album *Let It Bleed*, London Records, New York.

37   "In Buddhist Literature . . ." Will Durant, *Our Oriental Heritage, Story of Civilization, I*, Simon and Schuster, New York, 1954, p. 435.

38   "How lucky you are . . ." Lucien Stryk and Takashi Ikemoto, *Zen: Poems, Prayers, Sermons, Anecdotes, Interviews*, Anchor Books, Doubleday, 1965, p. 74.

41   "Don't get involved . . ." ibid., pp. 81-82.

42   "Now it was . . ." ibid., p. 78.

50   Dr. Heinrich Rosendahl is a fictional character. Belzoni, however, existed; an account of his exploits appears in C. W. Ceram, *Hands on the Past,* Knopf, New York, 1966.

60   "Evidence for a domestic cult . . ." James Mellaart, *Earliest Civilizations of the Near East*, McGraw Hill, New York, 1965, p. 106.

151   "Vin Vitae . . ." quoted in *New England Flavor: Memories of a Country Boyhood*, Norton, New York, 1961, p. 87.

171   "Demonstrators tried to . . ." *Everywoman* (newspaper), Los Angeles, 1/15/71.

"The girls, all trained . . ." *White Mountain Times,* 3/19/71.

218   "Skin Diving in Winter . . ." *New Hampshire Vacationer*, 12/24/71, p. 12.